Praise for the National Bestselling
Bookmobile Cat Mysteries

"Charming.... Librarian Minnie Hamilton is kind-hearted, loyal, and resourceful. And her furry sidekick, Eddie, is equal parts charm and cat-titude. Fans of cozy mysteries—and cats—will want to add this series to their must-read lists."
—*New York Times* bestselling author Sofie Kelly

"With humor and panache, Cass delivers an intriguing mystery and interesting characters."
—*Bristol Herald Courier* (VA)

"A pleasurable, funny read. Minnie is a delight as a heroine, and Eddie could make even a staunch dog lover more of a cat fan." —*RT Book Reviews*

"Charms with a likable heroine, [a] feisty and opinionated cat, and multidimensional small-town characters."
—Kings River Life Magazine

"Almost impossible to put down ... the story is filled with humor and warmth." —MyShelf.com

continued ...

Also by Laurie Cass

Lending a Paw
Tailing a Tabby
Borrowed Crime

Pouncing on Murder

A BOOKMOBILE CAT MYSTERY

Laurie Cass

AN OBSIDIAN MYSTERY

OBSIDIAN
Published by New American Library,
an imprint of Penguin Random House LLC
375 Hudson Street, New York, New York 10014

This book is an original publication of New American Library.

First Printing, December 2015

For more information about Penguin Random House, visit penguin.com.

ISBN 978-0-451-47654-8

Printed in the United States of America
10 9 8 7 6 5 4 3 2 1

Penguin
Random
House

To Jon.
Always.
FYI, this is your fifth
dedication. Not that it's
a contest or anything.

Chapter 1

Throughout the long winter, I'd often dreamed about the month of April. It would be warm, I'd thought. Sunny. There would be baby lambs and fluffy white clouds and daffodils and we'd be able to walk outside without boots and hats and thick coats and mittens.

In the northern part of Michigan's Lower Peninsula, however, the reality of April was a little different.

I switched on the bookmobile's windshield wipers. They groaned as they tried to move against the slush spattering the glass, but inch by inch they gained speed and finally arced across, shoving the white stuff away.

"Remember the April eight years ago?" Julia Beaton asked. There was an element of wistfulness in her expressive voice.

"Nope," I said cheerfully. "This is only my fourth spring in Chilson." I'd spent many a youthful summer with my aunt Frances, but I hadn't lived in Chilson until I'd had the great good fortune to be offered the job of assistant director at the Chilson District Library. The decision had taken less than a second to make.

A job in my favorite place in the world? In a region teeming with lakes of all sizes, in a land of forested hills, in a small town filled with outstanding restaurants and eccentrically original retail stores, and in a library building lovingly converted from an old school? Sure, there was winter to deal with, a season that could last a solid five months, but I loved to ski, so where was the downside?

"It was the best April in the history of Aprils." Julia sighed. "The April to beat all Aprils."

"No snow?" I nodded at falling flakes.

"None whatsoever," she said dreamily, rearranging her long strawberry blond hair into a loose bun. "Blue skies, warm air. It was a page from *Anne of Green Gables*."

Right then and there I decided there was nothing better than a coworker who knew the same children's books that you did. Julia was the perfect bookmobile clerk and I would be forever grateful to my aunt for finding her for me.

Back in December, the library had received a large donation to fund the bookmobile operations. The gift had almost made me weep with gratitude. Chilson's bookmobile was my pet project, which meant it was my responsibility to find the money to run the program. Once the check cleared, I'd immediately started the hunt for a part-time bookmobile clerk, and the sixtyish Julia had been my happy hire.

Born and raised in Chilson, she'd moved to New York

City right out of high school to find fame and fortune as a fashion model. That particular career path hadn't worked out, but her fallback career as an actor had worked out just fine. She'd found a satisfying amount of Broadway fame, saved her money, and waved good-bye to the bright lights as soon as the offers of leading roles slowed to a trickle. These days she taught an acting class at the local college, turned down every community theater role offered to her, and was always looking for ways to expend her considerable energy.

My aunt Frances, who taught woodworking classes at the same college, had made a paper airplane of the clerk's job description and sailed it into her classroom. Julia, one eyebrow raised, had unfolded the paper and scanned the text. When she started to nod, Aunt Frances had smiled and walked away, dusting off her hands at a job well done.

Now I grinned, not taking my attention off the road. "If you don't like winter, maybe you should consider moving to Hawaii."

"Winter I like just fine," she said. "It's April that's the trouble. No matter what temperature it is, you always want a little bit more." She sighed, then looked at the large plastic carrier snugged up next to her feet. "What does Eddie think about April?"

"I don't know," I said. "Why don't you ask him?"

Julia leaned forward, looking into the cat carrier through the wire door. "Good morning, young sir. How do you feel about the current weather conditions of cold, slushy, and wind tossed?"

"Mrr," said my black-and-white tabby cat.

Eddie and I had been together for almost a year. It had been an unseasonably warm day last April that lured me from inside chores to a long walk outside that ended at the local cemetery. Which sounds odd, but this particular cemetery had an outstanding view of Janay Lake and beyond to the bulk of the massive Lake Michigan.

While relaxing in the sun on a bench next to the gravestone of one Alonzo Tillotson (born 1847, died 1926), I was startled by the appearance of a large black-and-gray cat. He'd followed me home, where I'd cleaned him up as best I could, turning him black-and-white. I had responsibly run an ad in the newspaper and had been relieved when no one claimed him. Because of my father's allergies, I'd grown up without pets. Eddie, who my vet estimated was now roughly three years old, was my first pet, and I wasn't sure how I'd ever lived without my opinionated pal.

There'd been a little issue when my new boyfriend turned out to be allergic to cats, but after trying a series of various medications, he'd found one that worked just fine. Then again, since we were now in the midst of a long-distance relationship, he had probably let the prescription lapse. I made a mental note to send a text to remind him.

"Eddie," Julia told my furry friend, "you must learn how to enunciate more clearly. Theatergoers in the top rows will never grasp your nuances unless you work on the consonants."

"Mrr!"

Julia sighed and settled back. "He does not take advice well, does he?"

The interviewing process for the bookmobile job had included a tour of the bookmobile and an introduction to Eddie, because Eddie had been part of the bookmobile from the beginning. He'd stowed away on the maiden voyage and quickly become an integral part of the services we offered. Books, magazines, DVDs, video games, and Eddie hair, not necessarily in that order.

For months I'd felt the need to hide the feline presence on the bookmobile from my follow-the-policy-or-else boss, Stephen Rangel, but it turned out that Stephen had known about Eddie's adventures from the beginning.

I really should have known better.

And I really should have known to stop interviewing after I'd talked to Julia. She was the best candidate for many reasons—and had the bonus of being eight inches taller than five-foot-nothing me, making the job of re-shelving the top rows of books easy to delegate—but the buttercream frosting was how she'd immediately started talking to Eddie in the same way I did, which was as if he understood what we were saying.

We agreed that this was ridiculous, of course, but there were times when his comprehension of human speech seemed to go far beyond his name and the word "no." Not that he paid any attention to either, but the twitching of his ears proved that he heard us.

"Cats aren't big on taking advice," I said. "They'd much rather give it."

I flicked on the turn signal and started braking. It was time for our first stop of the morning, in the parking lot of what had originally been a gas station and was now a ... well, I wasn't sure exactly what it was. A store, sure, but a store that defied description. The owner stocked everything from apples to taxidermy supplies. On the surface, it fit the definition of an old-fashioned general store, but there was also a corner with tables, copies of the *Wall Street Journal*, and free Wi-Fi.

"General stores don't stock the *Wall Street Journal*," I muttered, bringing the bookmobile to a stop.

Julia laughed. "Wake up and smell the twenty-first century, Minnie Hamilton."

I pretended to sniff the air, then frowned, shaking my head. "I like my stereotypes and I'm going to keep them."

"Mrr," Eddie said.

"You two are quite the pair." Julia unbuckled her seat belt and reached forward to open the wire door. "There you go, Mr. Edward. You are free to move about the bookmobile."

"Mrr."

"You're very welcome," she replied.

Julia and I fired up the two computers, emptied the milk crates we used to haul books from the library to the bookmobile, un-bungeed the chair at the rear desk, and unlocked the doors. Eddie watched our activity from his current favorite perch, the driver's seat headrest, and made the occasional critical comment.

"What do you think he's saying?" Julia, who was straightening the large-print books, cast a glance Eddie-ward.

I didn't need to look to know. "That he wants a cat treat."

"Maybe," she said in the tone indicating she was about to get creative, "he's saying that every day is a gift. That today, especially, is a gift and we should—"

The back door opened, and a few sturdy-sounding footsteps later a man came into view. Henry Gill could have been a young-looking eighty or an old-looking sixty, but with his bald head, fit frame, and almost complete crankiness, he was one of those people you just didn't think of in terms of age.

"Good morning, Henry," I said.

The look he gave as his return greeting made me wonder if my hair, which was black, shoulder-length, and far too curly, had gone up in flames without my noticing.

Eddie gave Henry a long visual examination, then jumped off the headrest and trotted down the aisle. He bonked Henry's shin with the top of his hard, furry head, then started twining around his ankles in the feline-standard figure eight.

Henry reached down and gave Eddie a few pets. Then, when he realized I was watching, he stood up. "Doesn't do to make cats too happy," he muttered. "Next thing you know you'll be feeding them bits of prime rib by hand."

I grinned. Henry was undoubtedly a curmudgeon, but he liked cats, and Eddie appeared to like him back, so it was easy for me to overlook his cranky attitude and see down to the man underneath, a man I liked quite a bit.

"You have an excellent point," I said. "If you're in the market for biographies again today, there's a new Theodore Roosevelt you might like."

Henry grunted, but didn't nod, so I wasn't sure

whether he'd said, "Why, yes, Minnie, that sounds wonderful. Thank you for being such an outstanding librarian" or "Whatever." I gave a mental shrug and left Henry alone, or as alone as you can leave someone in a bookmobile.

Other people came on board, and the time passed quickly. Julia and I were kept busy with helping people find books and checking them out, and at the end of the forty-five-minute stop, Henry was the last patron to leave.

I checked his books into the computer and slid them back across the counter to him. "Would you like a plastic bag?"

He picked up the books without answering, then put them back down again. "Here," he said shortly and, reaching into his coat pockets with both hands, he drew out two brown paper bags and handed them to me. "For you and her," he said, tipping his head toward Julia, then picked up his books and tromped down the steps and outside.

"What are those?" Julia asked.

"No idea."

"Everyone says Henry Gill has turned a little strange since his wife died," Julia said, not opening her bag. "Rock, paper, scissors to who opens theirs first?"

Patrons bearing questionable gifts were something no one had warned me about in college. Before I could scare myself into imagining what could lurk inside, I opened the bag, reached in, and drew out a Mason jar filled with a golden liquid.

"Oh, my." Julia's voice carried reverence and awe. "It's maple syrup. I take back every unkind thought I ever had about that man."

I held the jar up to the light, admiring the liquid gold, and, once again, came up against the reality that we never really know what goes on inside people's heads. Henry as a maple syrup Santa? "Who would have guessed?" I murmured.

"What's that?" Julia asked.

"Henry," I said. "I don't think I've ever met anyone like him."

She nodded. "He could have made a fortune as a character actor. Never would have gone a day without work."

"You're probably right," I said, laughing, although I couldn't imagine Henry living anywhere but northern Michigan.

"Oh, I am. He has that sparkle." She used her fingers to make imaginary fireworks. "It's hidden, but he has a hard kernel of personality that is bedrock and unchanging. A good director would draw that out of him in two rehearsals."

"So you've thought about this."

"I cast everyone I meet," she said. "Occupational hazard."

"Even him?" I nodded in Eddie's direction. At that particular moment he was curling himself up onto the computer keyboard, and I made a mental note to vacuum it at the earliest opportunity.

"Eddie is the levity that every drama needs," she said. "The humor that allows the tragedy to be felt deeper. The dose of reality in every fantasy."

I walked away before she could cover every type of play in existence. Eddie as everyman? Please.

My cat lifted his head an inch, met my gaze, and winked.

The next morning, I settled into my office chair, a steaming mug of coffee in hand. I absolutely had to talk to Stephen, and to do that, I needed to be fortified by copious amounts of caffeine.

Stephen, in many ways, was an excellent boss. He laid out concrete goals, he made his expectations known, and he didn't micromanage. However, his goals were usually impossible to meet, the expectations nearly so, and his support skills were of the "Don't bother me unless the sky is falling" variety.

The current situation was typical. Back in December, one week after Stephen had told me that he was grooming me to take over his job when he retired, he'd summoned me to the second floor. Stephen's was the only office up there; the rest of the floor held conference rooms, a computer training lab, storage, and the Friends of the Library book sale room. Stephen's corner office had a stupendous view of Janay Lake, and it stayed warm even in the buffeting winds of winter, thanks to thick curtains and a radiant heater, but I found it a lonely place.

"Ah, Minnie," he'd said as I'd walked in that December. "It's time to start thinking about a book fair."

I'd blinked at him. "A book fair?"

"Yes." He'd frowned. "Surely you know what a book fair is."

Of course I did. I'd just never heard of one being held in Chilson.

"Book fairs," Stephen had gone on, "are events held

to promote the sale of books. Publishers, booksellers, and authors all come together. There can be author readings, contests, prizes, giveaways, story hours, any number of things to promote books and reading."

It wasn't a bad idea. Every time I turned around, it seemed, I heard about another new small regional publisher. If the pace kept up, soon there'd be as many small publishers in the area as brewpubs. Plus, the region was blessed with a large number of outstanding bookstores, and there were authors everywhere, especially in summer, when the seasonal folks returned.

"Early May," Stephen had said, nodding. "That's when we'll hold it."

Two of those words had jumped out at me like an alien in a 3-D movie: "May," and "we." Both held dire implications.

"Early May?" I'd asked. "There's no one around that time of year. A summer book fair would have ten times the number of people attending."

"Don't exaggerate, Minerva," Stephen had said. "And you illustrate the point of a spring fair perfectly. Yes, more people would, perhaps, attend a fair in the summer months. But I want, and the library board wants, to hold an event that will bring locals to the library, people who wouldn't otherwise walk in."

It had sounded reasonable, but I didn't quite buy it. "Why would anyone walk in to buy a book on one particular day when they can walk in any old day to borrow a book for free?"

Stephen had checked the knot in his tie. "Because Ross Weaver will be here." He'd glanced at my face and chuckled. "Ross is a high school friend of mine. We've kept in touch over the years and when I told him I was considering a book fair, he said he'd be happy to make a public appearance."

At that point I'd realized my mouth had been hanging open. I shut it and wondered at the world. Ross Weaver was the author of twenty bestselling thrillers. He was good-looking enough to be cast as his own main character and by all reports was a genuinely nice guy. The notion that Ross Weaver was friends with my boss, who would always be cast as the nerdy guy who never gets the girl, was going to take some mental adjustment on my part.

"That's . . . great," I'd finally said.

"Yes." Stephen had handed me a piece of paper. "Here's an outline of what needs to be done."

The full import of the conversation had finally hit the inside of my brain. "You want to hold the book fair here at the library," I'd said slowly. "Five months from now. And you want me to plan the entire thing."

Stephen had sighed. "You must break that habit of exaggeration, Minerva. I've given you the date, the location, and an author who will draw hundreds, if not thousands, of people to the event. The rest should almost take care of itself."

Spoken like a man. I looked at the list he'd given me. He'd included the names of a handful of publishers and booksellers.

"That will give you a start," he'd said, reaching for his computer keyboard. "If you ever want to sit in this chair, Minnie, you must delegate. You can't do everything yourself. It's past time for you to learn how to manage a project properly."

I'd put on a smile and walked downstairs. When I reached my cozy office, the paper was a crumpled ball in my fist. I'd taken a deep breath, then another one, and pushed my thoughts back where they belonged. Back to books and libraries and bookmobiles and away from the idea of using Stephen's tie to . . .

"Never mind," I'd said out loud, tossing the small paper ball into the wastebasket. I'd thumped myself into my chair, pulled out a yellow legal pad of paper, and started my own list.

Now it was April. The book fair was edging ever closer, and it was time to update my boss on the progress. I looked over my notes, picked up the three-inch ring binder that contained said notes, slugged down the last of my coffee, and headed up to Stephen's aerie.

"Ah, Minnie." Stephen was taking off his coat. It was three minutes past nine and I'd caught him dead to rights at being late. It was an excellent way to start our meeting. "How are you this morning?" he asked as he sat behind his large desk.

I smiled politely. "Fine, thanks. Do you have a few minutes? I'd like to update you on the book fair plans."

"Yes, that's coming up soon, isn't it?"

"Five weeks, two days, and one hour," I said promptly.

Stephen laughed, but it was laughter that had a crinkly edge. "Are you sure you want to spend your time calculating that figure?"

I'd made it up, but there wasn't much point in telling him so. Stephen and my sense of humor weren't compatible. I placed a pile of stapled papers on the corner of his desk. "These are for the next board meeting. It's an update on the book fair."

Stephen eyed the stack. "Does it include financials?"

Of course it did. And none of the contents would be a surprise to Stephen. Early on in the event's planning, I'd handed him an estimate of the cost. His eyes had gone wide, and for a short happy moment, I'd thought he might cancel the whole kit and caboodle. But even as he'd been frowning at the bottom line, his face took on a glazed look and I knew he was running calculations in his head. He'd rearranged a few line items in the budget, told me to cut the event costs by ten percent, and waved me away.

After a few minutes of fuming, I'd come to the obvious conclusion that it was my job to make the fair a successful event that didn't drain the library's resources. So I'd obtained multiple estimates for every large purchase. I'd driven down to Traverse City to pick up items and combined the trip with personal chores so I didn't charge the library mileage. I'd asked for business donations. I'd asked for sponsors. I'd begged for free advertising.

And somewhere along the line, I'd become a passionate believer in the whole thing. Why not hold a book fair in May? Why not bring new folks to the library? It was an outstanding idea and I was grateful to have the chance to show off our beautiful building to new people.

Now, standing in front of my boss, I was practically bouncing on my toes with energy and enthusiasm. "Here's what's left to do," I said to Stephen, and launched into a lengthy narrative that started with confirming the number of vendor tables we needed to rent.

Stephen's eyes glazed over halfway through my recital, but my zeal carried me to the end. He blinked when I finished, then stirred and asked, "Have you considered a location for overflow parking?"

Of course I had. I'd figured that out weeks ago. "If the back parking area fills up—which it never did, but whatever—"I have permission from the Methodist church to use their lot."

My boss nodded, his attention drifting to the magazine on his desk. "And you have a plan if the weather is rainy? Or cold?"

"The tents have side panels," I said. "With them pulled shut, everything inside will stay dry and with people inside, it'll stay relatively warm."

"Sounds as if you have everything in hand." Stephen put on his reading glasses and picked up his magazine. "Thank you for the update."

Clearly I was dismissed. Since I hadn't been invited to sit down, I didn't have to stand up; all I had to do was walk out of the room. So I did. When I got downstairs, I dropped the binder on my desk and picked up my favorite mug, which was emblazoned with the perky logo of the Association of Bookmobiles and Outreach Services, and went in search of more coffee.

The break room was occupied by my best library friends, Holly Terpening and Josh Hadden. Holly was a couple of years older than my thirty-three and Josh was a couple of years younger, and we'd all been hired by

Stephen about the same time, Holly as a clerk, Josh as the library's IT guy.

Holly was married to a man who had a wonderful job over a thousand miles away. He came home to his wife and two small children whenever he could, but I dreaded the day that Holly would get tired of living without her husband and move the family out West.

"Want some?" Holly proffered a full pot of coffee. "Just so you know, I made it myself."

"True fact," Josh said, feeding a dollar bill into the vending machine. His caffeine intake was almost always of the carbonated variety. "Saw her take the scoop right out of Kelsey's hands." A can thudded out of the machine and he shoved it into one of the side pockets of his cargo pants as he pulled out another dollar.

For the thousandth time, I wondered why he didn't bring his own soda and put it in the fridge instead of spending so much money on the vending machine, and, for the thousandth time, I didn't ask.

"Thanks," I said to Holly, and held up my mug. Her brown hair was held back in a ponytail and, as she poured, I saw the method of ponytailing was via a sparkly pink hair fastener.

"Anna help you get ready this morning?" I asked.

Holly's daughter, Anna, was five. Her father sent the kids weekly trinkets, which for six-year-old Wilson tended to be baseball cards. Anna's presents were often hair related, which was getting a little awkward because she was more interested in building houses out of her brother's baseball cards than she was in accessorizing her hair.

"It was handy," Holly said. "Josh, when are you going

to stop wasting your money on that crap and start drinking coffee like an adult?"

Josh looked up. His dark hair was almost as curly as mine, since he hadn't bothered getting it cut in months. He pushed it out of his eyes. "Next month, probably."

"What?" Holly froze.

I lowered my mug and peered at my stocky coworker. "You hate coffee. You've always hated coffee. You've never even liked the smell."

He shrugged. "If I dump in enough sugar I should be able to get some down. Enough to do the job, anyway."

"But . . . why?" Holly asked.

Josh rubbed his thumb over his fingertips. "The coffee here is free. This stuff is a buck." He popped the top of a can and took a long swallow.

Holly and I exchanged glances. "It's been a dollar a can for years," I said. "Did you get a pay cut that I don't know about?"

"Nah." He wiped his mouth with the back of his hand. "I put in an offer on a house. If I get it, I'll move out of my apartment next month."

"Josh!" Holly shrieked, and ran to him, her arms outstretched. "That's great!"

I watched Josh submit to her hug with good grace and hoped the house-purchasing mentality wasn't contagious. "I didn't know you were looking to buy."

"My landlord's been raising my rent every year and not fixing half the stuff he should be. A house will cost me more, but at least I'll be building equity."

I blinked. The idea of Josh as a grown-up was a little frightening. "Well, congratulations."

"Thanks," he said, "but I don't have it yet. The deal could fall through."

"Oh, fish sticks." Holly went back to her coffee. "It'll be fine. And I'll tell you what. If you want, I'll help you decorate. If I lived in a city, I'd be an interior designer. I love decorating houses."

Josh frowned. "Decorate what? It's not Christmas."

"Don't be stupid." Holly rolled her eyes. "Minnie, tell him how much difference a little decorating can make."

"Um . . ." My home interior skills were limited to what colors were available in the cheapest brand of paint. Maybe someday I'd own a house, but now wasn't the time. Librarians had wonderful jobs, but the rewards were more intrinsic than monetary.

"Tell you what," Holly said. "I'll pick out some of my favorite decorating books and let you borrow them. Then we'll pick some paint colors. This will be so much fun!"

Josh's gaze darted toward me, a little bit of the deer-in-the-headlights look in his eyes.

I smiled and topped off my mug. "See you two later," I said, heading out. "Unless"—I paused in the doorway— "you'd like to help with the final arrangements for the book fair. What do you say?"

"So, Holly," Josh said, swinging away from me. "What do you think about the rag rolling technique for painting walls?"

Holly put her back to me. "I'd recommend sponging. It's a lot easier to do consistently."

"Funny," I muttered loudly, and left the room.

But actually they were funny, because they'd both

been a tremendous amount of help for the fair. So had the rest of the library staff. And almost everyone had agreed to help out on The Day. The only thing left was to carry out the plans already put in place. Plus, we'd spent hours dreaming up every worst-case scenario possible and figured out what to do for each one. I was confident that everything would be fine.

So why was a classic line from that poem by Robert Burns now sliding into my thoughts?

"The best-laid schemes o' mice an' men gang aft agley . . ."

I slugged down half of my coffee to wash away the worry and headed back to my office.

Chapter 2

That evening, I started hauling empty boxes down from the vastness of my aunt's attic. Eddie sat at the bottom of the lowered steps and stared upward, offering the occasional suggestion.

On the third trip down, my arms laden with dusty cubes of cardboard, I looked at him and said, "I'd take your comments more seriously if you were actually offering to help, but since all you're doing is criticizing, I don't see why I should listen to you."

"How, exactly," my aunt Frances asked, "do you think he could help? He doesn't have any thumbs and only weighs thirteen pounds."

My aunt was six inches taller than me, twenty-nine years older, and had lived in Chilson longer than I'd been alive. Her late husband, Everett Pixley, had been a Chilson native, but he'd died so long ago that I wasn't sure if my few memories of him were my own or were generated by photographs. Since then, Aunt Frances had made a living taking in summer boarders and teaching woodworking classes. In all the years she'd been a widow, she'd never once taken a serious interest in another man until December, when she started spending time with Otto Bingham, her new across-the-street neighbor, and I was crossing my fingers that the romance would blossom permanently.

Aunt Frances and I looked at Eddie, who was now inspecting the wall and voicing the occasional "Mrr." Finally I said, "If he's not going to help, he should at least keep quiet."

She laughed. "Are we talking about the same Eddie? Here, I'll take those to your room."

I handed over the boxes gratefully and went back up the creaking wooden steps for the last load because, in spite of the chilly weather, it was time for me to get packing.

My winter home was a large room in Aunt Frances's rambling boardinghouse, a place of pine-paneled walls, claw-foot tubs, ancient board games, and a massive fieldstone fireplace. My summer home was much different: a cozy houseboat that I moored in one of Chilson's marinas. Not one of the fancy marinas that came with spa and tennis court privileges, but one that normal people might be able to afford if they didn't eat out much all winter.

Yes, Uncle Chip's Marina was my summer neighborhood, and it was about what you'd expect from a name like Uncle Chip's. The marina office and shop had been built in the fifties and not updated since, and the amenities amounted to a small strip of grass next to the docks that held a couple of picnic tables and a metal grill box for anyone who wanted to haul out some charcoal.

In spite of all that—or perhaps because of it—the marina was a friendly place where someone always hosted a Friday night party, and even though the close quarters of living in a marina could get a little much by August, I'd forget about it by Thanksgiving, and come April I'd be longing for a warm evening on my small houseboat's front deck, reading and sipping the occasional adult beverage.

I gathered up the last of the boxes and descended from the murky attic. When I got off the last step, Aunt Frances collapsed the stairs and pushed them back up into the ceiling. If I'd tried to do the same thing, I would have needed a step stool, but I had become accustomed to my compact and efficient size years ago and it no longer bothered me to let the taller folks take care of things that those folks could do more easily.

Most of the time, anyway.

"Is Tucker coming up to help haul your things to the marina?" Aunt Frances asked.

I shook my head. "I talked to him last night. He's working on a big project and can't get away."

"So, when are you moving?" my aunt asked, dusting off her hands.

"Not that you want to get rid of me," I said, laughing.

"You can stay as long as you like—" she began.

"As long as I start paying boarder rate," I finished. "Don't worry. All my stuff will be out by the end of the month." Since I moved twice a year, I'd pared my possessions down to the minimum, but it still took a while to get settled. The houseboat cleaning itself was a chore of large magnitude. Chris Ballou, the marina manager, gave

me access to the warehouse where my boat was stored
out of season, and for the next couple of weeks I'd be
spending my spare hours in that cavernous space, dusting and washing and scouring.

"Speaking of boarders," Aunt Frances said, taking the
top boxes off my pile, "this might be the last year I take
in any."

I stopped. "What? Why?"

"Because I'm sixty-two years old," she said dryly.

"Sure, but you're a young sixty-two," I protested.
"And you've never said anything about it being too
much work before."

Although, since I was living on the houseboat, how
would I know if it was too much for her? I never saw her
clean and the only meal I ever stopped by to eat was the
occasional Saturday breakfast. This was a meal cooked
by one of the six boarders, which, in addition to often
being entertaining, was also a critical part of the board-
ing agreement.

"There's no better way to discover a person's true
character," Aunt Frances always said, "than to see how
he behaves in a kitchen emergency." And, since my aunt
had secretly match-made her boarders into happy couples for decades, I had to agree with her methods.

Now Aunt Frances rearranged her hold on the empty
box. "I make enough money from teaching during the
school year," she said. "I don't have to take in boarders if
I don't want to. And there are so many things I don't have
time to do in the summer. I can't remember the last time
I went to Mackinac Island, let alone Pictured Rocks."

Oh-ho! I grinned, then wiped it from my face before

my aunt could see. This was an Otto-induced change, I was certain. And while it might be the end of an era—children who were products of some of my aunt's earliest matches were traveling north with their own children—it was always better to leave a party while it was hopping.

"Well," I said, "I hope you're not thinking I'm going to take on your boarders."

My aunt snorted. "With your cooking skills? They'd make their regrets and abandon you within a week."

"Really?" I frowned. "You think they'd last that long?"

"Only if you get two different kinds of cold cereal."

She dropped the box on my bed, gave Eddie a fast pet, and scampered out before I could find a rubber band to shoot at her.

I stopped by the marina the next day after work to make sure Chris would have my houseboat set up for me to start cleaning that weekend.

"Hey, Mini Cooper," he said lazily. "What's new with you?"

Since his uncle Chip, the marina's owner, was almost seventy, Chris was probably somewhere in his forties, but if you went by his speech patterns, you'd think he was twenty. And though the marina was always spick-and-span and shipshape, I rarely saw Chris lifting anything heavier than a twelve-ounce can of beer.

My best friend, Kristen, was sure that he hired elves to do the real work, and I was starting to think she was right. Another of my good friends, Rafe Niswander, said Chris was one of the last of a dying breed of Up North men and that we should encourage him in all ways. Of course, Rafe and Chris were also friends, so I had a good idea of what kind of encouragement he meant—the kind that came in a six-pack.

How Rafe and Chris had become friends, I really didn't know. They had to be a decade apart in age, and in spite of Rafe's summery, laid-back attitude, he had a top-notch work ethic and was the best middle school principal Chilson had seen in years. When Rafe wasn't being the principal and wasn't wasting his time lounging in the marina's office, he was renovating a mess of a house that was next door to the marina. He was also taking his own sweet time about it. He kept saying he wanted it to be perfect and ignored me when I kept telling him that perfection was an unattainable goal.

"Hey yourself, Chris," I said. "My aunt was making fun of my cooking skills, can you believe it?"

He grinned. "Sure can. Good thing you're not running the boardinghouse, eh?"

"True fact. I'd run it into the ground inside of a week if I took over."

"Frances Pixley is giving up the boardinghouse?" Chris pushed back his Detroit Tigers baseball cap and stared at me.

From such conversations, rumors are born. "This is a purely theoretical discussion," I said. "Aunt Frances can't understand that I'm happy living on cold cereal for breakfast all summer long."

"Nothing wrong with that." His feet went back up onto the counter. "Especially if it's Frosted Flakes."

I squinted at him. "I always figured you for a Wheaties kind of guy."

"Too healthy." He took a long swig from a can of soda, then said, "I got some news. You're getting a new right-hand neighbor this year."

"Gunnar getting a slip out on the point?"

Why the wealthy Gunnar Olson had ever rented a boat slip at Uncle Chip's had always been a mystery to the regular marina renters. His massive boat dwarfed all the others in both size and price, and his flagrantly expensive lifestyle fit in more with the folks at the west end of Chilson.

"Other way around." Chris creaked back in his ancient canvas director's chair. "He's getting a divorce, and to pay off his wife he had to sell his boat."

"Oh." A year ago the news would have made me smile. I would have felt bad about it later, but I would have smirked a little and thought it couldn't happen to a nicer human being.

Late last summer, however, the famously bad-tempered man had done me a favor out of the blue. It had made me look differently at a guy who, previously, had seemed to go out of his way to make his nearest neighbor—me— miserable. After that incident, he'd returned to his annoying "I'm the only one who matters" attitude, but I got to carry the knowledge that underneath the crusty exterior he did, in fact, care about things other than keeping his boat shiny and his drinks cold.

I hoped that Gunnar and his soon-to-be ex-wife could make it through without too much anguish. "That's too bad," I said sincerely, earning a pair of raised eyebrows from Chris. Then a thought struck me. "Um, if Gunnar's not coming back, what's going to happen to my slip fee?"

My ability to afford marina space and still eat out on occasion was due to the fact that no one else wanted the slip next to Gunnar. There was no way that my budget could easily absorb the full cost of a slip rental.

I ran through some fast monetary calculations. If I bought the store-brand cold cereal, purchased Eddie's food in bulk, stayed away from Cookie Tom's, tossed out every single take-out menu in my possession, and slashed my book-buying budget . . . no, it still wouldn't work. I sighed and looked up at Chris.

Who was grinning.

"Ah, don't worry about it," he said. "What Uncle Chip doesn't know won't hurt him."

Relief and guilt washed through me in equal measures. "Chris, I can't let you do that. Besides, what if your uncle Chip comes up North this summer? You know I can't tell a lie for beans."

Chris nodded. "You're the worst liar ever except for the dog I had when I was a kid. That mutt would look guilty if he so much as looked at the couch."

Being compared to a dog wasn't exactly flattering, but I supposed it could have been worse. Somehow.

"Tell you what," Chris said. "Let's see what the new guy is like. He may be worse than old Gunnar was."

Possible, but not probable. "What if he's nice? What if he's friendly and holds the best Friday night parties ever and having the slip next to his would be a bonus and not a misery?"

"Huh." Chris rubbed the stubble on his jaw. "Let me think on that."

I looked about the office. A calendar from 1996 was

tacked to the far wall. "I could help around here. Do a little cleaning. Paint."

A horrified expression crowded Chris's weathered face. "Don't you dare. It's taken me years to get the place looking this good. You git before you get any more ideas. Out of here!" He shooed me away.

"Are you going to pull my boat out for me this weekend?"

"If you promise to stick to cleaning to that little tub, yeah, absolutely. Just keep your bleach and mops away from here."

"Promise," I said, laughing, and we did a mutual halfway-across-the-room high five to seal the deal.

The next few days, I spent all my free time down at the marina, getting the houseboat ready for moving into. Eddie had been giving me the cold shoulder for not giving him enough attention, so on Thursday, out on the bookmobile, I wasn't surprised to hear Julia ask in a puzzled tone, "What is your cat doing?"

I was kneeling on the floor, trying to stuff more returned books into a milk crate than the milk crate wanted to allow, so I happily gave up on the task and looked up. Eddie was lying on the bookmobile's dashboard and managing to take up the entire length of it. His front legs were stretched out Superman-style, his face was pressed against the dash, his back legs were behind him, and his tail appeared twice as long as it did most days.

"Dusting?" I suggested.

Julia lifted one eyebrow. "Wouldn't he be actually moving if he was dusting?"

She had a good point. I stood and studied my cat. If the day had been sunny, I might have understood Eddie's wish to soak up the sunshine with all possible body parts, but it was—once again—cloudy, windy, and wet.

"You know," I said, "I've never seen him up there like that." Which was odd, because we'd found Eddie in every other possible location on the bookmobile, and that included the top shelves. "Maybe he just wanted to see if he fit."

We stood side by side, watching Eddie not move. I had the sudden and scary thought that he might have had a kitty heart attack while I wasn't paying attention, but as soon as I had the thought he opened his eyes and picked up his head a quarter of an inch.

"Mrr," he said.

Julia sighed. "If only we understood cat."

"Eddie-speak is likely a whole different dialect," I said, watching Eddie's head drop back to the dashboard. "I'm pretty sure he's his own species." I was about to tell her that I'd considering applying to the science folks to get the name *Felis eddicus* established before someone else stole it away, when the back door was flung open and someone pounded up the steps.

"Oh, Minnie," Phyllis Chambers said, panting. "Have you heard?"

She reached out to grip my hands, her skin so cold to the touch that I almost flinched. Phyllis was another downstate transplant. She'd moved north from a state government job in Lansing last summer and, in spite of the long winter, she was loving the northern life.

"Heard what?" I asked.

"Oh, dear." Phyllis squeezed my hands, released them, and rubbed her face. Her short hair, a thick and glorious white, was in its normal disarray. She ran her fingers through it, but everything sprang back to where it had been before she made the effort. "Oh, dear. I hate to be the one to bring you bad tidings, but it's Henry Gill."

Julia and I exchanged a quick glance. "What's wrong with Henry?" I asked. "He was fine last week."

"I'm so sorry, Minnie," Phyllis said. "But Henry's dead."

That night, Aunt Frances was out with Otto at a wine tasting, so it was just Eddie and me on the couch in front of the fieldstone fireplace. I could have started a fire, and I could have popped a big bowl of popcorn, but instead I stared into space.

"Did you hear what Phyllis said about Henry?" I asked softly. Eddie had been mostly asleep the entire stop, so I wasn't sure what he'd heard. "A tree fell on him."

I shivered, hoping he hadn't suffered. Henry hadn't been the easiest person in the world to like, but part of my job was to learn about my patrons and bring them . . . well, if not happiness through books, at least something that would lighten whatever load they were carrying, because we were all carrying burdens of some kind.

What Henry's load had been, though, I didn't know. The only personal things I knew about him were his book choices, that he was a widower, and that none of his children lived in the state. Also that he tended to avoid conversation, most often preferring grunting and shaking his head whenever those could pass as communication.

I sighed, thinking about the exquisite maple syrup that Henry had given Julia and me the last time he was on the bookmobile. "Phyllis said he'd been out at his sugar shack." I put my hand on Eddie's warm back to feel his quiet reverberations. "He'd finished boiling sap and was cleaning up."

Last year I'd ventured out to a state park to watch a maple syrup cooking demonstration. Add maple sap to a large pan over a fire, boil, add more sap, boil. Add more firewood, add more sap. Repeat until the liquid turned into maple syrup, which was when it reached just above two hundred and nineteen degrees.

I'd happened to mention my park trip to Henry, and over the next few months, he'd dribbled out a lot of maple syrup–making information. For example, I now knew the large commercial operations had complicated systems of tubes that ran from the trees to large storage vats and fancy machines that processed the sap into syrup. I knew that Henry was old-school—no surprise there—and hauled his sap from the trees in buckets. I also knew that he cooked his sap in a massive and ancient pan that he'd inherited from his father, and I knew that he sorted his firewood by age and that he considered firewood stacking to be a fine art.

"Poor Henry," I whispered, pulling Eddie close to my chest and hugging him tight. For a change, instead of struggling to get away, my cat let me snuggle him close.

And never stopped purring.

The next day, I risked life and limb by venturing into the restaurant owned and run by my best friend. Kristen

Jurek was, physically, my complete opposite. Tall, where I was efficient. Blond and straight hair to my black and curly. She also had the easy grace of the natural athlete, while I had to practice the simplest activity over and over again before I got the hang of it, and she was so used to the admiring stares of men that she didn't even notice them. If a man stared at me, my first reaction was to wonder what food was stuck in my teeth.

I banged on the back door of the Three Seasons, using the same triple-knock pattern I'd used since we met, the summer we were twelve. We'd encountered each other on Chilson's city beach and, over cones of mint chocolate chip ice cream, had started a friendship that had endured time, distance, and even living in the same town seven months out of the year. Kristen closed down her restaurant just before winter—hence the restaurant's name—and spent the snowy months in Key West, tending bar on the weekends and doing as little as possible during the week.

She'd recently returned to Chilson and had immediately jumped into restaurant-readying preparations. For most people, the weeks before the summer season were a time of happy anticipation. Not for Kristen.

"Hey," I called, shutting the door behind me. "Are you here?"

A metallic crash, following by a sailor-quality curse, was answer enough.

Smiling, I picked my way around stacks of boxes and went straight to the kitchen, where a deeply tanned Kristen, with her hands on her hips, was staring at a large pan on one of the many gas burners. "I hate that pan," she said. "I've always hated it."

"Then get rid of it," I said, pulling a stool up to the work counter crowded with cooking and serving items, half of which I couldn't identify.

"Can't. Paid way too much money for the dang thing."

I could see how that would be a problem. "Has Scruffy touched it?" I asked. "Sell it on eBay, saying that it was used by the producer of *Trock's Troubles*."

Scruffy was Kristen's current love interest. He was indeed the producer of *Trock's Troubles*, a long-running cooking television show hosted by Trock Farrand that was occasionally filmed in Chilson because Trock owned a house in town. Scruffy was also Trock's son and the tidiest person I'd ever met. This was a man who ironed creases into his jeans. Who always carried a handkerchief. Who never had a hair out of place and always knew the right thing to say.

Kristen adjusted the burner's heat and glared at the pan. "No, but it could be arranged. He's flying in next week."

"That will be nice." I took a linen napkin off the top of a huge pile and tried to fold it into a pirate hat. "Have they scheduled you?"

The Three Seasons had been short-listed to appear on the show last year and had eventually risen to the top. Kristen had tried to pull out, saying it wouldn't look right to other area restaurateurs since she was dating the producer, but the avuncular Trock had blustered at her for being an idiot and had ignored her request.

"Yes," she said morosely.

"Hey, that's great!" I waved the napkin over my head the way I'd heard people did towels at sporting events. "Awesome, even. Why aren't you more excited?"

With a whisk, she poked at the contents of the pan. "Because it's set for a July filming. And an October airing."

Her moroseness suddenly made sense. "Oh." From the Fourth of July to mid-August, tourists and summer residents flooded the region in numbers so large that many locals didn't venture downtown at all. Having a TV crew in the restaurant during peak season would make things worse in ways I couldn't comprehend. And timing the show to be aired in October, right before the restaurant closed, was about as stupid as timing could get.

"Scruffy can't rearrange something?" I asked.

Kristen shook her head, causing her long blond ponytail to flip back and forth. "Prior and future commitments, blah, blah, blah."

The television world was a mystery to me, and the more I learned about it, the more I was glad I'd become a librarian. "Well, I'm sure it'll all work out."

Kristen made a *hmmph*ing noise, reached for a spoon, dipped it into the pan, and tasted whatever was in there. "God, that's awful," she said, squinching her facial features into something a five-year-old would have been proud of. "Want to try?"

"After that advertisement, how could I not?" I accepted the spoonful she held out. "What is it?" I sniffed the whitish sauce. Dark flecks that I assumed were intentional floated around.

"Bechamel."

"What's that?"

"White sauce."

I rolled my eyes and tasted. It was a glorious burst of

rich buttery flavor, heightened by the flavors of whatever herbs she'd tossed in. "This is awful?"

"You are the worst taster ever." She turned off the burner and poured the sauce down a sink. "Couldn't you tell that there were too many competing flavors?"

"Tasted fine."

"Why do I even try to educate you?"

I grinned. "Because while you enjoy pain, the recovery time from this is far shorter than if you banged your head against the wall."

"And involves exactly the same amount of reward." She filled the pan with warm water and went to the refrigerator. "However, you are to be rewarded for being the person who can keep me sane even after I've failed at that stupid sauce ten times in a row." She thumped two small white dishes on the counter. "Here. Eat."

"I get to eat both of them?" The thought made me start to salivate. Eating Kristen's crème brûlée was the closest I might ever get to heaven.

"Do you want to help me perfect the summer's signature dish, which will be topped by the new Three Seasons bechamel sauce?"

"Not really."

"Then you only get one." She took out two spoons. "Eat and be grateful for what you've been given."

Five minutes of silence ensued. When both dishes were empty, Kristen sighed. "Okay, I feel better now."

I rolled my eyes. "Took you long enough."

"Yeah, well." She grinned. "It was a good winter."

"How much of that is due to Mr. Scruff?" I knew he'd visited Key West at least half a dozen times since Christmas and would be in town all summer running his father's show.

She winked at me and spooned up the last of her custard. "And how much of those rosy cheeks is due to the attentions of your doctor?"

I scraped hard at the corners of the dish and licked a teensy bite of custard off my spoon. "Probably not a whole lot."

My boyfriend, Tucker Kleinow, known in Charlevoix Hospital's emergency room as Dr. Kleinow, and I had been dating since last summer. After that rough patch when we'd realized he was horribly allergic to Eddie, things had smoothed out and had been going reasonably well until he'd accepted a short-term job downstate.

"Still living with his parents, is he?" Kristen shoved our dishes to the side.

I nodded. Tucker's new job was a two-year fellowship position at the University of Michigan, and his parents lived less than an hour away from the university hospital. To save money, he'd chosen to move in with them instead of getting his own place. It made financial sense, but it also made my visits a little awkward.

"Ah, it'll all work out," Kristen said. "And it'll be easier this summer, when you're on the houseboat instead of at your aunt's boardinghouse. I mean, your aunt Frances is awesome, but it's not the same as having your own place."

Many people had said the same thing to me over the years, with additional comments about the need to build equity and a solid credit record. I ignored them all.

"Tucker's taking his vacation up here," I said. "Third week of June."

Kristen glanced at a wall calendar. "So you're going downstate soon?"

"Not that I know of." Her eyebrows went rose dramatically, so I dredged up a quick explanation. "With the book fair and moving to the houseboat and . . . and everything, I'm just really busy. The bookmobile needs a good spring cleaning and . . . and . . ."

"And you don't get along with Tucker's parents," Kristen said, making it a statement of fact.

I sighed. "I want to like them. I try to like them. But every time I go down there, I never know what to say."

Dinners were the worst. Tucker and his parents would talk about people I didn't know and places I'd never been and I'd sit there with a polite smile on my face with absolutely nothing to contribute. I kept myself entertained by picking cat hair off my clothes, setting them free one by one, and guessing where they'd land. Once, an Eddie hair had stuck to Tucker's dad's right sock and I'd laughed out loud, which had proven awkward since everyone else had been talking about the early demise of a neighbor.

"Talk about books," Kristen advised. "That will keep you going for hours, if not days."

But I was shaking my head. "The only bookshelves in the entire house are in the study, and those hold more knickknacks than books."

Kristen dropped her jaw, opening her eyes wide. "They don't read? Sacrilege! Have you warned them what might happen to their brains? Give them a librarian's citation. That'll shape them up."

I smiled. Kristen was the best friend a person could have, a tremendously hard worker, a brilliant chef, an outstanding employer, and had a tremendous sense of humor, but she was not a reader. "They have a lot of cookbooks in the kitchen."

"Ha!" She thumped the table with her fist. "Just as I suspected. You are a book snob. You don't think cookbooks are real books, do you? No, don't deny it. I've known you too long. I bet you've never even read a cookbook from cover to cover, so how can you pass judgment?"

She ranted on, and the tight feeling in my stomach eventually faded. Which was, no doubt, what she'd intended because she had known me for a long time.

And because she'd known me so long and so well, she eventually stopped talking and gave me a long look. "So, what's wrong? No denials, I can see you're sad about something. Save us both some time and tell me now."

I tried to smile, but it wasn't a big one and it didn't last. After a moment, I said, "Remember the guy on the bookmobile who gave me the maple syrup?"

"Sure." She nodded.

"He'd dead." I sighed. "An accident, they say. A tree fell on him and . . . and . . ."

"Oh, honey." My best friend stepped close and wrapped her arms around me. "You go ahead and cry. I'll hold you, and you cry."

So I did.

Chapter 3

The next bookmobile day was clear and bright and even though there wasn't a hint of green growth anywhere, the sunshine was enough to make me believe that someday summer would indeed come.

"Just think, Eddie," I said. "Soon we'll be on the front deck of the houseboat on the chaises, me reading the newspaper while you try to sleep on top of it." I did, on occasion, read parts of the paper out loud to my cat, but I'd drifted away from the habit while living with Aunt Frances. Some things are best kept private.

At this point on the bookmobile route, it was just Eddie and me. There were a number of housebound stops to make, and the library board had agreed that the inviolate rule to always have two people on the bookmobile didn't apply to the housebounds, as long as I kept a fully charged cell phone on my person.

"One of these days," I said to Eddie, "someone should revise the library's bookmobile policies." The set I'd drawn up a year ago, before the maiden voyage, had been a good start, but things had evolved, as things tended to do, and the policy should be updated to reflect that.

Of course, doing so would take time, and that was a commodity in short supply.

"How about you update the policy for me?" I asked Eddie as I made a right turn onto a gravel road. "You know how we do things. All you'd have to do is read over the existing document and make a few changes. I can help with the spelling."

Eddie's "Mrr" was half swallowed by one of his slurpy yawns.

"Nice," I said. "Hope you wiped your chin." I braked and made another right turn, this time into an empty barnyard large enough to accommodate tractors hauling pieces of large and expensive equipment.

"Don't get all excited," I said to the sleepy Eddie. "It's the neighbor who's getting the books. His driveway, because of its length and narrow width, is not what you might call bookmobile friendly and this farmer was kind enough to let us park here."

We came to a complete stop and I reached for Adam Deering's bag of books. Though I'd never met Adam, I'd met his wife, Irene, soon after the pair moved up North. The first time she'd walked into the library, I'd been at the reference desk and had smiled at her expression of happy awe.

I understood her look, because the Chilson District Library was flat-out gorgeous. After the town's middle school had moved into a brand-new building, the old one was converted into a stunning facility of wood-paneled walls, Craftsman-style light fixtures, mosaic-tiled bathrooms, spacious community rooms, and so many books that I sometimes felt light-headed when I looked at them all.

Irene's rapt face had been the start of an acquaintanceship that held the strong possibility of turning into friendship, given the right circumstances, so when she'd called and asked if the bookmobile could drop off some books to her husband, who was recovering from heart surgery, I'd been happy to help out.

I'd wondered, of course, about a woman who couldn't be much older than forty having a husband who'd had heart surgery, and was curious about meeting Adam. "They say that curiosity killed the cat," I said, unlatching Eddie's cat carrier, "so don't get carried away with your freedom, okay?"

He snuggled more deeply into the pink blanket that one of Aunt Frances's boarders had made him last summer, and purred.

To get around the fence that bordered the two properties, I tromped out to the road, down to the Deerings' mailbox, and up the long, narrow, winding driveway that would have been a challenge to maneuver in anything larger than a VW bug. The plastic bag of books got heavier and heavier, digging deep into the insides of my fingers. "Onward and upward," I muttered, and hoped that Adam's recovery wouldn't last until next winter.

Half a century later, their two-story log-sided house came into view. I heaved a sigh of relief, climbed the steps to the wide front porch, and knocked on the door.

From inside, I heard a male voice call out, "Come on in."

I pushed open the wood-slab door and poked my head inside. "Hi, I'm Minnie Hamilton. Your wife asked me to bring you some books."

The front door opened straight into the living room. Plaid blankets were draped over the back of the couch and over armchairs, the large hanging light fixture was a clever driftwood sculpture, and botanical prints hung on the walls. Instead of the braided oval area rug I'd expected to see on the wooden floor, there was a faded Oriental carpet. It wasn't too Up Northy and it wasn't too Transplanted City Folk. It was just right.

There was a fortyish man sitting in a recliner with his feet up. His dark hair had just a touch of gray, and from what I could tell of what showed above the blanket, he looked to be tallish and in the could-use-some-exercise category. "Hi," he said, waving. "I'm Adam. Sorry for not getting up, but—"

"But Irene, your cardiologist, your general practitioner, and the entire nursing staff at Munson Hospital will scold you if you do." I smiled at him. "How are you doing?"

"Bored," he said. "There's only so much ESPN even I can watch."

"ESPN?" I gave him a puzzled look. "That's a new cooking network, right? Extra Special Potato Noodle."

He laughed. "I can see why you and Irene have hit it off. She's not what you might call a sports fan, either. Actually she's mostly a city girl, though she's taking to life up here like a duck to water."

A woman after my own heart. I emptied the books onto the table next to Adam's chair and made a mental note to look into the purchase of a wheeled book carrier. "Irene said you like to read," I said, "but that you haven't had much spare time for years. I brought a wide selection today, but if you let me know what you like and what you don't, I can do better next time."

Adam reached for the books, then winced. "Piece of advice," he said, grimacing with pain, "avoid emergency heart surgery at all costs. The recovery time is brutal."

"Can I get you anything?" I stood there, helpless, watching as he took fast, shallow breaths. "Water, or . . . anything?"

He laid his head back against the chair. "Do you have time to give me some quick book summaries? I'll choose one, and then you can hand it to me so I don't rip open my staples."

I blinked away the vision of a doctor using the latest Swingline product to tidy up a surgical incision and glanced at my watch. "If it means luring you away from a twenty-three-year-old football game played by two teams you don't care about much, then sure."

The top book on the stack was *The Tipping Point* by Malcolm Gladwell. I'd done no more than cite the title when Adam started smiling. "How did you manage to bring the one book I've read in the last fifteen years? My boss, down in Chicago, loved it so much that he bought me a copy and wouldn't let up until I'd read it."

I tried to remember if Irene had said what Adam did for a living, but I came up dry. "What kind of business are you in?"

"Numbers," he said, shifting a little in his chair. "I'm an accountant. And yes, you'd think I could manage to sit at a computer while recovering from heart surgery, but they don't want me working for at least two months."

I thought about how that much enforced inactivity would mess with my head and reached into the pile of books for *Atlas Shrugged*. "Eight weeks should give you enough time to read this."

He looked at the heft of the book. Laughed, then winced and sighed. "Forty-one years old," he said, "and I'm a mess. I can't work for two months, and I've been self-employed since we moved north, so that means no income for probably three months. I have medical bills up the wazoo thanks to our crappy health insurance, and my wife is working two jobs to make ends meet."

My heart ached for him, but there wasn't anything I could say that would help, so I just sat.

He sighed again, then put on a fake smile. "But I'll get better, right? And at least I found out about this congenital heart condition I didn't know I had."

"Alive is almost always better than dead," I agreed.

His mouth twisted. "Yeah. I could have ended up like Henry."

I blinked. "You mean Henry Gill?"

Adam blinked back. "You knew him?"

"He was a regular. I first knew him at the library, but when the bookmobile started up, he decided it was easier to let the books come to him instead of him going to the books."

Adam's smile was faint. "Sounds like Henry. I was there . . ." His voice faded away to nothing.

I didn't understand, and then suddenly I did. "You were there the day Henry died?"

"Yeah," he said quietly.

"That must have been awful."

"Yeah."

We sat there, each thinking things that were probably similar, thoughts along the lines of sudden death, of pain and suffering and tasks left undone, of tender feelings never spoken and wonderful places never visited.

"I'm so sorry," I whispered.

Adam shook his head, then started talking. "I met Henry early last summer. I'd gone out for a long bike ride and was in the far southeast corner of the county, you know, where the land isn't quite as hilly but there are all those little lakes?"

I nodded, but he wasn't paying attention to me, he was back in time, watching his memory spin out.

"There must have been some glass in the road or who knows what? I ended up with a really flat tire, so I stopped on the side of the road to fix the tube." He gave a wry smile. "I'd checked my patch kit before I left, but I hadn't made sure the glue was still good. Stuff was hard as a rock."

My knowledge of bike tube repair was hazy, but even I knew that hard glue was bad. "What did you do?"

"I didn't do anything." Adam grinned. "I was sitting there, staring at the tire, feeling like an idiot. I had my cell phone, but Irene was at work and there wasn't anyone I could call."

This, I knew, was what often happened when people moved north. New folks would have a few friends, usually coworkers and neighbors, but it could take a long time to forge relationships that allowed you to call someone half a county away to come save you from your own stupidity.

"What happened?" I asked.

"Henry," Adam said promptly. "He was out in that beater pickup of his. He slowed down, took a good look at me, and stopped. Asked where I lived, and when I said, he gave that grunt of his, you know?"

I certainly did.

"Anyway, he said he'd drop me off at my house, then told me to put my bike in the bed of his truck."

I smiled, knowing what was coming.

"Took Henry fifteen minutes to get it strapped down the way he wanted. I told him it wasn't an expensive bike and not to worry about it, but he said driving with an unsecured load was dangerous." He smiled. "Then we got into the truck and headed southeast."

"Um . . ."

"Yeah," Adam said. "The opposite direction from here. Henry had a guy he needed to talk to about a part for a lawn tractor and he wasn't about to quit the errand just because I wanted to get home."

"How long did it take you to get back?" I asked, laughing.

"About as long as it would have taken to walk." Adam gave a crooked smile. "After the tractor part, Henry stopped to see a guy whose dog had just had pups. Then it was close enough to lunchtime to eat at the restaurant out there. And you know what that means."

I nodded. "Coffee. Lots of coffee." A discussion regarding what made the perfect cup of coffee had been the first real conversation Henry and I ever had.

"Henry didn't drink it hot," Adam said. "And he wouldn't dream of diluting it with a single ice cube. We sat at that greasy table for more than an hour, drinking coffee, eating ham sandwiches, and hardly saying a word."

Classic Henry. I felt my eyes mist up. Cranky and crusty as he'd been, I would miss him terribly.

"And you know what happened next?" Adam asked.

"Yep," I said. "Henry wouldn't let you pay the bill, he thanked you for the best lunch he'd had in a dog's year, and he slapped you on the back so hard you almost fell over."

Adam's chuckle was quiet and deep. "So you've been out to eat with Henry, too."

"A couple of times." Chilson's downtown diner, the Round Table, was a congregating place for the entire area, and I'd run into Henry once or twice at Sunday morning breakfast. He'd wave me over, make me sit, and we'd have the same type of silent conversation. "He was one of a kind," I said.

Adam sighed. "I've felt awful about the whole thing."

"I'm sure you did everything you could."

"It wasn't enough," he said, looking at a vacant spot in the air. "And I wish the sheriff's office . . ." He stopped and shook his head.

I frowned. It wasn't that I believed the Tonedagana County Sheriff's Office didn't know what they were doing—in fact, I knew very well how dedicated and capable they were. It was more that I knew a little too much about the department.

For instance, I knew one of their two longtime detectives had recently retired and the new guy wasn't quite ready to roll out on his own. And thanks to my friend Rafe, who knew everything about everything in the city of Chilson, I knew that a number of deputies were out sick and on short-term disability. The whole place was understaffed and if that didn't change soon, the busy summer months were going to become a large problem for the sheriff.

"What's that about the sheriff's office?" I asked.

Adam looked at me. "Do you really want to hear this?"

Not a chance. "Yes, please."

His gaze drifted past me. "That day, out in the woods. The sap run was over, so I'd stopped by to help Henry clean up the sugar shack. He went out to stack some wood and when he didn't come back, I went out to find him."

I knew where Henry had lived, on a forty-acre parcel covered with maple trees. It was a beautiful piece of rolling land, not on the water but next door to it and bordering numerous cottages that fronted Rock Lake, most of which would be empty at this time of year.

Adam put his palm flat on his chest. "Henry was under a tree," he said, the words tumbling out. "I tried lifting it, tried pulling him out, digging him out, but then my heart kind of exploded. Next thing I know, I'm falling to the ground. I'm flat on my back. Could hardly breathe and the inside of my chest is on fire. I know my cell phone's in my pocket, and when I reach around for it, my head turns, and I swear, I swear . . ."

I was on the edge of my seat. "What?"

Adam's eyes focused on my face. "I swear I saw someone. Running away."

Chapter 4

As soon as the bookmobile had been stowed away for the night and Eddie returned to the boardinghouse, I marched straight to the sheriff's office and, standing at the tall front counter that almost reached the underside of my chin, gave my name, and asked if I could see Detective Inwood.

"Hang on," said a deputy. With no speed whatsoever, he reached for the phone, pushed a few buttons, and turned away to talk. He murmured a few words, glanced back at me—I smiled brightly—flipped back around, laughed, then hung up the phone. "Hal says to send you back to the interview room."

"Thank you," I said politely, trying not to wonder what had caused the laughter.

The deputy buzzed open the locked door that led to the interior offices. "It's down the hall, third office on the right."

"Thanks," I said, though I didn't need the directions. If this had been baseball, someone would have been keeping track of the number of times any given honest law-abiding private citizen had sat in the small window-less room. Last fall I'd lost count after using up all my fingers and had decided it was a silly number to try to remember anyway.

I sat primly in the chair that I'd long ago come to think of as mine, and kept my attention away from the stains on the ceiling tiles, especially the ones near the door. If I stared at them too long, they'd turn into fire-breathing dragons and fly into my dreams. As it was, I had enough problems with animals in dreams, thanks to Eddie's ten-dency to sleep on my head when the outside temperature dropped below sixty degrees. Why the outside tempera-ture should cause a change in his inside behavior, I didn't know. All I knew was that it was true.

"Ms. Hamilton." The tall, rangy, and gray-haired De-tective Inwood entered the room and stood next to the scratched laminate table. "Do I need to sit down for this?"

He showed a number of signs of a man with too much to do and not enough time to do it in. He glanced at the clock on the wall. Tapped his leg with his fingers. Glanced out to the hallway. If I tried to talk while he was standing, I'd never get his full attention.

I slid down and reached out with my toes to push out the chair opposite from me. "How nice to see you, De-tective Inwood. Did you have a nice winter? And how were your holidays?"

"Ms. Hamilton," he said, his patient tone slipping, "please don't tell me you're here for a social call. Dever-eaux retired last month and Wolverson isn't a detective yet, so I'm dealing with a double caseload. I have half a dozen cases going and—"

"It's about Henry Gill."

Inwood's tense impatience fell into lines of fatigue. He went to the chair and sat heavily. "Henry. I still can't believe the old bugger's gone."

Too late, I realized what I should have considered earlier, that the detective and Henry were near contemporaries, that Tonedagana County didn't have all that many people in it, and that the odds were good that any two men from the same generation knew each other. Hundred percent odds, really, if Inwood's reaction was a guide. It had been poor judgment not to think about the possibility, and I was sorry I'd been flip in the way I'd changed the subject.

After a moment, I said, "I was talking to Adam Deering earlier today."

The detective nodded. "The guy who found Henry."

"He was saying that he saw someone running away from Henry, after that tree fell."

"Thought that he saw a male figure," the detective corrected.

I bristled at the dissing of my new friend's reputation. "Well, he was having a heart attack."

"Exactly," Detective Inwood said. "Eyewitnesses are unreliable in the best of cases, and this certainly wasn't best."

"But—"

Inwood held up his hand against my protest. "Point number one. Mr. Deering was having a heart attack. Point number two. He was in an area with which he was not familiar. Point number three. The weather was windy with gusts up to thirty miles an hour, two inches of rain had fallen inside the previous twelve-hour period, and the heavy cloud cover made the light quality very poor. None of these created optimal conditions for observation."

Grudgingly I gave him credit for not ending the point-number-two detail with a preposition. "Okay, but—"

The hand went back up. "And point number four, the most pertinent point. Mr. Deering's statement was inconsistent."

My spine lost a little of its starch. "But that has to happen all the time. It's easy to get a couple of details mixed up, especially in . . . in a situation like that."

Detective Inwood didn't appear to care. "Initially Mr. Deering claimed there was thunder and lightning that day. Later, he said there'd been none. Then Mr. Deering said he went out to check on Henry because he thought he'd heard a strange noise. Later, he said he went outside to get some fresh air. At one point Mr. Deering said he'd seen someone else in the woods, someone wearing a brown jacket. Later, he said the jacket was dark green. Even later, he said it was navy blue. Later yet, he said it was plaid."

The intellectual part of my brain knew that what the detective was saying made sense, that Adam's emotional and physical state had been clouding everything to the point where his statement couldn't be trusted, but the other part of my brain, the part that cared deeply about puppies and kittens, wasn't convinced at all.

"But none of that means he was wrong," I said, trying to be calm and rational. "Even if he'd said the man's coat was bright purple with fluorescent green polka dots, that doesn't mean a man wasn't there."

Inwood smiled. "I'm surprised at you, Ms. Hamilton. Of all people, I would have thought you'd be open to gender possibilities."

I felt my cheeks warm. "Adam said he'd seen a guy. I was just going with his impressions."

"The same impressions that seemed to change every time we talked to him?" The detective sighed and looked at the ceiling. I wondered if the dragon looked like something else from that side of the table. Maybe next time I'd break out of my rut and sit in his chair.

A man about my age—a very good-looking man—hurried into the room. "Sorry I'm late. I got a phone call and . . . oh." Deputy Ash Wolverson looked at me. "Hi, Minnie. Is something wrong?"

"Ms. Hamilton stopped by to tell us that we should pay more attention to our eyewitnesses." Detective Inwood stood. "Please show her out." He gave me a marginally polite nod and left the room.

Ash settled into the vacated chair. "Is that why you're here? Did you witness a crime?"

Once again, I wondered how such a stunningly handsome man could be so unaware of how his good looks could affect the women around him. I, of course, was immune since I was dating Tucker, but surely Ash had grown up with girls throwing themselves at him. In my experience, that tended to make men annoyingly sure of themselves, but Ash came across as humble and almost shy.

I smiled at him. "No, I stopped by to drop some books

off for Adam Deering and heard what he's saying about Henry."

Ash folded his hands on the table and stared at them. "Mr. Deering stated, in various ways, that he'd seen a figure running away from Mr. Gill and himself."

"And you don't believe him," I said. "At least that's what Detective Inwood implied."

"Inwood is—" Ash stopped abruptly. Looked at his hands some more.

"Is what?" I asked. "Encouraging and sympathetic? Willing to take the time to teach you all you'll need as a detective? Supportive?"

Ash laughed. "Have you had Hal as a boss? Because it sounds like you know him pretty well."

No, but I did have a boss named Stephen. "I'm sure he loves his wife and children dearly and wouldn't dream of kicking a dog."

"Grandchildren, too," Ash said. "Have you seen the pictures? Cute kids."

The idea of Detective Inwood dandling babies on his knees was a little much even for my overactive imagination.

"But the problem," Ash went on, lowering his voice and leaning forward, "is he's city."

"He's . . . city?"

"Yeah. Hal grew up downstate in a big town, spent twenty-five years on a big-town police force, and moved up here to work until he got old enough to retire for good. So he's from the city and thinks city."

"I'm from Dearborn," I said a little stiffly.

"Really?" He caught himself and started again. "And

that's just what I mean. You're from the city, but you think small town. Hal Inwood, he's big city inside and out."

I wasn't understanding this at all. "What does this have to do with Henry and Adam?"

"Because once Hal gets out of town, he doesn't always see the possibilities."

"Like what?"

"Like the possibility that someone could have set up that tree to fall."

"Set it up?"

"Sure." Ash nodded. "Wouldn't be that hard. Find a tree rotted in the middle, tie a come-along to it, and start winching it. Bring it almost to the falling point, then back off and unchain it. Rig up a block and tackle to some upper branches, wait for your guy to get into the right spot, give a good yank, and the tree comes down."

I stared at him. "But you're talking about . . . about something worse than leaving two injured men behind. You're saying it was—" I didn't want to think about it, let alone say it out loud.

"I'm not saying anything," Ash said, shaking his head. "I'm just saying there are possibilities that need to be looked into."

"Possibilities of murder," I said.

"And another thing." Ash looked into my face, and for the first time I noticed that his eyes were almost gray. A little blue, but if I had to choose a color, it would have been gray.

"Another thing?" I asked faintly.

"If it was a setup, I'm not sure about the target."

"What are you talking about?"

"The light was bad," Ash said. "It was rainy and windy and cold and all-around crappy. If someone knew Deering was helping clean out the sugar shack, that someone could have expected Deering to go out to the woodpile, not Henry."

My mouth moved, but nothing came out. Finally I stopped trying and stared at Ash mutely.

He nodded. "If it was murder, Adam Deering could have been the intended victim."

"Wolverson!"

I jumped backward, Ash jumped to his feet. We'd leaned so close, talking so quietly, that our heads had been almost touching.

"Yes, ma'am!" Ash stood ramrod straight.

Sheriff Kit Richardson stood in the doorway, looking from him to me and back again. "Please tell me this little scene has to do with an investigation."

I stood and started talking, but Ash spoke over the top of me. Which was easy enough, since he was almost a foot taller to begin with.

"Yes, ma'am," he repeated. "Ms. Hamilton here had some information regarding the death of Henry Gill."

"Hamilton?" The sheriff faced me and I felt myself squaring my shoulders and standing as tall as I ever had in my entire life. "Minnie Hamilton?"

"Yes, ma'am," Ash and I said simultaneously.

If I hadn't been at eye level with her teeth, I might have missed the short, tiny quirk that one side of her mouth made. "Wolverson, you're still working the accident-by-design angle?"

He nodded, and a part of me loosened that I hadn't

even known was tight. Ash wasn't keeping anything from Detective Inwood; he was being up-front about his theory and had taken it all the way to the sheriff. The detective must not agree with Ash's theory, and that was why Ash had been whispering to me.

"All right, then," Sheriff Richardson said. "Carry on, you two." She nodded at us and as she turned away, she looked at me. "I'd date him myself if I wasn't married," she said softly, and this time her smile wasn't hidden at all.

I left the sheriff's office directly after that little incident, and spent the rest of the evening on the couch rereading *The Stand*. After all, there was nothing like eight hundred and twenty-three pages of a postapocalyptic Stephen King horror/fantasy novel to make you forget that not only did your county sheriff know your name, for unknown and probably scary reasons, but she might also be trying her hand at a little matchmaking.

"As if I didn't get enough of that from Aunt Frances," I told Eddie as I pulled a lap blanket to my chin. My aunt was teaching a night class, so Eddie and I had the huge house to ourselves.

Eddie glared at me and jumped down.

"Okay," I said, "I take that back. Aunt Frances hasn't ever tried to set me up." At least not to my knowledge. But given her summer tendencies, I lived with the fear that she was biding her time as far as her niece was concerned.

Eddie must have forgiven my transgressions during the night, because the next morning I woke up on my stomach with him sprawled across my lower back. A few stretches and a long, hot shower later, I was in the car with a piece of toast, heading east to the other side of the state for an interlibrary event in Alpena.

My regional counterparts and I had a nice time talking about cooperative ventures, new programming, and electronic difficulties. We ended the morning with a happy discussion about books, and, despite the invitation to lunch, I made my good-byes and pointed my car back west. There were things that needed doing at the library—book fair–related things—and they couldn't wait.

Halfway back, though, the piece of toast I'd eaten for breakfast and the mini blueberry muffin I'd had in the library wore off completely. I needed food before I got back to the library and I needed it before I turned cranky from hunger.

I didn't have time for a full restaurant meal, which was just as well because I was driving through a lightly populated part of the state, an area where towns were rare and commercial establishments of any type were more likely to be boarded up than occupied.

"There's got to be something," I muttered, tapping the steering wheel. I'd seen a gas station somewhere along this stretch of two-lane highway on the way over, hadn't I? I pictured it in my head, a concrete block structure painted a perky light yellow. Gravel parking lot. April-empty flower planters. Two gas pumps, no canopy.

I was starting to think my hunger-saturated mind had mixed it up with a stretch of highway I'd seen in the Upper Peninsula a while back, when the curving road straightened out and there it was. BUB'S GAS AND MORE, read the sign, its paint peeling away from the wood.

There were a couple of cars in the rutted parking lot, so at least the place was open for business. And all I wanted was something to eat. Gas station sandwiches were often suspect, and you had to especially wonder about a sandwich made by a guy named Bub, but Bub was bound to have protein bars. Potato chips, even. Or popcorn. A bag of cheese-flavored popcorn would tide me over nicely.

I was bumping my car across the parking lot, already dreaming of yellowed fingers, when two people, a man and a woman, walked out the front door.

My mouth fell open.

He was very tall and solid. Her head barely reached the top of his shoulder. He wore a baseball cap, a zip sweatshirt, and well-aged jeans. She wore an attractively styled jacket over tailored dress pants and low-heeled pumps. He opened the driver's door of a sleek sedan, waited while she got in, then shut the door and went around to the passenger's side.

And while I was pretty sure I'd never seen her before in my life, I knew exactly who he was.

"It was Mitchell Koyne," I said.

Josh shook his head. "Not a chance."

"Over there?" Holly asked. "That's almost a hundred miles away. I've never heard of him setting foot outside Tonedagana County."

Though I knew Mitchell occasionally went down to Traverse City, I also knew what Holly meant. Mitchell was a library regular and one of those guys who, if he'd wanted to, was probably smart enough to do pretty much anything. The only thing was, what he seemed to want to do most was nothing. He lived in an apartment his sister had created for him in her house and made a little money working various construction jobs in the summer and running ski lifts in the winter. Though he'd spent a few months handing out business cards that proclaimed him an investigator, I wasn't sure the business had ever, or would ever, generate actual income.

"And he was with a girl?" Josh laughed. "What self-respecting female would go out with Mitchell Koyne?"

"He's not that bad." I didn't know whether it was his height, his cluelessness about life in general, or his un-tapped intelligence, but there was something about Mitchell that was oddly charming.

"Yeah?" Josh smirked. "I don't remember you going out with him when he asked."

"She's made it a personal rule not to ever date anyone who's more than eighteen inches taller than she is," Holly said.

Josh squinted one eye in my direction. "I can see how that could be a problem."

"You know what else is a problem?" Holly asked. "You." She pushed a stack of books across the break room table. The pile shoved aside the plate of cookies she'd brought in and came to stop directly in front of Josh. "These are some great books on decorating," she said. "If you're buying a house, you need to think about some of this stuff. It's a lot easier to paint and whatever else be-fore you move in. And I know what you're like, once you're moved in, you'll never go to the trouble of doing anything." She stopped, but he didn't say anything. "Well," she asked. "Are you buying a house or not?"

Josh reached around the books for a cookie. "Closed on it yesterday."

"You what?" Holly shrieked. "Why didn't you say anything?"

Laughing, I said, "I'll see you two later."

By the time I reached the doorway, Holly was opening books and pointing at pictures. I walked down the hallway to my office, grinning, because I knew that, at the end of the day, when the library lights were shut down, the books would still be on the table.

Five minutes later, my smile was gone. Vanished. Obliterated completely, and it was all due to a single e-mail.

"Hey, Minnie," it said. "I'm so sorry, but I won't be able to design a flyer for your book fair after all. A couple of big rush jobs came in and I just don't have the time. I'm really sorry."

I rubbed my eyes and tried to think.

"Delegate," Stephen had said every time we talked about the book fair. Delegation is a fine art, he'd said, and I needed to learn how to do it well if I was ever going to succeed him as director of the library.

So I'd delegated, and one of the first things I'd given away was the creation of the book fair flyer. Amanda Bell was a regular library patron, and from the conversations we'd had, I'd judged her as cheerful, competent, and willing to help. She'd recently started a Web site and graphic design business, and I'd asked her if she'd be interested in designing an extremely cool and attractive book fair flyer as a donation to the library. She'd jumped at the opportunity, and now . . .

I flopped my arms on my desk and laid my head down.

Clearly there was a lot more to the art of delegation than I'd realized. What was I going to do? I had to e-mail the flyer to area newspapers soon or they wouldn't get printed in time to get inserted. And if they didn't get inserted in time . . .

I grabbed my already empty ABOS coffee mug and headed back to the break room. Maybe Holly or Josh would still be in there. And no matter what, caffeine would help. Plus, if there was a cookie or two left, how could that be bad?

The break room was empty, which was technically good, because Holly and Josh and everyone else all had jobs to do, but bad for me because I'd hoped for a temporary distraction . . . and there it was.

Mitchell Koyne, whom I'd recently seen dozens of miles away, was standing at the front desk. I could detect no outward sign that a woman was involved in his life; he looked the way he always did. Hands in his pockets, his baseball hat on backward, and stubble on his face. How he managed to have a constant eighth-inch of beard I didn't know and would never ask.

"Hi, Mitchell," I said.

"Hey, Min." He grinned. "What's cooking?"

I turned my empty coffee mug upside down. "Not a thing."

Mitchell's laugh was loud and deep. It was hard not to smile when Mitchell laughed, and I glanced around. Yep, every single person I could see was smiling, from Donna, a part-time desk clerk, to the ancient Mr. Goodwin, down to Reva Shomin's youngest, who was just learning to walk.

"So, what," I asked, "were you doing out at Bub's Gas this morning?"

His laughter ended and his smile faded. It was as if his face had stopped. "I ... uh ..."

"Come on." I winked. "I know it was you. That hat? That height? I was coming back from Alpena and stopped for something to eat." And there were still popcorn kernels stuck between my teeth. "What were you doing way out there?"

"Um." He stared at me blankly, then glanced at the clock on the wall. "Look at the time. I gotta go. Talk to you later, Minnie, okay?" He slouched off and was out the front door before my mouth could open.

"Wow." Donna was leaning on the counter, watching Mitchell. "I didn't know he could move that fast."

Not once, in all the years I'd known Mitchell, had I ever seen him pay attention to the time. I wasn't even sure his watch actually worked.

"You saw him out at Bub's?" Donna asked. "What the heck was he doing out there? I wouldn't have thought Mitchell even knew how to get out of Tonedagana County." She laughed.

I smiled vaguely and wandered back to the break room. I still needed coffee and I still needed a book fair flyer. But now I was also wondering why Mitchell was being so weird.

Mitchell was a constant in our library life, a fixture almost as permanent as the fireplace in the reading room. I didn't like it that he was acting so differently. I didn't like it at all.

Chapter 5

The next day was a bookmobile day, and because of some social arrangements of Julia's that were too complicated for me to I understand, near the end of the day I dropped her off in the retail area of a small town. She gave Eddie an air kiss good-bye and waved at me, and after I closed the door behind her, we headed off to make a few drop-offs to the homebound folks.

The afternoon had grown thick with fog and I drove slowly along the narrow, hilly, twisting roads, watching carefully for deer, cars, and any pedestrians silly enough to go for a walk late on a dank, thick April day.

Mrs. Koski was all smiles when I handed her a bag of history books about late nineteenth-century Asia, and Mr. Blake gave me a nod of approval when I gave him a hefty pile of Nicholas Sparks and Janet Evanovich.

"You're not judging, are you?" I asked Eddie when I slid back into the driver's seat. "Because you have that look on your face."

The look he had was more of sleep than judgment,

but it amused me to pretend that he had opinions about these things. "Reading across gender lines is a good thing," I told him. "Species lines, too. Tell you what, next book I check out for you will be *The Poky Little Puppy.*"

I glanced over and saw that his eyes had opened.

"Okay, you're right," I acknowledged. "You're past that reading level. How about *Old Yeller*? Because watching the movie doesn't count."

He didn't seem any more interested in that offering.

"Yeah, too depressing," I said. "How about . . . hey, I got it. The Chet and Bernie books. You know, by Spencer Quinn? Chet's a dog and Bernie's a private investigator. You'll love Chet. He failed K-9 school and—"

"MrrrOOO!"

Eddie's howl hurt my ears, and wincing, I glanced at the clock. When Eddie started howling like that, it meant one of two things. Either he felt like howling or he was about to urp up his lunch. "Are you okay, pal? Because if you're just being Eddie-like and not feeling sick to your stomach, I have a new bag of books for Adam I'd like to deliver."

Eddie didn't say anything, and when I sneaked a quick look over, his face was mushed up against the carrier's wire door. Half his whiskers were sticking out and he was staring at me with unblinking yellow eyes.

Truly he was the weirdest cat in the universe. But since he didn't look as if he was in distress, I stopped at a wide spot in the road and put on the four-way flashers. I pulled out my cell—Half strength! Hooray!—and called the Deerings' house.

"Hey, Adam, it's Minnie. I have a bag of books for you, if you want them."

"Does a drowning man want a rope?" he asked. "Does a starving man want bacon? No, that's a poor metaphor. A man wants bacon three times a day. Four if his wife would let him."

I laughed. "I'm about ten minutes away, but it'll take me about that long to walk up the hill."

"Timing is everything," Adam said. "I'll meet you at the mailbox. I was headed out there anyway. Someone from FedEx just called, saying they were dropping off a package. I didn't know they called ahead. Must be an Up North thing." He laughed.

I'd never heard of FedEx calling anyone, either, but then I always had things delivered to the library, so what did I know? Frowning, I said, "You're not walking, are you? I know you want to recover as quickly as possible, but—"

"Relax," he said. "I'm taking the car. The one with the automatic transmission."

"You're a smart man."

"Make sure you tell Irene, okay? She thinks I'm an idiot."

Since I knew for a fact that his wife thought he was handsome, brilliant, and the best husband in the world, I just said, "See you in a few."

But ten minutes later, I was still a quarter mile from his house. The fog had thickened to the point of opacity and I was driving at a rate that didn't even register on the speedometer.

I'd heard some explanations for the spring fogs. Some made sense, that the thawing of the winter-frozen earth chilled the adjacent air, causing a deep ground fog, and some didn't, case in point being Rafe's straight-faced story that spring fogs indicated how deep the snow would be the next winter.

"Who knew that fog could get so thick?" I muttered. "If the fog in London is thicker than this, I don't want to have to ever walk through it."

Eddie didn't comment, and I didn't dare look away from the road to see what he was doing. Slowly and carefully I found the barnyard entrance next to Deering's driveway without going past even once, turned in, and parked.

I unbuckled my seat belt. "I won't be gone long, so—"

"Mrr!"

"Eddie—"

"*Mrrrw!*"

"Okay, fine." I leaned over to unlatch the carrier door. "But if I find even one hairball on one book, you're banned from the bookmobile for a week."

Eddie bolted out of the carrier and, in long feline-fluid motion, jumped to the dashboard.

"Sure, you look innocent now," I said, "but I know that feline innocence is an oxymoron. There's no such thing."

My cat ignored me and began licking his hind leg.

"Well, back at you," I said, barely aware that I was losing an argument with a creature who couldn't talk. "And I'm taking the keys."

"Mrr."

I patted his head, which made him squint, picked up the bulging bag of books, and headed out into the mist. It swirled thick about my legs and I suddenly realized that my recent rereading of Stephen King was not a good preparation the present moment. Not that *The Stand* was horror, exactly, but I was familiar enough with Mr. King's books to know what his imagination could do with fog.

Creeping in on little cat feet, it was. Not Eddie feet, though, because Eddie's feet were big enough for a cat twice his size and he was only occasionally capable of moving silently. Any other cat would be as soundless as this fog, insidious and sticky, clever and . . . and what was that?

Had I heard a noise? What was . . . ?

"Adam?" I called. "Is that you?"

"Hey, Minnie," he said. "A real pea-souper, isn't it?"

His voice was coming from a different direction than whatever it was I thought I'd heard, but fog did funny things to sound. At least that was what I'd gathered from all those scary books I'd read as a kid.

"And I don't even like pea soup," I said. My toes hit the main road and I turned right, toward Adam and Irene's mailbox, where I assumed Adam would be. "That was the only bad thing about my mom baking ham. You knew pea soup was coming along in a few days."

"Love the stuff," Adam said. "Irene makes the best ever."

The disembodied noise of a car came toward us. I stepped off the asphalt onto the outside of the road's shoulder, just to be safe, and kept walking. An Adam-sized shape materialized. He was facing me, standing in front of a mailbox-shaped object, his back to the approaching car.

"Best pea soup ever?" I asked. "No such thing."

"Au contraire," Adam said, and went on to extoll the

virtues of what I considered the most unappetizing food in the world, next to all mushrooms. And it was because I wasn't really paying attention to him that I saw the car coming out of the fog.

Coming in our direction.

Straight toward Adam, who didn't see it, didn't hear it, didn't even know it was there.

There was no time to warn him, no time to do anything except act.

I dropped the books and sprang forward, head tucked, arms outstretched in my best imitation of the football player I'd never been or ever wanted to be. As I thumped into Adam with all my weight, I could have sworn I heard a faint feline howl.

We fell to the ground hard. I twisted my shoulders, trying hard to rotate my momentum, wanting desperately to roll us over and away from the car.

Over and over we went, off the road, off the shoulder, and half into the ditch. Was it far enough? Would the car swerve? Would it still get us? I pushed into the ground with my feet and sent us one roll farther.

The car whooshed past and disappeared into the gloom.

"Are you okay?" Adam's voice was weak.

"I'm fine. How about you?"

At the end of the last roll, I'd ended on my back. I pushed myself to my knees and looked hard at the fog, making sure the vehicle was really gone. I saw no sign of the not-quite-a-killer car and breathed a sigh of relief.

"I'm fine," Adam said.

His voice, normally full of laughter and bonhomie,

sounded thready and old. Guylike, he hadn't worn a coat on his trip to the mailbox, even though the temperature was only in the mid-forties. He wore jeans, sneakers, and a plain maroon sweatshirt that showed evidence of more than one painting chore. There were spatters of white, brown, and even a color that was exactly three shades darker than the sweatshirt itself.

It wasn't until he touched that particular shade that I realized it was in a vertical line on his chest and that it wasn't paint at all.

"Adam," I said as calmly as possible, "you're bleeding."

He looked down and made a move to pull up his shirt and sweatshirt, but I yelped at him, "Stop!"

"But I'm bleeding." He reached for the bottom of his sweatshirt again and I grabbed at his hand.

"Anything we do now won't help and could make it worse," I said firmly. "Your clothes might be sealing the wound, and if we pull it away, it'll bleed even more." I wasn't sure how much of that might be true, but it sounded reasonable. Maybe I'd learned some medical stuff through sheer proximity to Tucker.

Adam looked half convinced. At least he stopped trying to look at his incision.

"Can you get up?" I asked.

"Of course I can." He put his hands on the ground and moved one foot forward to stand. Halfway up, he swayed.

Adam was almost a foot taller than me and probably a hundred pounds heavier, and if I tried to hold him upright, we'd both fall to the ground again and injure who knew what, so I rushed to his side and leaned into his body, bracing him.

"You are not fine," I said, panting a little as I helped him stand upright, "so don't try to tell me so. You're going to go over to your car and sit in the passenger's seat. Then you're not going to move until I make a couple of phone calls."

"Don't call 911." He leaned on my shoulder as we shuffled off. "Our insurance hardly covers ambulance rides."

"We'll see," I said. Fifteen feet later, I opened his car door and waited until he eased himself down into the seat. The dark stain on his sweatshirt looked a little bigger, but not massively bigger. "My cell's in the bookmobile. I'll be right back."

He nodded and I raced off. Inside the bookmobile, Eddie was lying in a meat loaf shape on the console.

"Mrr," he said.

"Adam's fine," I told him as I rustled in my backpack for the phone. "At least I'm pretty sure he is. You going to be okay in here by yourself? It might be a while before I get back."

My cat closed his eyes and purred.

"For an Eddie, you are okay." I kissed the top of his furry head and, locking the door behind me, scampered back to Adam, picking up the bag of books on the way. "What's your wife's work number?" I asked, stowing the books in the backseat.

"What time is it?" Adam's face was pale and his eyes were closed.

"Um . . ." I glanced at the phone. "Half past five."

"Then she's just starting her night job. She's waiting tables at the Mitchell Street Pub."

I entered the popular Petoskey restaurant's name into a search engine and within seconds a voice on the other end was asking what he could do for me.

"Could I please speak to Irene Deering? There's been an minor emergency at her home."

"Sure. Hang on."

A few moments later, Irene's breathless voice came on the line. "Adam? Are you okay?"

"This is Minnie, and Adam is fine." I waited a beat for that message of comfort to sink in. "But there's been a little accident."

"Accident?" The word came out shrill. "What's wrong? I'll be there right away. I can leave right now and—"

"He's fine. Really. Here, talk to him." I handed over the phone.

"Hey, babe," Adam said casually. "No, I'm fine. I was down at the mailbox to pick up a FedEx delivery the same time Minnie dropped by with another bag of books. Some yahoo was driving down the road, not paying attention, and Minnie pushed me out of the way." He glanced at me. I nodded and gave him a thumbs-up. "I fell down and my incision got knocked a little loose, is all. I told Minnie I'm fine, but—" He listened, rolled his eyes, and handed the phone back to me.

"Minnie," Irene said, "I hate to ask, but . . ." Her voice tailed off. "No, forget I said anything. I'll see if I can get the night off. Thanks for calling."

"I'm happy to take him to the hospital." I waved down Adam's protest. "If it's okay to drive your car, that is, and if your neighbor won't mind if the bookmobile is parked next door for a couple of hours."

"Oh, Minnie," she said raggedly. "I don't know how to thank you."

"You'll think of something." I laughed. "Just don't make it a frozen batch of pea soup."

Forty-five minutes later, Adam was in the Charlevoix Hospital's emergency room and I was sitting in the waiting room, reading one of the books I'd brought him, *The Amazing Adventures of Kavalier & Clay* by Michael Chabon, and it was compelling enough to make me forget that the last time I'd been in this room I'd been waiting for Tucker to get done with his shift. I'd just started the third chapter when I heard a rustling noise at my left elbow. I kept reading, hoping the noise would go away and leave me alone. At least until the end of the chapter.

"Hey," Adam said. "Is that one of my books?"

I flipped it shut. "Not any more. You can have it when I'm done."

He grinned. "Fair's fair."

"You're all set?" I asked. "You know Irene's going to want a full report."

"The incision itself is fine, but they bandaged the crap out of it just to be sure." He made a face. "All that tape is going to pull on my chest hair something fierce when I take it off."

"Do it in the shower." I squared the book on my lap, but didn't stand. "So you're ready to go?"

"Sure am. I didn't even get a new prescription."

"Then there's only one thing to do before I take you home."

Adam frowned. "What's that?"

"Call the sheriff."

Detective Inwood sat on the edge of the chair he'd dragged over from the Deerings' dining table. "You say the car didn't swerve, but was heading straight for Mr. Deering?"

I nodded at Adam. He was sitting up in his recliner, but I wasn't sure how long he was going to stay awake. Actually I wasn't sure he had stayed awake through the previous fifteen minutes of questions, but at least he was home where he belonged, and not in the sheriff's office, which was where the detective had wanted to talk to him.

"Absolutely not," I had said. "The man had emergency heart surgery less than two weeks ago. He's exhausted. The last thing he needs is to sit in that little room for an hour, staring at the dragon on the ceiling tiles until you have time to show up."

Inwood sighed. "And I suppose you have an alternative plan."

Of course I did. "I'll drive Adam home. You can come and talk to him."

"And this can't wait until morning why?"

"No time like the present," I said briskly. "Besides, he shouldn't be driving and his wife can't take time off work to bring him to you. You're going to have to come out here one way or another. Might as well get it done now."

"My wife has dinner waiting."

I felt a pang of guilt, but squashed it down. "I'm sorry for that, but I'm sure she's used to warming things up."

He sighed. "We'll be out in half an hour."

And indeed, half an hour later Deputy Ash Wolverson knocked on the front door. Detective Inwood was behind him, his shoulders drooping. We settled into the living room in short order, and now I could feel the questions coming to a close.

"Absolutely," I said, nodding toward Adam. "It wasn't a gentle swerve that was corrected with a jerk, you know, like sometimes happens when you're reaching for something on the floor of the passenger's seat and drift over a little, then realize what you're doing and . . ." The three men were looking at me with identically disapproving expressions. "Not that I've done that," I said quickly. Not lately, anyway. "What I'm saying is that it looked intentional. Not like a mistake."

The detective gave a faint sigh, and I remembered the conversations I'd had the last time I showed up at the sheriff's office. About eyewitnesses, and how they can't be trusted to get details right.

I decided to go at it a different way. "I know this isn't proof of anything, but it just didn't feel like an accident."

Though Inwood kept looking at his notebook, his eyebrows went up. "Didn't feel like an accident," he said slowly, writing down the words. Or at least that's what I assumed he was writing. If he was writing "Minnie Hamilton shouldn't be allowed out by herself," I didn't want to know about it.

"That's right. It felt like . . ." I hesitated, then forged ahead with the inappropriate thought that had popped into my head. "It felt like Christine was trying to make Adam her next victim."

Inwood stopped writing. "Who's Christine?"

Ash laughed. "Book or movie?"

"Book. The movie is too scary." We smiled at each other and a warm fuzzy feeling wrapped itself around me. I'd tried to get Tucker to read horror books, but he'd pushed them away and asked why I wasted my time on that junk.

Inwood was frowning at the exchange. "Anyone care to enlighten me? Deputy?"

"Yes, sir," Ash said. "Sorry. It's the title of a book by Stephen King, later made into a movie. The title character is a possessed car who kills by a variety of methods."

Inwood turned the page of his notebook. "Is there anything else you can tell us, Mr. Deering?"

"No, I can't think of—"

I snapped my fingers. "FedEx. You said you were down at the mailbox to pick up a Federal Express package. Did you even order anything?"

"Not me, but I thought maybe Irene had."

"Call her," Detective Inwood said. "Find out."

Adam picked up his cell phone from the side table. "Hey, it's me. Have you ordered anything lately? Something that might have come FedEx?" He looked at the detective. "Okay, thanks, babe. No, I'm fine. I'll see you when you get home," he said, and thumbed off the phone.

"No order," Inwood said.

Adam shook his head. "She said she hasn't bought anything online for a couple of months."

"Would anyone else be sending you something?" the detective asked.

"Can't think who," Adam said. "But I can call around and check."

Inwood made a note. "Don't bother. I'll contact Federal Express and see if there was a delivery scheduled to your home."

"If there wasn't," I said, sitting on the edge of the chair, "then this is proof that someone killed Henry and tried to kill Adam, too."

Inwood looked at me. "Proof?" he asked, and I thought I heard sorrow in his voice. "The only proof in any of this is that Mr. Deering here has a tendency to get himself into accidents."

My face went warm. "Oh, really?" I asked. "You think all this is—"

The detective held up his hand. "Proof," he reminded me. "You were talking about proof. It's a very narrow definition, Ms. Hamilton. What we have is theories and suppositions, none of which would interest the county prosecutor in the least."

Since I didn't even know the name of the county's prosecuting attorney, I had to take his word for it. "But you have to admit that something weird is going on. I mean, what are the odds that two bizarre accidents would happen to the same guy in less than two weeks?"

Ash looked up from his notes. "I wouldn't call a tree falling on a man out in the woods bizarre. Unusual, sure, but accidents happen."

I frowned. Wasn't he supposed to be on my side? "Maybe not, but combine the falling tree with this car almost running him over. That can't be something that happens on a regular basis."

The glance exchanged by Ash and the detective confirmed the truth of my statement.

"We will explore all possibilities," Detective Inwood said, tucking his notebook into his pocket. "I know the deputy here has the sheriff convinced there's a possibility that Mr. Deering was, in fact, the intended murder victim all along." He smiled faintly. "I think he's nuts, but it's his theory and he's welcome to it."

"And what do you think?" I asked. "Two unlikely accidents or one murder and one attempted murder?"

"We will explore all possibilities," the detective repeated. "If Mr. Gill's death was murder, we'll find out. If Mr. Deering's accident was a murder attempt, we'll find out. Please assure him that we'll put as many hours as we can into resolving this."

My chin went up. "Why are you talking as if Adam isn't even here? He's not an idiot, he's just recovering from surgery."

"And he's asleep," Inwood said, gesturing in Adam's direction. "We'll be in contact, Ms. Hamilton. Tell Mr. Deering that if he thinks of anything else that's pertinent"—he stressed the last word—"he should let us know immediately."

The three of us got to our feet and I escorted them to the front door. It had been an odd little session, but at least they seemed to be taking the whole thing seriously.

Somewhere in the house, a clock started chiming the hour. I matched my steps to the beats and got to nine just as I reached the door. Nine o'clock? How could it be that late? At least I had an excuse for being so hungry.

And that reminded me. I looked up at Detective Inwood. "Sorry about your evening. Um, what was for dinner?"

"Pea soup," he said. "Hate the stuff, to tell you the truth." He flashed a sudden smile. "And by the way, it's not a dragon."

I stared at him, uncomprehendingly. The poor man. He'd clearly lost it.

"Sit on the other side of the table next time. You'll see what I mean."

He opened the door and was gone before my brain caught up and remembered my earlier reference to the interview room ceiling tiles. Ash nodded at me and followed his boss. I closed the door behind them and watched out the side window as they got into the unmarked car and drove away down the hill, their taillights disappearing fast.

"Proof," I murmured. Inwood had said it was a narrow definition. One of the phrases I'd heard most often as a child had been "Look it up, Minnie." That simple instruction had probably steered me in the librarian direction from the time I could read. Not only because I loved to learn, but also because I loved to look at the explanatory pictures and diagrams in my parents' dictionary. For a librarian, this was a little embarrassing to admit, so I tried not to mention it. Ever.

I glanced around for a dictionary, half hoping to see the same one I'd grown up with, but didn't see any reference books. On the other hand, I had a smart phone. A few finger taps later, I had a definition in front of me. "Something sufficient to establish something else as correct or true."

It didn't sound narrow to me. Matter of fact, it sounded wide-open. How could Inwood need more proof that

Henry had been murdered than an attempt on Adam's life?

But it was obvious that he didn't think Adam's almost-accident was anything other than an accident. Oh, sure, he'd paid lip service to the idea and said the right things about exploring all yada-yada-yah, but he didn't really mean it, not down deep.

For a short instant I heard my mom's voice in my head. *"Now, Minnie, don't go thinking that you know for certain what anyone else is thinking or feeling. No matter what, all you have is a guess."*

I snorted. My mother wanted proof, too. Maybe she should have been a detective instead of a historian.

Mom kept on going. *"Respect other points of view, Minerva Joy. Only then will others respect your own."*

How that particular set of Mom Wisdom was going to help in this circumstance, I wasn't sure. Then again, more than once Mom's advice had proven useful when I'd least expected it to, so I probably shouldn't discount any of it, which would please her to no end.

If I ever mentioned it, that is.

Now that the room had two less law enforcement officers in it, I unlatched Eddie's carrier. I'd carried him in from the bookmobile when I brought Adam back home and he'd been sleeping the entire time. "Ready to come out?" I asked.

Eddie picked up his head and blinked. "Mrr?"

"Until Irene gets home," I said. "Shouldn't be much longer."

He closed his eyes and curled up into a ball half the size that he should have been able to curl up into.

"They're gone?" Adam was blinking and scrubbing his face with the palms of his hands. "Sorry, I must have fallen asleep."

"They left a few minutes ago," I said, getting up from my crouch and moving into the sofa across from his recliner. "Do you want anything? Food, drink, television?"

He shook his head. "I'm fine. Thanks for everything, but there's no reason for you to stay. It's getting late. Why don't you go on home?"

I shrugged, not wanting to tell him that his wife and I were conspiring to keep him quiet and comfortable. "My aunt isn't home tonight and it's a big house for one." Which was true. What I didn't add was that I didn't mind being alone every once in a while. Needed it, really. "If you don't mind, I'd just as soon hang out here for a while."

"No problem," he said, yawning. "If you leave, I'll just flop here and think too much, so stay, by all means."

"Is it possible to think too much?" I asked.

He moved his head in something that wasn't quite a nod, but wasn't exactly a head shake, either.

"C'mon," I said, sliding down into a lazy slouch. "There's no one here but me and Eddie. He won't talk, and I won't, either, not if you don't want me to."

"It's nothing," he muttered.

Right. And I was going to grow six inches next year. But I didn't say anything, just sat back and let the silence grow more comfortable. My own thinking drifted away, off to Tucker, and the upcoming summer. Then I thought about Henry and how summers for his children would be different from here on out, and—

"I think someone is trying to kill me," Adam said suddenly.

"You . . . do?" Maybe he hadn't been as asleep during that last part of the conversation as the three of us had thought.

"If that car really was trying to hit me, and it sure seemed like it, how can I think anything else? If it wasn't an accident, and I don't see how it was . . ." He stopped.

I completed the sentence in my head. *It was attempted murder.*

"So here I am," he said, "supposed to be resting so I can recover from surgery as quickly as possible, but someone might be trying to kill me. How do I figure out what's going on?" He slapped the arm of his chair. "From this recliner, how can I find out who killed Henry and tried to kill me? How will I ever be able to find out who was the real target? Was I the target and Henry was killed by accident? Was Henry the target and someone's trying to kill me because of what I might have seen? Could someone have wanted to kill both of us?"

They were all excellent questions, and I had an excellent response ready. "Tell you what." I sat up from my slouch. "I can do a little research about all this. Do some digging on Henry. Ask a few questions about him, maybe about you."

Adam's face brightened, but the look faded and he shook his head. "I can't let you do that. Besides, Detective Inwood and Deputy Wolverson will be doing the same thing. Thanks for the offer, though."

Behind me, I heard a familiar *pad-pad-pad* noise. "Eddie, where are—" My cat jumped on the back of the couch. "Ah. There you are." I reached back and pulled him around to sit on my lap, but he struggled away from me and walked up onto the arm of the couch closest to Adam.

He sat. "Mrr," he said, staring straight at Adam. "Mrr."

Adam moved his head so he could see around the large furry creature. "You speak cat. What does he want?"

"Pretend he's a Magic 8 Ball." I nodded in Eddie's direction. "Ask him a question, any question."

"Are you serious?"

"Try it."

Adam put on a serious expression and stared straight into my cat's yellow eyes. "O wise Eddie, should I have leftover pizza for dinner or leftover macaroni and cheese?"

There was a short pause, and then Eddie said, "Mrr?"

"The pizza is from Sunday," Adam replied. "Irene made the macaroni and cheese yesterday."

Eddie's stare was intent.

"Yeah, you're right. I should have finished that pizza days ago." Adam smiled. "Here's a tougher question—should I let your Minnie help me, or should I—"

But he didn't get to finish his sentence, because Eddie made a long leap to the arm of his recliner, head-butted his shoulder, and started purring.

Loudly.

Adam laughed in a gentle sort of way and reached out to pet my cat. "Apparently Eddie thinks it's a good idea that you help me out."

"Eddie's wisdom knows no bounds," I said. Which was

true, but I was pretty sure the lower boundary, the one of minimal wisdom, was the edge he was pushing. Though I loved my cat dearly, I wasn't about to grant him great powers of mental acuity.

"Well . . ." Adam pulled his head out of the way as Eddie flipped his tail around. "If you're sure it's not an imposition, it would be great to have someone I know and trust do a little research."

For a second I didn't know what to say. Yes, I was pretty sure I was a trustworthy person, but that was because I knew myself on the inside. To have someone else say so was a compliment so deep I wasn't sure how to respond.

"Mrr," Eddie said, flapping his tail against Adam's ear.

"Yes, of course I trust you, too," Adam said. "That goes without saying."

"Mrr."

"You're welcome."

"M—"

"All right, you two, enough already," I said.

Adam grinned.

Eddie glared at me and swiped his tail across Adam's face.

On Friday, I spent a large share of the day trying to design a book fair flyer. An hour past quitting time, I stared at mess I'd created and came to the not-so-profound conclusion that I was a much better librarian than I was a graphic designer.

I told Eddie all about it that night as I emptied the contents of my dresser into a cardboard box. He gave me a blank look that clearly meant he thought I had my priorities messed up, then walked out into the hallway and *thud-thud-thudd*ed down the wooden stairs.

"What do cats know about graphic design, anyway?" I asked, and finished packing without the help of my cat. Packing was at this point a near imperative, because my aunt's spring-cleaning crew would descend on the boardinghouse first thing Monday morning. It was a little early for them to show up, but their schedule was crowded this year and this was the best slot available for my aunt. She'd said I could stay for the duration, but I'd rather endure a few chilly nights on the houseboat than endure the sounds and astringent smells of a thorough housecleaning.

I'd scheduled myself to work all Saturday because of various staff members taking spring vacations, so I didn't have time to move the last of my things down to the marina until Sunday. The very last things I put in my car were a small suitcase, my backpack, and Eddie's cat carrier.

Aunt Frances stood on the sidewalk, her arms wrapped tight around her since she hadn't put on a coat and her light cardigan wasn't enough to keep out the chill.

"Are you sure you're going to be warm enough down there?" she asked, rubbing her hands over her upper arms.

"Just because you're cold because you're not dressed properly doesn't mean I'm going to get hypothermia." I buckled Eddie and his carrier into the front seat and shut the car door. "I have a space heater, Eddie has a fur coat, and it's supposed to warm up in a few days. We'll be fine."

"If you get cold, you have to promise you'll come back until it gets warmer."

"Promise," I said, giving her a hug.

"You're a good girl," she murmured, hugging back.

I gave her a last squeeze and climbed into the driver's seat. "Leave the worrying to my mother. She's a lot better at it than either of us. Might as well give the job to the best-qualified candidate, don't you think?"

Aunt Frances laughed and waved—"Bye, Eddie!"— as I backed out of the driveway. When I reached the road and braked to put the transmission into drive, I glanced up the drive to my aunt. She was still standing there, arms tight around her, only now she looked . . . well, sad.

I sat there in the middle of the street, unsure. Aunt Frances had lived alone for years before I moved north, so I'd never once thought about how lonely she might be when I left in the summers. Sure, the boarders would arrive in a few weeks, but it could be a long few weeks for her. Maybe I should stay. I owed her so much; enduring a cleaning crew was nothing compared to all she'd done for me. Yes. I would stay. I would keep her company until—

Aunt Frances looked up and past me. Her face lit up with a wide, happy smile and she called out something I couldn't hear.

I turned my head to see the object of her happiness. It was Otto, striding down the sidewalk, heading straight toward my aunt.

My foot came off the brake. "What do you think of that, Eddie?" I asked, smiling. "We're barely out of the house and her boyfriend comes over. Kind of makes you think we were cramping her style, doesn't it?"

Eddie bonked his head against the side of the carrier and flopped down.

"No comment? Well, I can understand that. Your little kitty feelings are hurt. You thought you were Aunt Frances's best beau, didn't you?"

"Mrr," he said somewhat sulkily.

Shaking my head, I flicked on the blinker and turned left. There were days when I really did wonder if he knew what I was saying.

Eddie and I arrived at the marina in short order. I left everything behind except the carrier, and it was me and my cat who walked down the wide wooden dock and stepped aboard my summer residence, which was the cutest little houseboat possible.

Made primarily of plywood long ago in a Chilson backyard, it boasted one bedroom with two bunks, a tiny bathroom, and a small kitchen with a dining area. As much as I loved the tidy interior spaces, I loved the view from the outside deck even more. The sheer pleasure of being able to see Janay Lake on my doorstep morning, noon, or night was worth the work of moving twice a year.

I set the carrier on the dining bench and opened the door. "We're home, Eddie."

"Mrr," he said, and zoomed out of the carrier, down the steps, and onto the bed, where he would get cat hair on the comforter before I'd slept in it even once.

I sighed a happy sigh. Home was indeed a good place to be.

Three hours later, I'd finished unpacking and hauled all the flattened cardboard boxes down to the storage bin that went with my slip.

After texting Tucker—*Eddie and I are all moved in. Miss you!*—and receiving a quick *Don't get 2 cold up there see u soon* in return, I came in the houseboat's door and stood in the small kitchen, surveying my home for the next few months.

"What do you think, pal?"

Eddie was already in one of his favorite spots from last summer, the back of the bench seat that was half of my dining area. He'd already prowled around the whole place a dozen times, sniffing and stretching and poking into things that he had no reason to poke into. Behind the small dresser I used as a nightstand, for one. Underneath the small kitchen sink, for another. Now he was lying, meat-loaf-shaped, on the seat back, looking over the houseboat as if he were the ruler of all.

"You're not the king, you know," I told him. "This is a partnership, remember?"

Which reminded me of the odd partnership Adam and Henry had shared, making maple syrup and who knew what else? I'd told Adam I would try to help, to do some research. But useful research requires a pointed question; otherwise it's only information-gathering.

"Which is usually interesting," I said, "but not always immediately useful."

Eddie stretched out one paw and rested his chin on the seat.

"Yeah, I know. It's up to me to figure out the right questions." I slid onto the bench opposite Eddie. "How about this? Let's assume . . . I know, you don't like assuming, but work with me on this. For right now, let's assume that Henry was killed by the same person who tried to run over Adam. What could a lifelong resident of Tonedagana County have in common with a newcomer with no family roots in Michigan who is more than twenty years younger?"

My cat's response was a heavy sigh.

"Okay, maybe that's not the right question." I thought a minute. "Here's another one. Henry was an insurance agent for a company in Petoskey before he retired. Adam is an accountant who works remotely for companies in Chicago. What could tie them together?"

Eddie moved his other front leg. Now both of them were stretched out in front of him. Supercat.

"The only thing they seem to have in common is a lack of friends. Adam hasn't been here long enough, and Henry didn't seem to have any." At the library, Donna had told me that when Henry's wife was alive they'd been very social, but since her death he'd retreated more and more. "I just don't see how that could matter to—"

Eddie stood and, without a backward glance, jumped down. I turned to watch as he stalked through the kitchen, down the few steps, and into the bedroom. He jumped up and out of view. This didn't bother me until I heard a rustling sound that I didn't recognize.

And then I suddenly did.

I bolted off the seat, ran through the kitchen, jumped over the steps in a single bound, and was in the bedroom in seconds, trying to reach my cat before he destroyed the library books I'd laid on the spare bed.

"Eddie! Leave that alone!"

My cat turned. Blinked straight at me. And sat down right on top of a book Stephen had handed me to read. "Funny," I said, pulling the copy of *101 Ways to Improve Your Communication Skills Instantly* out from underneath him. "If you're nice, I'll read it out loud to you at dinner. That way we'll both learn something."

Eddie stared at me for a long moment. Then he jumped down and marched into the back of my tiny closet.

"If you're going to be like that," I said, "I'm going to the restaurant. Kristen likes me just the way I am, poor communication skills and all."

From out of the closet came a muffled "Mrr."

"The cat food dish is where it always is," I told him. "On the floor next to the kitchen sink."

"Mrr."

"You're welcome," I said and, smiling, headed out for a night of watching Kristen cook. And with any luck, I'd also come up with some ideas for a reason someone might want to kill two men who were different in almost every way.

Chapter 6

The next morning I woke up with the feel of cat fur against my right ear. "Eddie," I said, "I love you dearly, and I'm pretty sure you have kind feelings for me, but do you really have to be this close?"

Other than starting up a quiet purr, he didn't reply. Just then the alarm clock started beeping. I reached outside the cocoon of covers to turn it off and was suddenly wide-awake. Of its own volition, my arm made a quick retreat to the warmth it had previously been enjoying. No wonder Eddie was wrapped up around my only exposed skin—it was freezing out there!

If it was actually freezing, I could have some serious issues with frozen pipes and engines and who knew what, but last night's forecast hadn't called for anything close to thirty-two degrees. However, I didn't like leaving the space heater on overnight, and the forty-three-degree low they'd called for last night was a lot lower than the sixty-five degrees I was used to up in the boardinghouse.

Eddie and I snuggled together until the alarm went off a second time. I reached out to slap it off. "You with the fur coat," I said to my cat. "How about getting up and turning on the space heater in the bathroom?"

"Mrr," he said sleepily.

"You're not moving," I said, pointing out the oh so obvious.

He burrowed deeper.

"Okay, I can see that I'm going to have to do this all by myself." I took a deep breath and, like ripping off a bandage, tossed back the covers and jumped out of bed. The cold hit hard and it took an act of supreme courage not to jump right back into where I'd been.

"I'm up," I told Eddie, my skin prickling as I quickly pulled on fleece sweatpants and sweatshirt over my pajamas. "How about you?"

He opened one eye and stared at me with it. I could almost feel the thought coming out of his little kitty brain: humans do the darnedest things.

"With you, pal," I said, my teeth chattering. "I am definitely with you." I fled for the bathroom, knowing that my upcoming shower wouldn't last long enough to thoroughly warm me. My houseboat was wonderful in many ways, but the size of its water heater was on the highly inadequate side. Eddie was right; humans—at least this human—weren't always very smart.

"Morning, sunshine," Holly said, pushing a cartful of books past the reference desk. "Say, didn't you move to the marina this weekend? Bet it was cold down there this morning."

"It wasn't so bad." After all, once I arrived at the library, it had only taken an hour and three cups of coffee to stop my shivering. "A little cold is good for the soul," I said virtuously.

She snorted. "Right. And eating peas will turn my hair curly."

I looked at her shiny, smooth hair. The overly curly black locks I'd been handed at birth had been the bane of my existence for years. "My mom told me that eating bread crusts would make my hair go straight."

A tall woman with dark blond hair and a quiet smile had come near the desk while we'd been talking. She nodded and said, "My mom told me I'd get sick if I ate chocolate chip cookie dough."

Holly smiled at Irene Deering. "Did you?"

"Only time was when I grabbed half the batch and ate it in the attic before anyone found me."

We laughed, Holly moved on with her cart, and Irene stood in front of the desk. "Do you have a minute?" she asked.

"I live to serve. Ask away." Then a worrying thought struck me. "Is Adam doing okay?"

"He's fine. And thanks again for your help the other day. I don't know what we would have done without you. No, don't wave away my thanks," she said. "I'm going to show my appreciation whether you like it or not."

"Not," I said.

"Well, I want to thank you for everything you've done. It means the world to us."

Whatever. I squirmed. "How's Adam doing with those books I dropped off?"

She smiled. "Already done with most of them, if you can believe it."

I started to stand. "Then you're here to get some more. I have just the—" But she was shaking her head. I sat down and saw the tension around her mouth. Noted the rigidity of her thin shoulders. "What's the matter, Irene?"

She swallowed. "I'm scared," she whispered.

My heart went out to her. Of course she was scared. Her husband had just had emergency heart surgery and then had almost been killed. Who wouldn't be scared? "It'll be okay," I said softly. "Adam will get better; he's young and strong and will come out of this fine. And the police will figure out who—"

She was shaking her head again. "It's not that. Well, it is, but I'm scared it's all my fault."

The idea sounded ridiculous, but I didn't laugh. "How could that be?" I asked.

There was no one within earshot, but she looked left and right and then edged up to the very front of the desk. "Adam's an accountant." She was talking to the countertop, but I nodded anyway. "He's a very good accountant and he was making a lot of money in Chicago working for a big firm. Now that he's on his own he doesn't have many clients, but he's getting there and someday everything will be fine."

"Okay," I said, drawing out the word a little, and not having any idea where this was going.

She blew out a breath. "One of the things Adam does really well is find bookkeeping anomalies. It's what made his reputation. Companies came to the firm he worked for just to get his opinion."

I waited for her to go on, because this was clearly leading up to something.

"Anyway," she said, "a few years ago, Adam turned someone in to the IRS. He'd found evidence of fraud and was obligated by law to report this guy, Seth Wartella, who was ultimately convicted of tax fraud and sent to jail."

I wanted to ask a question, but I could tell that Irene had started the real part of the story and I didn't want to interrupt before it was over.

"For a long time I barely thought about it," she said in a crowded rush. "It was years ago. It was history. It was over and done with and Wartella had never really been in our life; he'd just been a client's employee that, by law, Adam had to report. Adam testified and I went to watch, but that was it. Wartella had committed tax fraud and embezzled, and went to jail because of it, and none of that was Adam's fault," she said in a fierce whisper.

"Of course it wasn't," I said. "It would be ridiculous to think otherwise."

"The only thing is . . ." Irene's voice was strained. "A couple of Saturdays back, I could swear I saw Seth Wartella."

"A couple of weeks ago?" I asked, trying to summon a mental calendar.

She nodded. "The same weekend Henry died."

Detective Inwood's pen wrote for a long time before he looked up again. When he did, his gaze settled on me for a brief moment before he went back to Irene. "All right, Mrs. Deering. Please continue."

Right after Irene had told me about Seth Wartella, I'd called the sheriff's office and made an appointment with Inwood. "Is this urgent?" he'd asked tiredly. Which wasn't a good thing, since it was still morning.

"On a scale of one to ten," I'd said, "with ten being a falling rock about to hit my head, I'd say this is a seven."

"Come down at noon," he'd said, sighing. "I'll fit you in."

So here we were, in that old familiar interview room. I'd made the strategic error of letting Irene enter first and I ended up in my regular seat. While we'd waited for the detective, I'd craned my head around, trying to see the ceiling dragon from the point of view of the table's other side without moving over there, but all I got was a crick in my neck and an odd look from Irene.

Now Irene was sitting up close to the table, staring at her folded hands. "I called the arresting officers," she said, "and they told me Seth Wartella had been released from prison in January. I didn't want to tell Adam, because it was right after his heart surgery and I wanted him to focus on getting better, and not worry about Seth."

The detective eyed her. "Have you told him?"

She nodded. "Last night."

Inwood wrote, then asked, "Do you have any reason to believe that Mr. Wartella would want to injure your husband?"

She hesitated. "At the trial Wartella denied everything, but the evidence was obvious. He was angry when the verdict came in and I'll never forget the look he gave Adam." She hunched her shoulders.

"He never verbally threatened or accosted your husband?" the detective asked.

"Not as far as I know."

Inwood wrote some more. "All right, Mrs. Deering. Thank you for the information. It's a pity you didn't come to us earlier, though."

"I . . ." Irene's shoulders hunched a little more. "I was scared," she said in a small voice. "I just wanted him to go away. And maybe I was wrong. Maybe it wasn't him that I saw. Maybe it was someone who looked like him."

This seemed unlikely, since she'd told us Seth Wartella was about five foot five and had bright red hair and ears that stuck out, but I supposed it was possible.

"Possible," Inwood said, "but unlikely." He slid his notebook into his shirt pocket. "We'll be in touch. Ms. Hamilton, I assume you can find your way out?" He nodded to us and left.

"You've been here before?" Irene asked.

"Never in handcuffs," I said, and was rewarded with a glimmer of a smile.

Outside, the April sun was doing its meager best and I shied away from wondering how cold it would get that night. Irene got her car keys out of her purse. "Thanks for all your help, Minnie. I didn't know who to talk to about Seth, that day a couple of weeks ago. I guess I just tried not to think about it. But now that someone might be trying to . . . trying to . . ."

I took the keys from her fumbling hand, beeped the car doors unlocked for her, and handed back the keys. "I understand why you didn't want to tell Adam about Seth."

She looked at me ruefully. "That detective didn't."

"Mr. Sympathy? No. He didn't. But then he's not a wife who's stretching herself thin to hold her husband

and their life together. You were trying to protect Adam and I don't blame you a bit."

Her shoulders released some of their tension. "Thanks, Minnie. That means a lot."

A brilliant idea sparked into my brain. Hooray! I'd been wondering how to tell her that I'd promised her husband I'd do a little Minnie-type investigating, and here was the perfect opportunity. "Tell you what," I said. "I can do a little research on that Seth guy. See what I can find out."

"Minnie, you've already done so much for us." She shook her head. "I can't let you do that."

She and her husband were definitely two of a kind. "Ha!" I said. "Try to stop me. I'm a librarian, remember? Research is one of the things I do best." That and collect Eddie hair upon my person. "From safe and sound inside my snug office, I'll do a little digging. If I can find out that Seth was in, say, Australia last weekend, we'll know he had nothing to do with that car." And likely not with Henry's death, either.

Irene reached out and gave me a hard hug. "Thank you," she whispered.

I watched her get into the car and drive away, glad to given her a little peace of mind.

Then I walked back to the library and went to work.

After leaving the library the next day, I walked back to the marina, wondering how private investigators did their investigating. I'd spent part of the previous evening with my laptop, browsing the Internet for information about Seth Wartella, and had found essentially nothing.

I'd found an eighty-two-year-old Seth Wartella in Phoenix and an eighteen-year-old version in the greater Washington, D.C., area, both of whom were interested in dating active women who enjoyed long walks and sunsets, but I'd found nothing about a forty-something Seth. Admittedly I didn't spend too much time online, because the marina's Wi-Fi connection was abysmally slow, but to not find anything seemed strange.

"What do you think?" I asked Eddie after opening the front door.

He was sitting on the dashboard, studying the passing seagulls, most of him in the evening sunshine, some of him not, and was apparently too busy to talk to me.

I looked at him. "You know, if you went to the effort of sliding forward three inches, all of you would be in the sun."

He opened his mouth in a large yawn.

"None of that," I said through an answering yawn. "There's work to do."

"Mrr," he said, still looking outside.

"Ha." I walked into the bedroom, texting Tucker, *Home at the houseboat cleaning the deck, wouldn't mind some help* and got back a text reading, *Love to, but have chance 2 assist on emergency knee surgery. Next time?* Smiling, I changed out of school clothes and into grungy apparel, then came back to the kitchen and reached under the sink for the plastic bucket and scrub brush, talking to my cat the entire time.

"Just because you don't have thumbs doesn't mean you can't contribute to the running of this household. Oh, don't give me that innocent look. I know you're perfectly capable of cleaning." Not that I wanted my socks washed with Eddie spit, but he didn't need to know that. "There are all sorts of things you could do around here and it's past time that you started doing your share. I mean, did you catch a single mouse for Aunt Frances last winter?"

He turned to stare are me, and once again I was glad that cats didn't have the power to summon spontaneous combustion.

"Oh, come on." I added a little soap to the bucket and ran it full of hot water. "I'm just giving you a hard time." I went to kiss the top of his fuzzy head. "To tell you the truth, I don't blame you about the mice. They can't taste very good."

"Mrr."

"Better with mayonnaise? You're probably right." I lifted the bucket out of the sink. "Ready, Eddie Freddie? It's time to swab the decks."

For the next hour, I was on my hands and knees scrubbing the deck clean of the dust and grime it had accumulated while in storage. How a flat surface that was under a tarp and inside a building could get so dirty I didn't know, but the dark gray color that the water was turning was clear proof.

"Or not so clear," I said to Eddie, who was supervising from the small table I'd brought out for him to perch upon. I sat back on my heels and pushed my hair out of my eyes for the zillionth time. My hands were encased in thick plastic elbow-length gloves, so my dexterity was limited and I was undoubtedly getting soapy water all over my hair, but Eddie was the only one around to see and he wasn't overly critical of my looks. "Get it? The water is dirty, so it isn't clear."

Eddie blinked at me.

"Not sure what that meant," I said. "Do you think I'm not very funny, or do you not understand the joke? Because I could explain it again, if you're not sure about parts of it."

"More of a pun than a joke, isn't it?"

I spun around—which is hard to do while you're kneeling—lost my balance, and flopped over onto my back with a loud *thump*. From my new position, I could see blue sky and the beginnings of a setting sun. And if I waited long enough, maybe Ash Wolverson would go away and forget everything he'd seen.

"Are you all right?" Ash vaulted the boat's railing and crouched down beside me. "You're not hurt, are you?"

So, not going away. "I'm fine." I rolled onto my side and sat up. "Honest. You just startled me, that's all." I felt dirty water seep into the seat of my sweatpants. There was no way I was going to stand up in front of Ash Wolverson with a wet hind end, so I kept talking and tried not to think about my tangled wet hair and the dirty soapsuds on my face. "What brings you down to the marina? Any news about Henry or Adam?"

"Oh." Still in a crouch, Ash leaned back onto his heels and held his arms loosely across his thighs. It looked like a comfortable position for him, but I was pretty sure that if I tried it, my legs would start screaming at me within seconds. "No, sorry. No news." He looked at the wet deck. "Detective Inwood did tell me that Mrs. Deering had stopped by, with information about a Seth Wartella. So I'll be looking into that."

"Oh. Good." I almost told him that I hadn't been able to find a trace of Seth on the Internet, but decided to keep quiet. That might be considered interfering in police business and . . . then I decided to heck with it. "Just so you know—"

But Ash's words ran over mine. "Minnie, I heard your boyfriend moved downstate a few months ago. It's not like I was stalking you," he said hurriedly. "I just happened to hear from a friend. And I'm sorry things didn't work out between you, but if you're doing okay and you're ready to go, you know, go out again, I was wondering if maybe you'd like to go out with me."

For a moment, the only thing I heard was the soft wash of waves against the side of my boat. A few months ago, when Tucker was still living in Charlevoix, Ash had asked me out and I'd had to tell him I was seeing someone else. And now I had to tell him all over again.

Or . . . did I?

The instant the thought oozed into my head, my mother's voice chased it out. *Minnie, don't you dare think about cheating on that doctor of yours. You agreed to a long-distance relationship, didn't you? Well, then you'd best keep that agreement. Hamiltons don't go back on their word.*

Mom's words zipped in and out of my thoughts in a heartbeat. I looked up at Ash and tried to smile. "Thanks so much for asking, but—"

He stood up fast. "But you're not interested. Hey, don't worry about it. I just thought maybe there was a chance. I won't bother you—"

"Mrr!"

Ash whipped around. "Hey, Eddie. Sorry, big guy, I didn't see you there." He scratched my cat behind his furry ears. "How are you doing these days?"

"Just fine, thanks."

Ash and I turned to see Rafe grinning at us from the dock, his teeth white against a skin that appeared tan even in April. Of course, his distant Native American heritage helped that look, but it still seemed inherently unfair. "How are you?"

I glanced from the slim, black-haired Rafe to the near-movie-star square-jawed looks of Ash. "You two know each other?"

"My man Ash?" Rafe saluted him with an index finger shaped into a pistol. "We go way back. Say, how's your sister doing?" He waggled his eyebrows. "Still hot as ever?"

"Please tell me you're here for a reason," I said. "If you'll notice, I'm trying to get some work done." I'd had time to clean the houseboat's inside before moving, but hadn't had time to touch the outside until now.

Rafe looked down at the dirty, soapy mess I'd made. "Huh. You know it might freeze tonight, right? Better get that cleaned up or it could be nasty slippery in the morning." He pointed at Ash again. "You doing anything? Because if we don't get out of here, Ms. Hamilton here is going to dragoon you into helping her clean."

Ash almost, but not quite, looked at me. "I was just leaving."

"Perfect!" Rafe gave him a thumbs-up. "Tell you what. I could use some help drywalling a ceiling. Pizza and a six-pack of whatever you want when we're done."

"Sounds good," Ash said. Then, not quite looking at me: "I'll, uh, see you later, Minnie."

"Yeah. Later."

I stood there, watching them go, listening to their male banter as they went down the dock and onto the sidewalk that would, in a couple of hundred feet, take them straight to the front door of Rafe's fixer-upper.

"Mrr," Eddie said.

"You're a male," I said. "You tell me: Why are guys convinced to help a friend with a construction project at the mere mention of pizza and beer, but all they can think of when faced with a friend's cleaning project is to leave as quickly as possible?"

Eddie turned his back to me and didn't say a thing.

Men.

Chapter 7

"Why, *why* did I ever try to do this?" I grabbed two fistfuls of my hair, a move I would regret almost instantly for what it would do to what might be loosely called a hairstyle, and I pulled tight enough to thin my vision to slits. "Why?"

Once again, I looked at the computer screen. Sadly, the flyer design I'd come up with still looked downright awful, even with my skewed eyesight.

I released my hair, and my vision went back to normal. Flopping back against my chair, I stared at the dragonless ceiling and tried to think. The flyer had to be to the printer absolutely no later than Monday noon. If today was Wednesday, that meant ... I counted on my fingers ... there were three business days in which to get this done.

"Three days," I said to the computer in the deepest, most threatening tone I could summon. The computer ignored me and I tried not to consider its continued display of my absolutely awful flyer design as a taunt.

At that point, I realized I'd been ignoring my own hunger pangs.

I got up, grabbed my coat, wallet, and cell phone, and headed out. Everything would look better after a walk and some lunch. And even if it didn't look better, at least I would get outside for a little bit and get some food in my stomach, a win-win situation if there ever was one.

Half an hour later, my tummy was happily full with an Italian sub and chips from Fat Boys Pizza, but I still didn't have any idea how to figure out if Seth Wartella had ever set foot in northern Michigan, I still couldn't think of any reason why someone would want to kill both Henry and Adam, and I still hadn't a clue of how to get a designed flyer.

"Hello, Minnie."

I looked up from my contemplation of the sidewalk to see Pam Fazio. Her short black hair was as smooth as ever, and even though she had to be in her mid-fifties, not a single wrinkle showed on her face. She was standing just outside the door of her antique shop, Older Than Dirt, wearing a cheerful dress in a flower pattern topped with a shawl, and smiling at me with an odd expression.

"Do I have tomato sauce on my face?" I rubbed the corners of my mouth, just to be sure.

"No, it just that's the third time I said hello," she said. "You seem a million miles away."

Henry's house was a little more than ten miles southeast of Chilson, actually, but I didn't make the clarification. "Just thinking," I said.

"Nice footwear." Pam nodded at my shoes.

I turned them this way and that, displaying each foot proudly. "Yes, indeed, thank you very much." Last winter I'd purchased the high-topped black lace-up shoes from Pam and they were my favorite footwear of all time. Whenever I put them on I felt like Laura Ingalls Wilder but without the locusts and the scarlet fever and the backbreaking labor.

"What are you thinking so hard about that you didn't hear me calling?" she asked.

Most of it wouldn't be appropriate to tell her, but there was one thing I could share. "I've just come to the conclusion that I am, without a doubt, the worst designer of a book fair flyer in the history of the world."

Pam laughed. "Don't be so hard on yourself."

I eyed her. "Hang on." I'd e-mailed myself a copy of the flyer so I could look at it while I ate. I'd taken one look and decided it would give me indigestion, but it was still on my phone. I opened the image and showed it to her.

She took the phone from my hand, peered close, and snorted with laughter.

"Gee," I said dryly, "thanks for the support."

She grinned. "If you want, I could try my hand at a little redesigning." She looked at the image, turning it this way and that. "When do you need it?"

"Monday noon." I winced, preparing myself for her reaction.

"No problem. I'll send you something Monday morning."

It sounded good, but then so had Amanda's offer. "Are you sure you want to do this? I don't want to take up a lot of your time. You have a store to run." Because I could always make a flyer of text on brightly colored paper. It was what the library had always done before and no one would think twice about it; I'd just hoped for something outstanding for our first-ever book fair.

Pam made a rude noise in the back of her throat. "It's April. I was warned about the April lull up here, but I didn't know I was going to get so bored. I'll be glad for the chance to do something other than dust all my merchandise. Again."

I thanked her and, as I walked back to the library, I wondered what talents and skills might be hidden inside the people I thought I knew. Then I wondered if talents and skills might be hidden inside cats. Eddie, for one.

"Something funny?" Cookie Tom was in front of his bakery, cleaning the windows and looking at me.

I tucked away my Eddie-induced laughter. "Almost everything," I said, and headed back to the library.

The next day, I spent my lunch hour deep in the bowels of the Internet, chasing down any wisps of information about Seth Wartella. When I'd come up completely dry for anything since his incarceration, I hunted down what I could find for Henry and Adam and added everything I found to a spreadsheet.

Once the spreadsheet was as full as I could make it, I categorized every item at least two different ways, then sorted and resorted the data in an effort to jiggle useful thoughts out of my brain.

Sadly nothing jiggled loose by the end of my lunchtime, but when five o'clock came, I was officially off the library's clock. I closed my eyes and ears to the work-related things I could be doing and plunged even deeper into the two separate worlds of Henry and Adam, trying to find something that might connect them.

My rumbling stomach chased me out of my office, but I continued thinking about the problem the entire evening, was still thinking about it as I went to sleep, thought about it first thing when I woke up to another chilly morning, and then as I walked into Cookie Tom's to get a dozen doughnuts for the staff. It was a Friday, after all, and I'd skipped breakfast because I couldn't face eating a bowl of cold cereal when the houseboat's interior temperature was only fifty-one degrees.

Eddie, of course, had no such compunctions and stared at me gravely until I poured him a tiny bowl of milk to replace the leftovers that he usually got from the bottom of my bowl.

The smell of baked goods had me salivating the second I walked into Cookie Tom's. "Morning, Minnie," Tom said cheerfully. "What do you need today?"

It was more a question of want than need, but I wasn't going to enter into that kind of debate with the guy who gave me a deal on cookies for the bookmobile. And, in summer, sold them to me from the back door, letting me avoid the long lines.

"Box of doughnuts," I said. "A dozen, any kind you'd like."

He surveyed the contents of his glass cases. "Apple fritters, custard-filled long johns, glazed doughnuts, cinnamon twists?"

There was no way I was going to be able to choose. "Let's do an assortment."

"No problem." He unfolded a white cardboard bakery box and got to work, whistling as he went.

I watched him place the bakery yummies in the box, wondering how on earth he could run a bakery and stay so skinny. If it had been me, I'd have put on so many pounds that—

"Good morning, Ms. Hamilton."

I looked up. "Detective Inwood." I started to make a bad joke about cops and doughnuts, but stopped—Mom would have been so proud—and said, "How are you this fine morning?"

He held up an empty travel mug. "Looking for my first fill-up of the day." He glanced at the work Tom was doing. "I suppose I could make a bad joke about librarians and doughnuts, but I think I'll let it go."

I was simpatico with a man who was at least twice my age and probably hadn't read a work of fiction since high school. The idea was a little frightening. "So, I've been thinking," I said. "About what could possibly connect Adam and Henry Gill."

"And?" Detective Inwood walked around the end of the glass cabinets and filled his mug from the half-full pot on the back counter. Clearly the man knew his way around the bakery. "Any conclusions?"

"Nope."

He added two spoonfuls of sugar to his mug, screwed the top on, and walked back around. "Wolverson got the same results. I'm sure he'll be pleased that he wasn't bested by an amateur."

I'd never thought of it that way, but perhaps I should have. So I considered it for a moment. Then I stopped worrying. After all, if I found something they didn't that led to the jailing of a killer, how was that a problem?

I also briefly considered telling the detective about the connection theories that I'd kicked around. Very briefly. The briefest of briefs. Inwood did not need to know that I'd tried to research the notion that Adam was Henry's illegitimate son and that Henry's legitimate children were out for revenge because Adam was trying to steal their inheritance. Melodrama was all well and good in its place, but it didn't fit comfortably inside the borders of Tonedagana County.

Inwood put the mug on the counter next to the cash register and pulled out his wallet.

"Do you think," I asked, "it's at all likely that Seth Wartella tried to kill Adam?" *And,* I didn't add, *might have killed Henry by mistake?*

The detective looked at me with a completely blank expression.

"Seth," I said a little louder. "Wartella. The guy Adam put in jail for tax fraud."

Inwood nodded as he pulled out a bill and put it next to the cash register. My respect for him went up a notch, because Tom willingly gave free coffee to police officers. "It's extremely unusual for white-collar criminals to commit violent crimes. Not unheard of, but certainly on the far end of unusual."

I wasn't surprised. "The only thing Henry and Adam seem to have had in common, other than being friends, was they both regularly had breakfast at the Round Table." Tom held up the box of doughnuts for me to approve and I nodded absently. "Maybe," I said, "maybe the restaurant itself was a contact point. Maybe one morning they ate together and heard somebody say something."

Inwood gave me a pained look and picked up his mug of coffee. "All avenues of investigation—"

"Will be explored," I said, finishing his sentence for him.

He nodded once, said good-bye to Tom, and headed out into the crisp spring air.

"Anything else?" Tom asked, sliding the flat white box onto the counter with one hand and ringing up my total with the other.

I blinked away from my own exploration avenues. "All set, thanks."

Then I noticed the money that the detective had left on the counter for his ninety-five-cent cup of coffee.

A ten-dollar bill.

I pushed it over to Tom. "The detective left this for his coffee. I can run after him with his change, if you want."

Tom smiled and put the bill in the register's drawer. "That's what he always leaves. I gave up trying to return his money years ago."

"A fine celebration this is," Russell McCade said, startling me out of my reverie.

"Yes," said Barb McCade, his wife of many years and the mother of their children, who were grown. "I was thinking the same thing a mere moment ago."

"Are we doing *M* words?" he asked. "Let's start with Miss Minnie."

"Sorry," I said, laughing. I'd met the McCades last summer when Barb ran in front of the bookmobile, waving me down because her husband was having a stroke. We'd bundled her husband into the bookmobile and raced him to the hospital, and it wasn't until I was relaying patient information to the emergency room via my cell phone that I realized my male passenger was none other than painter Russell McCade, more commonly known as Cade to his thousands upon thousands of fans.

His critics dismissed his work as sentimental schlock; his fans defended it as accessible art. I'd loved his stuff since I was a kid, but had never dreamed I'd actually meet the famous man, let alone get to be his friend via the hospital trip and a murder investigation and the letter *D*.

For reasons now lost to the mists of time, the McCades had a habit of randomly choosing a letter and then finding words starting with that letter to fit into the ongoing conversation. This had happened the first time I'd visited Cade in the hospital, and when I'd joined in the game, our acquaintanceship moved into solid friendship.

The McCades, in their late fifties, owned a home on a small lake not too far from Chilson, but spent the winters in a place with plentiful sunshine and no snow. They'd returned to Michigan a few days ago, and the Mitchell Street Pub in Petoskey was their restaurant choice for a return celebration.

Now Barb looked at me keenly. "You seem distracted, my dear."

Cade clicked his tongue. "Not an *M* word in the bunch. You're going to get behind."

She ignored him. "Is it Tucker? I know you told me you were working things out, but long-distance relationships are difficult at the best of times."

"We're fine," I said, trying not to think how long it was going to be before we saw each other. "It's just ... well, there's this friend of mine who's in a little trouble and ..." The McCades looked at each other, exchanging one of those glances that long-married couples can use as communication. "What?" I asked.

Cade cracked open a peanut shell and popped the nut into his mouth. "We were wondering how long it would be before you involved yourself in another one."

"Another what?" I asked. But before either one of them could say anything, I spotted Irene Deering. "Sorry, I see someone I have to talk to. I'll be right back, okay?" I scooted the bentwood chair back and got up before they could exchange another communicative glance.

"Hey, Minnie." Irene smiled at me from behind the long wooden bar. She was pulling back on a tap and filling a tall glass with beer. "I saw you over there a minute ago. Are those your parents?"

As if. My parents left Dearborn only on holidays, and not even many of those. And since I was growing less and less inclined to leave the calm of northern Michigan for the noise and bustle of the Detroit area, our face-to-face visits were growing few and far between. There were regular phone calls, but I hadn't seen them since Christmas and wasn't sure when I was going to see them again.

"Friends of mine," I said to Irene. Most people knew that an internationally famous artist lived in the area, but I wasn't about to broadcast his present location. "I wanted to tell you that I ran into Detective Inwood this morning."

Irene looked up, her face suddenly taut and still. "Any news?"

Sort of, but not really. "He said it would be very unusual for someone like Seth Wartella, a white-collar criminal, to start doing violent crimes." I nodded at the glass in her hand. "You're about to overflow there."

Shaking her head at herself, Irene released the tap. "So, is that good news or bad?"

"Good in that even if it was Seth you saw, he most likely didn't have anything to do with the car that almost hit Adam. Or anything to do with Henry's death."

As my friend pulled in a slow breath, I saw how her cheekbones poked out sharply into her skin. The woman was working too hard, worrying too much, and not taking care of herself.

"But it's not unheard of," she said. "For a guy who did tax fraud to branch out. Into worse crimes, I mean."

I hadn't pressed the detective for statistics, but I had the feeling that even if there was even the tiniest percentage, she would lie awake tonight, worrying that she'd put her husband in danger by not reporting her maybe-sighting of Seth.

"No," I said. "I'm sure it's happened at least once. But maybe it wasn't Seth that you saw. You said you just caught a glimpse, and you haven't seen him for years, so maybe it was just someone who looked like him."

She frowned, thinking it over, but I could tell she wasn't buying it. "Promise me you won't worry for, say, seven days," I said, holding up the requisite number of fingers. "Business days, mind you. Weekends don't count. I'm bound to find something by then."

Irene actually smiled. "Thanks, Minnie. Very, very much."

"She won't take thanks," Cade said, slinging an arm around my shoulder. "Never has, probably never will. It's a horrible character flaw, you know." He nodded at Irene. "Just let her go ahead and do whatever it is she wants, and force gifts upon her later. It'll be easier for both of you."

I put my chin up. "I can take a thank-you just as well as anyone."

Barb, who had joined us at the bar, smirked. "Oh, really? Minnie, let me tell you once again how grateful we are that you and Eddie got Mr. McCade here to the hospital so quickly. Without you, I don't know what I would have done."

Cade nodded solemnly. "And without your assistance with finding an attorney, I might have—"

I put my hands over my ears and fled from the Mc-Cades.

But Irene had been laughing, so it wasn't all bad.

The next morning. I woke to sunlight streaming in through the white curtains of my bedroom. I twisted my head around to see what I could of the sky and saw nothing but blue, blue, and more blue. A full-out sunny day in April? A giddy first-day-of-summer-vacation kind of feeling filled me with happy expectation.

"And it's Saturday," I told Eddie. "What are the odds?"

My cat, who was curled up between my right hip and the wall of the houseboat, didn't move any muscles except the ones that were beating his heart and helping him breathe.

"Look," I said, putting my bare hand outside the covers. "It's not even cold out there. See, no goose pimples."

Eddie still didn't care, so I slid out of bed and tiptoed to the shower without any more disturbance of his beauty sleep. But even after I was clean and dry and dressed, Eddie showed no inclination to take part in any morning activities. Since I was a considerate kind of person, I decided that making my own breakfast would be too noisy for him. Clearly it would be best to go out.

Sabrina, the Round Table's forever waitress, brought me a glass of water and a mug of coffee.

"I don't get a menu?" I asked.

She snorted. "When was the last time you ordered anything other than sausage links and either cinnamon apple pancakes or cinnamon French toast?"

"I might if I ever get a menu. I don't even know what else you have."

Sabrina wrote something on her waitress pad and tucked her pencil into her bun of graying hair. "About what you'd expect. Now, do you want me to turn in your order for sausage and French toast, or do you want to go hungry because you're trying to make a point?"

I grinned. "Good to see that marriage hasn't changed you any."

She put a hand on one of her padded hips. "Did you really think it would?" she asked, and sashayed away.

Smiling, I watched her go, remembering the events of last summer. She and Bill D'Arcy, a restaurant customer and newcomer to Chilson, had gotten engaged after a short romance. They'd married at Thanksgiving and, as far as I knew, were still happily in the honeymoon phase.

Sabrina came back, going from booth to booth with a fresh pot of coffee. When she came near, I pushed my mug to the edge of the table and asked, "How's your Bill doing these days?"

Her soft smile told me everything I needed to know. "The new treatments are helping him so much that he's looking to invest in the company. Not that he'll ever get his old vision back, but they might be able to stop the deterioration."

Bill, at age fifty-six, had an advanced case of macular degeneration. He made scads of money by doing complicated things with financial markets, and for a while the talk around town had been that Sabrina would quit working at the Round Table. After all, why would anyone keep working if she didn't need to?

I'd kept my opinion to myself but hadn't been surprised that, as the months passed, she showed no signs of leaving the diner. No matter how deep and true the love she shared with Bill, there was no way his taciturn self would satisfy her need for human contact.

"That's great," I said, thinking about the time Bill crashed his car into the side of a building. "My fingers are crossed for him." I looked around at the mostly empty restaurant. "Say, do you have a minute?"

She scanned the room. "Got an order coming, but until then, sure. What's up?"

"Do you remember seeing anyone new in here the last few weeks?" I wouldn't have bothered asking the question during the summer, but April wasn't exactly top tourist season. "A guy in his mid-thirties, red hair, with ears that stick way out." I cupped my hands around my ears and flapped them around.

But Sabrina was shaking her head. "Why, did he skip out on paying library fines?" She grinned. "What is this world coming to?"

"No, he's . . ." How to explain this one? "He's someone that a friend of mine knew a long time ago. She thought she might have seen him around, that's all."

Sabrina's face lit up. "A blast from the past? Do I smell the revival of an old flame?"

Not in the least. "If you see anyone like that, will you let me know? It's important."

Sabrina winked. "Gotcha. Anything else?"

I stared at my coffee. "Still sad about Henry Gill, I guess. I know he was kind of a pain, but there was something about him I really liked."

"And what might that be?" she asked, starch in her voice. "That I couldn't ever bring him a cup of coffee that was good enough, or that no one could ever cook him hash browns as good as the ones his wife made?"

"He liked Eddie," I said.

"Anyone with a lick of sense likes Eddie." She rolled her eyes. "And don't mind me for speaking ill of the dead. Henry was a grumpy old man after his wife died, but he was one of ours. We're going to start up donations, you know, to fund a scholarship to the high school in his name."

Tears pricked at my eyes. "That's great. Let me know when you have it set up."

"You know," she said musingly, "he was different

when his wife was alive. Back then, the only person who didn't like him was Davis Thumm. And that was because Henry bought the same color truck he did." She grinned. "In 1975."

I blinked. As a motive for murder, surely that was the lamest one ever, but you never knew.

Sabrina put more coffee in my mug. "But Davis moved downstate to be closer to his kids back in the nineties. He died last year, I heard, the old bugger."

"Did you ever see Henry in here with Adam Deering?" I asked.

"Adam who?"

I started to explain the relationship between Henry and Adam, but before I got all the way through, she was shaking her head again.

"Last couple of years, I never saw Henry sitting with anybody other than you," she said.

Which pretty much destroyed the Round Table theory I'd proposed to Detective Inwood the day before. "Well," I said, sighing, "after what happened to Adam, I was just wondering, that's all."

"What do you mean?"

And that was when I remembered that Sabrina never read the local paper. She didn't need to, she'd said time and time again. "Right here is where I get all the news I need, and a lot that I don't." But since Adam was new to the area and lived out of town, he wasn't yet connected to the town's talk.

I told Sabrina about Adam's near miss with the car and she was appropriately shocked. "That's Irene's husband, right?" Because, since Irene worked in Chilson for her regular job as a bank's loan officer, she was connected to the town.

Nodding, I almost started talking about the oddness of Henry's being killed by a tree one week and, less than two weeks later, the guy who'd been with Henry that day being almost killed by a car. But then I remembered where I was and to whom I was talking. There was a time and a place to encourage the spread of rumors, but this wasn't it. Not yet, anyway.

A bell rang in the kitchen. "Order's up," Sabrina said. "Got to go."

I wrapped my hands around the warmth of my mug and opened the book I'd brought to read, but even Louise Penny's evocative prose couldn't keep me from thinking about Henry and Adam and what might really have happened that day out in the woods.

Chapter 8

Up above me, trees were just starting to bud. Tiny bits of color showed at the ends of thousands of branches, and if I squinted, the entire forest canopy fuzzed out to a light green, the color of spring.

I tried not to think that, downstate, spring had sprung almost three weeks ago and that it was still possible, up here, to get another snowfall. Late springs were a hazard of Up North life, and it didn't do to whine about the situation, since we were all in the same metaphorical boat. And at least it was sunny and warm. Well, nearly warm.

My hands, encased in warm wool gloves, were shoved into my coat pockets, and my feet were inside high hiking boots. I'd stuffed a fleece hat onto my head, knowing my obstreperous curls would be escaping all around in an unattractive manner, but I didn't expect to run into anyone out here at Henry's.

It had been while I was swiping the last piece of my Round Table sausage in the last of the maple syrup that the idea to come out to Henry's house had popped into my head. Maybe I wouldn't find anything, probably I wouldn't, but how could it hurt to have another pair of eyes taking a look at the place where he'd died?

Besides, it was a glorious April day and I wasn't scheduled to work. If I didn't go somewhere and do something, it was likely that I'd end up in my office, and all work and no play might make Minnie a miserable mess.

"*M* words," I said out loud, and shook my head at myself. Barb and Cade had infected me with their word game and I had the feeling it was a permanent contamination.

I studied Henry's house. The curtains on the two-story home of fieldstone and white clapboard were drawn tight and it had that forlorn look houses get when they're not being lived in. In my fanciful moments, of which I had many, I was sure that houses could feel the difference between their people being on vacation and never coming back.

This house knew. And Henry's front door? It knew for sure.

Turning away, I hoped I'd remember to never say any of that out loud to anyone, because I'd get a patient nod and, soon afterward, concerned phone calls about my well-being would be exchanged.

I looked up the hill. Somewhere up there was Henry's sugar shack. Which meant there had to be a trail, because there would be a lot of traipsing back and forth. I wandered around the yard for bit and found a narrow path by the back of the garage.

The winding way took me up the hill by a circuitous route, around this big tree and that big tree, and it wasn't until I noticed a dribble of damp coming out of a small hole in a tree trunk that I realized I was following in Henry's ghostly footsteps.

I stopped and fingered one of the holes, which were smaller than the diameter of my finger and about four feet off the ground. In the cold of February, Henry had drilled those holes, inserted a small metal spigotlike thing, hung a bucket on the spigot, and waited for the weather to warm. When the sap started to drip, he'd lugged pails from tree to tree, emptying the tree buckets into the bigger pails and hauling it all to storage vats.

I laid my gloved hand over the hole and wished for things to be different. Henry shouldn't be dead. Adam shouldn't have had to watch a friend die to learn that he himself had a heart condition. And Irene shouldn't have to be so worried about her husband and their finances.

"It's not right," I told the tree, and I was pretty sure it agreed. Or at least it didn't disagree, and that was almost the same thing. I gave the tree a pat and went back to walking the trail.

Around more trees I went, and next to a creek. Then the trail turned steep, and when I was almost out of breath, it went flat again, and that was when I saw the sugar shack.

I'd somehow thought the term was more traditional than accurate. That the word "shack" was a holdover from the old days, and that the locations for cooking maple syrup were, in fact, brightly lit structures of modern construction.

Not so. At least not here at Henry's.

I eyed the cobbled-together conglomeration of wood siding, vinyl siding, and aluminum siding and stopped wondering why the sugar shack was so far from the house. Henry had, for a long time, been married to someone who everyone said was a lovely woman, and no lovely woman I'd ever met would have allowed something like Henry's shack within sight of the kitchen window.

"Score one for Mrs. Gill," I said, and wished I'd had the chance to meet her. And to meet Henry when she'd been alive.

More wishes.

I walked to the front door—the only door—of the shack. There was no knob, just a latch. I opened it and went inside.

And promptly came back out again. I pulled my cell phone out of my coat pocket and fired up the flashlight application. It wouldn't light very much for very long, but any light would make that darkness more friendly.

The dim light played over what little was in the shack. A vast rectangular pan sat atop a homemade arrangement of bricks and blocks, filling most of the space. At the pan's far end was a metal chimney that rose to the roof. In one corner lay a neat stack of split wood, two corners had uncomfortable-looking stools tucked into them, and a cluster of tools occupied the fourth corner.

It could have been a scene from fifty years ago. A hundred years ago, even, if you forgot about the vinyl and aluminum siding outside.

I danced the light on the walls, ceiling, and dirt floor, and saw nothing except for a few spiderwebs. There was very little dust and dirt, which was good for a place where food was cooked, but surprising for a shack in the middle of the woods. The darkness seemed odd, but I supposed once the fire underneath the pan got going, there'd be light enough to work.

I stood there for a moment, imagining Henry sitting on a stool, the room warm from the heat of the fire, his coat hanging on a nail, getting up to pour sap into the pan, then sitting back down and picking up the library book he'd laid down, turning pages and reading from the light cast by the fire's glow.

It felt a little Abraham Lincoln–ish, and I wondered if Mr. Lincoln had ever made maple syrup back in his Illinois days. Things like that rarely make the biographies, which was a pity, really, because—

"Who are you?"

I jumped high and whipped around, dropping into a crouch, aiming the only weapon I had—my cell phone in flashlight mode—directly at the intruder.

"Who are you?" I countered, backing toward the corner where the tools stood. The man blocking my exit wasn't huge, but even an average-sized man was a lot bigger than I was. If I could grab the poker, or even the shovel, I could do him enough damage so I could make my escape. I inched back, reaching behind me with my free hand.

"Felix Stanton," the man said. "Northern Development." He reached into his pocket and I grasped a tool. Whatever it was, it had to be better than nothing. "Here's my card," he said, holding the flat rectangle in my direction. "Are you a real estate agent? Because I've already talked to the family."

Everything fell into place. I looked back at the tool I'd grabbed. A leaf rake. Well, it might have worked. "Minnie

Hamilton," I said, taking his card. It was made of thick paper stock and was emblazoned with a logo so professional I almost asked him for the name of his graphic designer. Then I shoved the designed-to-impress card into my coat pocket and looked at Felix. Or tried to; the light was so poor that all I was seeing was a silhouette in the doorway. "Let's go outside."

"What? Oh, sure." He walked out and my shoulders released a bit of tension. My brain hadn't really thought I was under attack, but my tummy had been concerned.

Outside, the sky was still blue and the air still fresh. I'd probably only been in the shack for ten minutes, but time had shifted while I was in there and I wouldn't have been surprised to see a complete change of seasons and different decade.

Felix Stanton looked to be in his early fifties. He was about five foot ten, broad-shouldered, broad-faced, and had a little bit of a paunch. His cloth driver's hat, a canvas jacket, navy blue pants, and leather hiking boots looked comfortable and expensive. He also looked familiar.

"Do I know you?" he asked. "Because you look familiar."

"I'm a librarian in Chilson, but I don't think that's where I've seen you. And I drive the bookmobile, but that's not it, either."

He shook his head. "No time to read, these days. I keep meaning to, but you know how it goes."

I didn't, actually, but I smiled anyway. We started playing the Up North game of How Do I Know You? and it wasn't long until I snapped my fingers, which doesn't work all that well when you're wearing gloves. "Shomin's Deli." The deli had booths with hooks for coats at the ends and I remembered seeing that hat hanging from one of the hooks.

"That's it." He nodded. "They have the best Reubens in the county."

"Swiss cheese and green olives on sourdough for me."

He winced. "To each his own," he said, then looked at me speculatively. "So, what's a librarian doing on Henry Gill's property on an April morning?"

Now, that was an excellent question, and if I thought a minute, I could probably come up with something he might believe. "Not much," I said. Lame. So very lame. "Henry used the bookmobile, so I'd gotten to know him the last few months." Sort of. "He brought me maple syrup and I just kind of wondered what his sugar shack looked like."

It was still a seriously sad answer, but Felix was actually buying it. "He made a great syrup," he said, nodding. "That smoked flavor was something special."

I put my hands back in my coat pockets, and his business card poked into the middle of my palm. "Henry's heirs are looking to sell the property?"

Felix smiled. "Just looking into the possibilities."

A light breeze pushed the upper branches of the trees around in small swirls, and I thought about Henry and his father and his grandfather and who knew how many generations back, all harvesting maple sap from these trees. "You're not thinking about condos, are you?"

"No lake access to this property," Felix said, but it was a fast answer and even I knew enough about developing to know that just because one parcel didn't have lake access, it didn't mean that parcels with lake frontage couldn't be purchased.

"It's been nice talking to you, Minnie." Felix smiled. "Next time we run into each other at Shomin's, at least we'll have names to match the faces." He nodded and headed out, walking back toward the driveway.

I watched him go. While I understood the need for new homes and new developments and understood that growth was prosperity, I also wished that some things didn't have to change. Wished that some things, at least a few things, could stay the same forever and ever.

More wishes.

But happily, since wishes weren't and never had been horses, I wouldn't have to think about where I'd stable mine. Or what I'd feed them. I'd grown up in the city, just as Ash said Detective Inwood had, and I was essentially clueless about what, or how much, a horse ate. And they were big, so they'd probably eat a lot more more than Eddie did.

I shook away the thoughts that wanted to distract me and tried to remember what Adam had said about finding Henry that day. After all, the reason I'd come out here in the first place was to see if I could find something that might point to who'd killed Henry and tried to kill Adam.

What I might find that the police hadn't found, I didn't know, but it would have been embarrassing if the answer was right there, lying about, waiting to be found, and no one bothered to pick it up.

Then again, the only things I could see lying on the

ground were last year's leaves, a few blades of grass poking up, and sticks and branches of various sizes.

I kicked halfheartedly at the leaves, sending them flying in short arcs. Nature girl, I was not. I'd been kidding myself if I'd thought I'd find anything out here. I couldn't tell a maple tree from an oak tree if the leaves weren't all the way out. Woods were pretty much woods, as far I could tell, and—

"Wood," I said out loud.

Adam said that Henry had gone out to stack some wood. Which would lead pretty much anyone to think that there was a stack of wood somewhere out here. Which meant I was looking for wood in the woods, and might be sillier than bringing coals to Newcastle, but I had to try.

I trudged around the sugar shack in ever-widening circles, looking for anything close to resembling a pile of wood. I found brush piles that might have been made by Henry or might have fallen into heaps naturally and I found fallen trees that might have dropped to the ground via natural means, but how was I to know for sure? Women who weren't nature girls had no way of telling.

Still. I had to try, and I would try.

My circling walk grew to a radius so large that I started to lose sight of the shack. The leaves on the short, scrubby trees in the understory were farther out than the treetop version, and I took off my gloves to feel their softness. Spring. In spite of the recent snow and the cold mornings, it really was spring. Daffodils were budding and would soon be in bloom and—

And there was a tidy stack of wood. I walked around

all four of its sides, looked at it from various angles, frowned at it, even smiled at it, but the only thing it looked like was a plain old stack of wood.

So much for this brilliant idea. I might as well have—

"Hello. Who are you?"

I jumped high and to my left, away from the large man standing next to a massive tree trunk. And here I'd figured Henry's place would be empty today. I would have had more solitude if I'd stayed home.

"A friend of Henry's," I said, trying to sound casual and not like I'd just had the bejeebers scared out of me. And for some reason, scared I definitely was. I inched backward, away from the guy. "He used to bring me maple syrup. I'm . . ." My throat was suddenly too tight to talk. I gave it a quick rub and tried again. "I'm going to miss him."

The man nodded. He was probably in his mid-forties, was more than six feet tall, bulky as a football player, and dressed in jeans, work boots, and a hooded fleece sweatshirt from a private university. "Cole Duvall. I have a summer place over there." He tipped his head, covered with carefully cut white-blond hair, in the direction of Rock Lake. "Sure is a shame about Henry."

I introduced myself and said, "He and his wife had children, didn't they?"

"Three boys." Cole Duvall leaned against the tree, his hands tucked into the hand-warmer part of his sweatshirt. "Don't remember what any of them do, but they're scattered all over the country. We've had this place five years now and I've never met any of them."

"Do you think they're going to sell the property?"

Cole shrugged. "No idea. Like I said, I've never met them. But it's hard to figure them keeping it, being so far away and all."

Though that made sense, it made my heart droop a little. "There was a developer here a few mintues ago. He said he'd talked to the heirs."

"Oh?" The expression on Cole's face sharpened the slightest bit. "Any idea who it was?"

"Felix Stanton, Northern Development. Um, are you okay?" Because Cole had an odd expression on his face.

"He didn't waste any time, did he?" Cole asked, disgust thick in his voice.

"What do you mean?"

"Stanton has been trying to talk Henry into selling since last fall. The poor guy is barely in the ground and already that vulture is poking his nose around, trying to make a buck off Henry's sons." He made a rude noise in the back of his throat. "Hard to believe some people, you know?"

We chatted a little more, said amiable good-byes, and I walked back down the hill via the two-track that Cole had pointed out, thinking all the while.

Hard to believe some people, you know?

"I do know," I murmured. "I absolutely do."

Because, after all, I was a librarian, and librarians knew a lot more about people than what kinds of books they checked out.

Chapter 9

After a late lunch at the houseboat—peanut butter and jelly for me, cat food for Eddie—I drove to the boardinghouse to pick up a few things.

"You do this every year," Aunt Frances said. She was sitting at the kitchen table, paperwork spread out around her.

"Four years in a row," I answered cheerfully. "Moving with the seasons, out with the old winter, in with the new spring, opening myself up to new horizons and new adventures, opening my bedroom here for new boarders."

"No, I mean every year you leave things behind."

I looked at the cardboard box into which I'd been tossing items. A book, a magazine, a handful of hair bands, a comb, a bottle of liquid soap that had been a Christmas present from my sister-in-law, and a package of instant oatmeal. "Not a lot, percentage-wise."

She laughed. "I'm just saying that maybe it's psychological. That you leave things behind because you want to come back."

"Well, of course I want to come back. You're my favorite aunt in the entire world."

"I'm your only aunt," she said.

"True, but even if you weren't you'd still be my favorite."

"And you know this how?"

I grinned. "Going with the odds, that's all. You've met my uncle, haven't you?" My mom's bachelor brother was a fine man, but there were common qualities in everyone born to the Rivard family, including my mother, and a keen sense of the absurd was not one of them.

Aunt Frances nodded, conceding my point. "Speaking of favorites, how's Tucker doing?"

"Fine," I said vaguely, repacking the box. Which didn't need repacking, but with any luck she didn't know that. My aunt, however, had the eyes of an eagle and suddenly didn't seem very interested in her paperwork, so a fast distraction was needed.

"Ash Wolverson stopped by the marina the other day," I said. I'd found out last fall that Aunt Frances was a friend of Ash's mother.

"He's a nice boy," my aunt said.

"Boy" wasn't a term I would have thought applied to the very masculine deputy, but whatever.

"Are you two becoming friends?" she asked.

I'd met Ash last year, during the bookmobile's maiden voyage, but almost all of our interactions had been law-enforcement-based. "I doubt it," I said. "He asked me out."

"And you turned him down?" Aunt Frances frowned.

"Of course I did." I frowned back. "I'm dating Tucker."

"Exclusively?"

I looked at her. "Aunt Frances, what's going on here? No, don't deny it, I know from the way you're pursing your lips that you're holding back on me. What aren't you telling me? Have you heard something about Tucker?"

She blinked at me. "Good heavens, no. How would I hear anything about him?"

"Because you have amazing powers that, thankfully, you use only for good. And you have a vast network of contacts. I wouldn't be surprised if you'd been getting reports from a former boarder all winter about Cade's recovery."

Smiling, she said, "You make me sound like a spymaster. A career choice I never considered. But to answer your question, what I'm holding back is about Ash. Though it's an old story, and public knowledge, I still feel a little squirmy telling you."

"Then don't," I said promptly. "I don't want you to feel squirmy."

And I certainly didn't want to feel squirmy myself, the next time I ran into Ash. My face warmed a little as I pictured a physical running-into episode: Minnie, trundling head-on into the sturdiness of Ash, his hands gripping my shoulders to keep me from falling to the ground, my face turned up to his. A nice image, but I was seeing Tucker. Every once in a while.

Aunt Frances sighed. "No, I think you need to know."

"Okay." I pulled out a chair and sat. "Spill."

She toyed with the corner of an envelope. "I met Lindsey, Ash's mother, the first year I moved here. I know you don't remember Everett very well, but he and

Lindsey's husband had grown up next door to each other and were good friends up until the day Ev died."

"So you got to know Lindsay because Uncle Everett and Ash's dad hung out together?"

Aunt Frances nodded. "Dinners, card games, cookouts. You know the kind of thing. Ash was the cutest little toddler imaginable."

Oh, I could imagine all right.

"Anyway," she said, "it wasn't until Ash started to talk that anyone realized there was something wrong."

"What do you mean?"

"The poor boy stuttered." She sighed. "It was awful. He couldn't say two words in a row without one of them getting stuck inside his mouth. The other children were horrible to him."

That, too, I could imagine. "There isn't a trace of it in his speech now. How long did it take for him to get over it?"

She gave me a long look. "Almost eighteen years."

I stared at her. "You mean, he stuttered all through elementary school?" I winced. "And middle school?"

"High school, too," she said sadly. "Lindsey finally found a speech therapist who could help when he was a junior."

I pictured a younger, shorter Ash. Tried to imagine that Ash being a natural target for bullying. No wonder he didn't realize how good-looking he was. In high school, the popular girls would have turned up their noses at him. Then I realized a piece of the story was missing. "What happened to Ash's dad?"

Aunt Frances pushed her papers together in a sloppy pile. "Not my story to tell," she said briskly. "Do you have everything?" She nodded at my box.

I wanted to ask whose story it was to tell, but let it go. "Everything but an answer to one question. If you can ask me how things are going with Tucker, I get to ask you how things are going with Otto."

The faintest blush of pink gave her cheeks a spring-like look.

"Never mind," I said, holding up my hand. "I think I figured it out."

We made our good-byes and I hefted my box. I went out through the dining room and the living room, and it was then that I noticed an addition to the long-standing arrangement of framed photos on the narrow table behind the sofa. Uncle Everett. The same photo that had, until recently, been on her bedside nightstand.

I gave my aunt a silent cheer and headed home.

That evening, an unaccustomed fit of domesticity overcame me and I went all out in the dinner department, to the extent of stopping at the grocery store and buying specific ingredients.

"Mrr."

"Lettuce is, too, an ingredient," I said to my feline critic. "It's listed right here." I leaned down and held the cookbook in front of his face. "See? Right there under Caesar salad. And don't get excited about the anchovies, because I didn't buy any."

Once upon a time, Kristen had made me try them, and they were okay, but I knew that if I bought them for this meal, I'd use half a dozen and then the rest would turn moldy in the refrigerator. Unless I shared them with Eddie.

"Sorry, pal. I didn't think about that. Next time."

He sniffed at the cookbook, then jumped up onto the back of the dining bench to criticize from a distance, but that must have turned boring because he started snoring five minutes later.

I stirred and whisked and cut and broiled and soon I was sitting at the table with a nice meal of salad, brown rice, and shish kebabs. "See?" I pointed at my full plate. "I can, too, cook. Don't let anyone tell you different."

Eddie opened one eye, then shut it again.

"Yes, I can tell you're confused." My fork went into a marinated and broiled chunk of green pepper. "See, it's not that I can't cook; it's that I don't like to."

Eddie's head popped up. He stared at me with wide-open eyes.

"Yeah, I know. I've been scamming people for years with the Minnie-can't-cook theory. But I didn't start that story. Because I don't cook, people assume I can't. The story grew all by itself."

"Mrr."

I nodded. "Sure, early on I could have explained myself, but I didn't, and now the fiction is being taken as fact." I ate my salad and thought about the myth that I'd accidentally perpetuated. It had its benefits, but there was an element of hovering deceit that was starting to bother me.

"What do you think, Eddie?" I asked. "Should I make sure everyone knows that I'm perfectly capable of, well, maybe not baking, but of cooking as well as the average single person? Should I clear this up? Eddie?"

His snores grew louder. I rolled my eyes at him and reached for a book.

By the time I'd washed the dishes and cleaned up the kitchen—tasks that fulfilled nothing in me and were part of what drove me to cold cereal and takeout—a warm wind had blown up from the south. The temperature had skyrocketed, and there was no way I was going to stay inside on the first evening of the year that you could round up to sixty degrees without cheating too much.

I zipped my windbreaker and looked at Eddie, who was sitting on the dashboard, watching seagulls flap past. "Want to come with me?"

Eddie turned and almost, but not quite, looked in my direction.

"Come on, it'll be fun. We don't have to go far. A mile at most. I can put on your harness and your leash and—"

My cat hurled himself to the floor, raced across the kitchen, and bounded down the stairs in one leap. He pushed open the bifold closet door and the last I saw of him was the tip of his tail snicking into the closet.

"I take it that's a no on the walk?" I tipped my head, listening for an answering "Mrr," but there was nothing.

"Fine." I took a marker and wrote where I was going on a small whiteboard, just as I promised my mother I'd always do as long as I lived alone, shoved my cell phone into my pocket, and headed out.

Two minutes later, it was clear that I wasn't the only person in town who wanted to get out into the warm sun. Half of Chilson was out and about on the downtown streets and waterfront. Families with children in strollers, families on bikes. A few singles, like me. Couples walking hand in hand. Friends walking in loose groups. And absolutely everyone was smiling.

"Minnie, hello!" Aunt Frances and Otto—a hand-in-hand couple—strolled toward me.

"Long time no see," I said. "What's up with you two?"

Otto, the man I'd practically had to push into my aunt's arms, smiled. "Why did no one tell me how sudden a northern Michigan spring could be?" He gestured toward the blooming forsythia bushes and the blossoming daffodils. "Didn't it snow last week? This is glorious!"

I grinned, suspecting that his enthusiasm was due, in large part, to the growing relationship between him and Aunt Frances. "We don't want everyone to know," I said in a stage whisper. "Even more people would move up here."

Otto laughed. "You're a transplant yourself. Isn't that a little hypocritical?"

"Didn't you know?" I looked at him with mock impatience. "It's okay if *I'm* hypocritical." A couple sitting on a nearby bench waved hello in my direction. "Excuse me," I said to my aunt and her paramour. "I need to go talk to these nice folks."

"Hey, Minnie," Irene Deering said. "Want to sit a minute?"

Adam slid over a few slow inches. "Have a seat," he said. "We have an excellent spot for watching people launch their boats." Their car was at the nearest curb behind the bench—Adam hadn't walked far.

I sat. The friendly criticizing of boat launching was a

popular pastime. "Anyone back into anything yet?" The previous year I'd watched a guy jackknife his pontoon boat into a piling. It had happened so fast that no one had had time to stop him, and the results hadn't been pretty.

"Not so far," Irene said. "But there was this huge cigarette boat that—"

"Shh!" Adam waved her to silence. "Would you look at that?" His voice was full of reverence. "Perfection. Pure perfection."

It would have been an excellent time to call out for *P* words, but Irene was rolling her eyes. "Don't mind him," she said. "He gets like that around wooden boats."

"Well, he's not the only one." I was wide-eyed myself at the mint-condition Chris-Craft being backed down the boat ramp. Twenty-eight feet if it was an inch, in the classic runabout style. "That one's a beauty."

"One of these days I'm going to get my own," Adam said.

I smiled. "You want a woodie?"

"With all his heart and all his soul," Irene said. "He's been talking about it for years. I'm pretty sure it's one of the reasons we moved up North, so it would be easier for him to find the right fixer-upper."

"Not sure I'll have as much luck with that now." Adam pulled in a short breath as the owner of the Chris-Craft climbed into the boat and started the engine. "Henry said he'd find me a boat."

The backs of my hands tingled. "Oh?"

"Sure," Adam said. "We used to drive around, looking. Henry was one of those guys who knew guys with boats sitting in their barns. You wouldn't believe some of the wrecks we saw. But I've never restored a boat, so for my first one I need something a little easier."

Irene elbowed me. "Did you hear that? 'My first one,' he says."

"That implies there's going to be at least two," I said.

"Probably won't even be one, without Henry." Adam sighed. "I didn't get the last names of half the guys we talked to, and Henry drove so many back roads I don't know where most of them were."

"But you remember the boats," Irene said, rolling her eyes again.

"Well, sure. There was this Century that would have been great, but the engine was blown. I mean, I can do some mechanical, but a whole engine? Not my thing. I want to do the woodwork. Take this Hacker-Craft. If there'd been less hull rot, I would have picked it up in a minute."

Irene nudged me. "He'll go on like that for hours," she whispered. "You'd better escape while you can."

"I'm good," I whispered back. And I was being completely truthful, because it was a fine night, and I couldn't think of a better place to be than sitting there in the warm night with my friends, watching boats go in and the sun go down.

It was all very good indeed.

Except for that tapping sorrow for Henry.

And that nagging worry about Adam.

The next day was another day off for me, which made two in a row and would be the last time I had two days off in a row until after the book fair, so I wanted to make the most of it. I'd go for a long bike ride or maybe a long walk, wash the outsides of the houseboat's windows, even eat outside if it was warm enough.

So when I woke to a steady drumming of rain on the roof, I heaved a huge sigh.

"Mrr," Eddie said, sleep heavy in his voice.

"Yeah, I know." I turned sideways, which made him slide off my collarbone and onto the bed. "Oh, stop whining. Maybe you didn't want to move, but you don't mind this." I snuggled him close and kissed the top of his fuzzy head. "There. Any complaints now?"

He yawned and rolled over.

I gave him another kiss. "You'd complain if you were served your favorite stinky wet food every day for a week, saying you wanted more variety." I slid my arm out from underneath him and got up. "If every day of the entire year was warm and sunny, you'd complain that it was too hot." I padded to the shower, talking back over my shoulder. "If I stayed home every single day, you'd complain because I'd disturb your naps."

At the door to the shower, I paused and looked back.

He'd already moved and was curled up onto a loose Eddie-shaped ball on my pillow.

Cats.

I ate a bowl of cereal and a piece of toast for breakfast, then spent a happy couple of hours reading. Some might call rereading Cynthia Voigt's *Jackaroo* for the fifty-second time a guilty pleasure; I called it therapy.

At noon, I went all out and made a fried egg sandwich with a side of steamed broccoli for lunch.

"Don't tell, okay?" I said to Eddie as I picked up the sandwich. "About the cooking thing, I mean."

He was sitting on the bench seat across from me, and the bottom of his chin was level with the tabletop. I was pretty sure he was hoping to get his own plate at the table, but I was equally sure that was never going to happen.

After chewing and swallowing, because I always tried to maintain my table manners, even if my dining companion was a cat, I asked, "So, what should we do with the rest of the day?"

Eddie didn't say anything, so I picked up my phone and sent Tucker a text.

Day off for me. Recommendations?

A couple of minutes later, my phone dinged. *Assisting on a hip resurfacing,* Tucker wrote. *Come watch — we start in 30 min.*

Which meant that the surgery would start three and a half hours before I arrived.

Maybe next time, I texted back. I started to type, *Good luck,* but stopped. Maybe surgeons were like actors and being wished good luck was bad luck. Of course, texting *Break a leg* didn't seem appropriate, either, so I sent my standard *Miss you!* and set aside the phone.

"I still don't have any plans for the day," I told my cat, who looked at me intently.

"No," I said, "I'm not going back to bed to nap away the afternoon. You can do that if you'd like, but I'm going to do something productive."

A bright light flashed. Half a second later, thunder crashed overhead.

Eddie's yellow eyes didn't blink.

"Nice try," I said. "But just because I'd be risking life and limb by going outside right now doesn't mean my only alternative is to do what you want. And stop that. Your sighs don't influence me at all."

Which was a downright lie, but he didn't need to know that.

Eddie jumped up onto the back of the bench and flopped down onto the lap blanket I'd had on my legs when I was reading. My brother and sister-in-law, Florida residents, had given the beach-themed cotton throw to me for Christmas, and Eddie seemed to particularly like lying on top of the palm trees.

I watched Eddie settle down at the base of his favorite tree and thought about snapping a cell phone photo and sending it to Matt, my brother. I could ask him if—

"Brothers," I said out loud, and reached for my phone.

Half an hour and four phone calls later, I had the numbers for all of Henry's sons. While living in a small town can limit some of your options, it can also make it relatively easy to get the information you need.

From oldest to youngest, their names were Mike, Dennis, and Kevin. Ages went from forty-three down to thirty-nine. Occupations were a firefighter, a computer programmer, and a piano tuner. Locations were upstate Maine, Denver, and Southern California.

Three sons, three different time zones. I pondered the wisdom of calling, then decided that thinking too much might stunt my growth, and dialed.

When Mike Gill answered, I introduced myself, saying that I'd been a friend of his father's, was sorry for his loss, and that I was calling because I'd heard a developer was trying to convince the heirs to sell the property.

"Same old Chilson," Mike said, chuckling. "Rumors run around up there faster than the speed of light."

"Well, I don't know how much people are really talking. I ran into Felix Stanton yesterday and he happened to mention it, that's all."

"If Felix told you, he's probably telling everybody."

Which sounded like a fair assessment of Mr. Stanton. "If you do sell, I hope you give someone a chance to buy your dad's maple-sugar-making equipment. There's a lot of history there, and I'm sure someone would love to have those things."

"Not going to happen," Mike said.

"Oh." The light around me went flat. "I see."

"No one's going to get Dad's things," Mike said confidently, "because next year we're all going to be up there."

"You mean . . . you're not going to sell?"

"I won't lie to you—we thought about it. We got together via Skype the other day and hashed it out. With Mom and Dad both gone now, it's on us to make it a point to get together. We've talked about it for years, especially now that we all have kids, but it never seems to happen."

"Scheduling can be hard," I murmured.

"Absolutely. But the three of us used to help Dad with the syrup every spring—it's not rocket science, just a lot of wood and a lot of time—and we figured it's time to start doing it with our own kids."

He went on, describing the plans they were making to get a neighbor to collect the maple sap—"We'll let him take at least half"—and how they were going to time their vacations, since syrup making was so completely weather dependent, and how they were already collecting canning jars.

I wished him and his brothers the best and hung up, hoping that Felix wouldn't be able to convince them differently. Money was a smooth talker, and the lure of making maple syrup might not hold up against the lure of a lot of zeros on a check.

"What do you think, Eddie?"

My cat, who was still on top of the palm tree, opened his eyes a small fraction, then closed them again.

"So you're saying you don't want to go outside for a walk with me?"

As I spoke a gust of wind buffeted the window. Though I didn't exactly see the glass flex under the wind's pressure, it probably should have.

Eddie jumped to the floor and made a beeline for my closet. I followed him and found him wedged into the closet's back corner, wrapped around my rain boots. "You are the weirdest cat ever," I told him.

He burrowed his head deeper toward the bottom of the closet and didn't say a thing.

"Have a good nap, my fuzzy friend." I packed my backpack with cell phone, wallet, and a couple of books because you just never know, pulled on my raincoat, and headed out into the wild weather.

Outside, another buffet of wind almost made me change my mind, but I knew it would do me good to get out and do something, even if it was just driving around.

And I could even do something marginally useful, such as check out possible bookmobile routes. I never took the bookmobile down a road without vetting it first with my car—what looked fine on a map had the potential of being problematic for a large, tall, thirty-one-foot-long vehicle with the turning radius of a semi-truck.

I pointed the front bumper of my car south and east of Chilson, and a dozen miles later, once I got around the east end of Janay Lake, I headed straight south to farm country. There were roads down here I'd never driven, and who knew what fun things I might see?

There were all sorts of possibilities, really. Barns with murals painted on their sides. Fences made from stacks of fieldstones. Garages made of hundreds of short pieces of wood stuck together with concrete. Wide vistas of hills and woods and lakes and sky. Deer. Turkeys. Grouse. Woodpeckers. Bald eagles. Black bears, even, and I'd heard rumors of mountain lions, which seemed unlikely but you never knew.

Though it was still windy, the rain had stopped. I pushed in a CD of a Canadian group, the Bare Naked Ladies, and was happily humming along about having a million dollars, enjoying the countryside that was starting to fuzz with green, when the rattletrap pickup that had been a couple of hundred yards ahead of me for the last few miles took a left turn.

"That's Mitchell's truck," I said out loud. Mostly trucks all looked alike to me, but Mitchell's had the unusual attribute of having one color for the bed, another for the body, another for the hood, and yet one more for the passenger's door.

For no other reason than sheer curiosity, I decided to follow him. Maybe I'd figure out why he was acting so oddly. A weird Mitchell was acceptable and even desired, but Mitchell's current weirdness was so out of the ordinary that it needed explanation.

At least that was what I told myself as I followed him onto a narrow gravel road. Far ahead, I watched the back end of his truck run over the ruts and potholes at a much faster speed than I dared push my little sedan. The only thing I knew about oil pans was that they lived on the bottom of vehicles and were a bad thing to thump upon.

My teeth chattered together as my car bounced down the road. Every so often I'd wince in preparation of a pothole too big to go around and sigh in relief when the hole didn't suck me in forever.

It wasn't long before I lost sight of Mitchell altogether. While the number of road crossings in the last bumpy mile were zero, there had been a number of long driveways that he could have turned down and been lost to my sight.

When I reached the top of a long hill and saw no car on the road, either in front of me or behind, I knew I'd lost him. "Rats," I said, and came to a stop. I reached into my glove box for the Tonedagana County map and opened it up.

"Huh." If I turned around, I'd drive the same two and a half miles of rotten roads before reaching asphalt. If I kept going, I'd drive two miles of gravel road before I reached asphalt. The odds of the gravel ahead being in better condition were minimal, but at least it would be different gravel, and half a mile less was half a mile less.

I folded the map and tucked it away. "Onward," I said, and forged ahead.

The next mile and a half of road was, if anything, worse than the road behind. It was wetter, for one thing, and mud spray soon covered the hood and spattered the windows. "Stupid weather," I muttered.

The weather up North was, I'd found, not what you'd call predictable. It could be raining buckets down at the marina, but not raining at all a mile away at the boardinghouse. On the east side of the county, snow could be coming down at a rate that would guarantee a school closing, and the west side would get a dusting. The temperature near Lake Michigan could be ten degrees different from what it was a quarter mile inland. It was odd, but also wonderful in a weird sort of way.

I bounced down into, and up out of, a hole that wanted to swallow me whole, and when my head stopped bobbing, I saw something that made me brake to a complete stop.

Not too far from the road, parked under a tree and covered with a tarp, was a wooden boat. Back farther in the trees was a farmhouse so dilapidated that I doubted it was still being occupied.

I tapped my fingers on the steering wheel. Had this been one of the boats Adam and Henry had come across? If Adam had already rejected this one as too much work, there wasn't much point in me getting out into the mud to take a look, but if he hadn't, maybe this could be the boat of his dreams.

"Buck up," I muttered. "What's a little mud?"

I pulled the car as far off the road as I could and got

out, immediately stepping into a puddle. I sighed; I'd left my rain boots in the closet because I hadn't wanted to disturb the sleeping Eddie, and was wearing old running shoes.

But it was just a little mud and would clean off—eventually—so I kept going.

Closer to the boat, I could read the label. Hacker-Craft. The company had been building boats in New York for more than a hundred years, and every one was a beauty. Expensive, too, so it was unusual to see one in a place like this. Adam had mentioned seeing a Hacker, hadn't he? Was that the one with the hull rot? I crouched down.

"Hey! You!"

I looked up to see a thin, white-haired woman hobbling toward me. "Oh, hello. I was just looking at your boat. I have this friend who—"

"Get away!" She lifted her hands and I belatedly realized that she was holding a long-barreled gun. "You get away right now! You're trespassing!"

Fear jumped into my throat and I backed away. "S-sorry," I said, holding up my hands. "I didn't . . . I wasn't . . ." My rear end thumped against my car and I fumbled for the door handle with one hand as I continued to hold up the other.

She pointed the gun at my feet. "Get away!" she shouted.

I fell into the car, started the engine, and got.

Chapter 10

The deputy at the front counter took lots of notes. Or he did until I got to the point where I told him exactly where I was when I'd been threatened with certain death.

"You were out on Chatham Road?" he asked. "Just north of County Road 610?"

I nodded. "Half a mile north, probably. Her house was on the east side of Chatham."

"Uh-huh." He put down his pen. "Hang on a second, okay?"

It wasn't okay, but that didn't seem to matter. The deputy left me alone in the stark lobby. I leaned against the high counter. Decided it was too high to do that comfortably. Wandered around, studying the scarred plastic chairs and decided that I didn't want to sit in any of them. Stood looking out the tall, narrow window and decided that I didn't like looking at the world through glass with wire mesh through it. Sighed, and stood near the counter, listening to the hum of the fluorescent light.

I'd just decided that the rhythm of its humming was close to the beat of "In-A-Gadda-Da-Vida" when I heard footsteps coming my way.

"Ms. Hamilton," Detective Inwood said. "I had a feeling it was you."

Since I was sure the desk deputy had described who was up front and since there probably weren't many other five-foot-tall women in the county with curly black hair named Hamilton, I didn't applaud his extrasensory powers. "Don't you ever get a day off?" I asked. "You do know it's Sunday, right?"

He plucked at his golf shirt. It was a faded maroon and had paint spatters of numerous colors across the front. "This," he said, pointing to a light yellow, "is the color in the paint can that's still open in my downstairs bathroom. I hope to return before it dries."

I squinched my eyes at him. "You didn't leave the brush out, did you?"

"Wrapped in plastic and in the refrigerator. Now. I hear you ran into Neva Chatham."

"Hang on," I said. "Please tell me you didn't come in just to talk to me."

"Sorry, Ms. Hamilton." The detective smiled faintly. "You are not the sun around which my world revolves. Another situation demanded my attention. This is just a little bonus for me."

I almost laughed out loud. In another five years or so, the detective and I might come around to having a decent working relationship.

"Neva Chatham," he said. "What were the circumstances?"

So I told the story again, starting with driving down the road, minding my own business, and ending with me sending my car far faster down a rutted road than was good for it. Or me.

"Uh-huh." Inwood leaned against the counter and put his hands in his pockets. Which meant he wasn't writing anything down. "So you were trespassing."

"You'd have to get a surveyor out there to be sure," I said a little sharply. "There's a strong possibility the boat was inside the road right-of-way."

Inwood's grin came and went so quickly that I wasn't sure I'd even seen it. "Ms. Hamilton, what exactly are you here for? To press charges? And what would those be? Mrs. Chatham didn't touch you, so there's no bodily harm involved. And she didn't damage your vehicle, so there's no property damage."

My mouth opened and shut. What was going on? "A woman threatened me with a firearm," I said carefully.

Detective Inwood smiled. It was a good look on him; he should do it more often. "And if you hadn't been poking around her boat, this never would have happened, now, would it? All you have to do to avoid a situation like this in the future is to stay away from that Hacker-Craft."

I frowned, wondering how he knew what kind of boat it was, but strong-mindedly stayed on topic. "Aren't you concerned that she'll hurt someone? What if she goes after a child with that gun?"

Inwood's smile went even wider. "I don't think we have to worry about that, Ms. Hamilton. Now, please don't tell me you want me to spend my Sunday afternoon trudging out to see a little old lady and then writing up a long report."

"She threatened me with a firearm," I said again.

"Did she really?" Inwood asked. "What were her exact words?"

"That . . ." I thought back an hour. "She said to get away." And there it was. Not a threat, not really. Although you'd think having a gun in her hand would make it one.

"So that's it." The detective nodded. "Not sure something like that will come to anything. You're welcome to talk to the prosecutor, of course, if you'd like to pursue the case."

Oh, right. As if that would get me anywhere. First thing the county prosecuting attorney would want was the police report, and since the pertinent police didn't look as though they were about to move a muscle, getting a report was going to be a bit of a problem.

"That sounds like a fine idea. Hope your paint hasn't dried up," I said politely, and was rewarded by watching his face go from patronizing kindness to one of anxiety. Ha! Score one petty point for Ms. Minnie Hamilton.

Outside, the wind and wet was still going on, but I stood there and let it whuff against me. For whatever reason, the detective and the deputy were protecting Neva Chatham. And while I could appreciate their concern for an elderly woman who might be a touch unhinged, I was more than a little concerned about what she might do to anyone who stopped to look at her boat. Or what she might do to herself, for that matter.

Again, I saw that small black hole at the end of her

gun. A shiver ran over me, top to bottom, and I was fairly sure it didn't have anything to do with the weather.

Because I'd just realized what I should have realized earlier. If Neva Chatham could charge after me with a gun, she might not have been far from firing it. And if she could shoot at me, could she have dropped a tree on Henry? Could she have tried to run over Adam?

I stood there, staring out at the wind-whipped Janay Lake, and wondered.

The next morning I bounced out of bed five minutes before the alarm went off. "Good morning, sunshine," I said to Eddie.

My furry friend opened his eyes, then closed them again. Firmly.

"Come on, get up." I tapped one of his white paws. "It's a brand-new day out there. The wind has dropped, the clouds are gone, and it looks like it's going to be a stunning spring day."

Eddie squirmed around and put one paw over his eyes.

"Fine." I gave him a head pat and stood. "I'll leave you alone. But don't blame me if you get bedsores, okay?"

Less than an hour later, I'd showered, breakfasted, and walked up to the library, while sending a morning text of *Beautiful morning, wish you were here* to Tucker. After a moment, I got a *Stuck in traffic, wish I was there, too* text back, so my perky mood continued all the way into my office.

The first thing I did when I sat at my computer was start up Google. I typed in *Why don't cats get bedsores?* and frowned at the lack of results. Really? I was the only one who'd wondered? Surely the question had occurred to every cat owner at least once. Clearly someone needed to get going on their cat research.

Grinning at myself, I started checking my office e-mail.

"Uh-oh," I said. Because there was an e-mail from Pam with an attachment, dated late last night, subject line *Book fair flyer.* Happily I'd managed to tuck the Flyer Fiasco into the back of my mind over the weekend. My index finger hovered over the mouse button for a long moment.

"Be brave," I said out loud, and clicked open the attachment.

When it appeared in front of me, I stared at it for a long time before I did anything. Since that lack of anything included breathing, it wasn't long before my lungs burned and I was sucking in air while reaching for the phone.

"Pam," I said, when she answered groggily. "It's Minnie. Call me when you've finished your coffee, okay?"

The minutes ticked past slowly, but the phone eventually rang. "Hey, Minnie," Pam said. "What's up?"

"What, exactly," I asked, eying the flyer she'd sent, "did you do in Ohio?"

Pam had moved to Chilson a year ago, and though we got along wonderfully, I didn't know much about her. I knew that she possessed more fashion sense than I ever would and that she loved coffee with a passion that bordered on scary, but I knew very little about her background.

"Worked for a large corporation that shall remain nameless," she said.

"Doing . . . ?"

"Graphic design," she said, and I could hear the grin in her voice.

"You are a scammer," I said.

"Every chance I get."

The design she'd sent was eye-catching, readable, and fun without being overly cute. It was perfect. "This is the best graphic that's ever come out of this library," I said, "and I'm sorry, but I absolutely can't pay you. There's nothing in the budget."

She made a gagging noise. "It's April. I was glad to have something to do. There's just one thing," she said sternly. "Don't tell a soul I did this. Lie if you have to, but if word gets out that I've done something for free, my days are numbered. I mean, it was fun now, when there's nothing else going on, but in summer I won't have time for it."

After vowing to keep her involvement a complete secret, I thanked her, thanked her again, and hung up.

I printed the flyer and tacked it to my bulletin board, which was right next to the portrait of Eddie that Cade had forced upon me as a thank-you gift. For the ten thousandth time, I admired the painting, and then I moved on to admiring Pam's flyer; not only the design, but also the name of thriller writer Ross Weaver. Yes, indeedy, Ross

Weaver was coming to the Chilson Library and yours truly would get to meet him in less than two weeks.

Less than two weeks?

A small alarm of panic went off in my head. There were a million things I had to do between now and the fair date of Friday after next. Flyers to distribute. Authors to confirm. Tent rentals and catering issues to finalize. Make that two million things. What was I doing, just standing there?

I flung myself into my chair and got busy.

Late in the day, so late you could call it evening, I'd finished as much book fair business as I could get done that day, but I wasn't ready to walk back to the houseboat. Not by a long shot. The library's Internet connection was much faster than the marina's, and there was research to be done.

I pushed up my metaphorical sleeves, typed the name "Seth Wartella" into Google, and hit the Search button. With the faster connection, I wouldn't stop looking after the top twenty searches. No, indeedy, this time I would keep looking at Seth Wartellas to the end of all the listings. Plus, there was Facebook to try, LinkedIn, Pinterest, and all sorts of other social media sites where I might catch a glimpse of the man.

Maybe he was completely innocent of all wrongdoing, except for that tax fraud thing along with a side order of embezzlement, so maybe I was wasting my time. But if there was any chance of finding evidence that Seth had been in, say, Hawaii, when Adam was almost run over, then I had to try. I'd promised Adam and I'd promised Irene and I'd promised myself.

And on the bright side, at least he wasn't named Bill Smith. Things could always be worse, right?

I nodded to myself and started clicking.

The long rays of the sinking sun flared onto my computer screen. Hunger pangs gnawed at me, but those were easier to ignore than the emotion that was creeping into the back of my throat. I swallowed down the feeling and it went into my stomach, where it didn't mix at all well with the emptiness.

"Not a good plan," I muttered to myself, and took a long drink of water from my coffee mug. Which helped a little, but not very much.

Sighing, I pulled out my cell phone and made the call. Better to get the task over with now than to stew over it.

"Hi, Minnie," Irene Deering said.

There was a lot of noise in the background, so I figured she must be at her waitressing job. "Can you talk a minute?"

"Sure. I'm on break. What's up?"

"I've been trying to track Seth Wartella online," I said. "I've been looking at Facebook, Pinterest, all those."

"What did you find?" Irene asked, her voice tight.

"Nothing," I said. "Absolutely nothing."

"What do you mean, nothing?"

"Exactly that." Suddenly I couldn't sit still any longer. Phone in hand, I stood and paced around my office. "He wasn't anywhere. I couldn't find any sign of him on the Internet at all."

"You know," Irene said slowly, "that sort of makes sense. Before he went to jail, he was all over the Internet. That's part of the evidence they used against him, the timing and content of some of his Facebook posts."

That did make sense. I stood in front of my office window. It was dark enough now that what I mostly saw was myself looking back at me. "There's been no trace of Seth Wartella since he walked out of prison." I pulled in a deep breath and let it out. "He's vanished."

Chapter 11

My uneasiness about Seth didn't dissipate overnight. It didn't go anywhere as I showered and dressed the next morning and it didn't go away as I crunched through my cornflakes.

It was only after I'd hauled Eddie's carrier up the steps of the bookmobile and finished the pretrip checklist that my mood started to shift, because I'd finally looked around and seen that it was going to be a beautiful spring day. Janay Lake was flat calm, the sky was blue, and though the morning was a little chilly, it was supposed to get close to sixty degrees later on, and who could ask for more than that?

"Mrr."

"It's April," I told Eddie as I strapped his carrier into place. "It's pointless to ask for summerlike weather in April. You'll doom yourself to disappointment. Can't you be happy with the blue sky?"

He didn't say anything, as he was busy rearranging himself on his pink blanket. It had been crocheted for him last summer by one of my aunt's boarders and he'd taken to the soft fuzzy thing as if it had been a long-lost brother.

"Cats always want more." Julia laughed as she came up the steps. "Life with a cat is one long negotiating session."

"No wonder I'm tired all the time," I said, glancing back at the books. All shipshape and seaworthy. Ready to go, Captain!

Julia slid into the passenger's seat. "You're tired because you're working too hard."

"Not true. I didn't go into the library the entire weekend."

"When was the last time you did that? And when's the next time you're going to take off two entire days in a row? Even better, when are you going to take a full week of vacation and get a true rest?"

"Mrr," Eddie said.

"See?" Julia asked. "I'm not the only one who wonders these things."

I snorted and turned the key in the ignition. The bookmobile's engine started with a happy rumbling sound. "Eddie only wants me to take time off so he can get me to let him in and out and in and out all day long."

"Eddie?" Julia looked down at the carrier by her feet. "Is this true? Are you really that self-centered?"

There was a long pause; then came a quiet "Mrr."

"Told you," I said, grinning, and I dropped the transmission into drive, starting another day on the bookmobile.

*   *   *

At the end of the day, we pulled into the farm drive next to Adam and Irene's house. "I'll just be a minute," I said to Julia. "I talked to Irene last night and she said Adam was on a John Sandford kick." I picked up a plastic bag that held half a dozen of the thrillers set in Minnesota. "Are you okay here with Eddie?"

Julia unbuckled her seat belt and stretched, which made her look a little bit like a cat herself. "Me, Eddie, and three thousand books." She smiled. "I think I'll manage to find something to do."

The Deerings' driveway seemed shorter that day, but maybe that was because I was carrying a smaller bag of books. I knocked on the front door and poked my head in. "Adam? It's Minnie."

"In the kitchen," he called. "Come on in."

Adam was sitting at a square wooden table. Nothing was in front of him; he was just sitting there. He had the look of a man who'd tried to walk a little too far and had dropped into the closest chair available.

I gave his face a quick study. He was pale, but not sweating and not shaking. "Doing okay?" I asked, emptying the bag onto the table.

"Better now," he said, reaching for *Buried Prey*. "Thanks for stopping by. Irene said you might."

"Did she tell you what I found out about Seth?"

He nodded. "Yeah. Not that weird, I suppose, but here I thought all that social media stuff was supposed to make it easy to find people."

"Not if you don't want to be found," I said. "And if . . ." My voice faded away.

"What?" Adam asked.

"Where did Irene think she saw Seth?" I couldn't remember her saying, and I'd neglected to ask.

"Chilson," he said. "Downtown, somewhere. She was driving through town and saw him on the sidewalk."

Downtown? Excellent. It would take time, but I could work with that.

"Why?" Adam asked.

"Another possible area of investigation," I said vaguely, sounding even to myself as if I were spending too much time with law enforcement officers. Then I remembered the other thing I wanted to tell him. "I think I found one of those wooden boats that you and Henry found."

Adam immediately brightened. "Where? Do you know what kind it was?"

I told him about my bumpy, rutting time and finding a tarped-over Hacker-Craft on the side of Chatham Road.

"Sounds right," he said, nodding. "Was there a cranky old lady with it?"

"She came at me with a gun," I said crisply.

"What?" Adam's eyebrows shot up. "You're kidding. Neva?"

"You know her?"

Adam shook his head. "Henry did. Back in the day, she used to date his older brother. He went downstate to college and really never came home. Got married and moved to Virginia, Henry said, and died a few years ago of a heart attack."

"Neva didn't come at you with a gun?" I asked. "Did you look at the boat?"

"Henry did, mostly. Once I saw that hull rot I got a little nervous." He stared off into space. "But now that I think about it, what's a little rot? That could still be restored to a beautiful boat."

I headed back to the bookmobile, thinking.

Maybe Henry had earned the wrath of Neva because of her long-ago failed relationship with his brother. It seemed odd that a romance from fifty years ago could have anything to do with what was happening now, but who knew? And though Adam had said he didn't look at the boat, he'd been close enough to note the hull rot. If he'd been that close, Neva would surely have seen him, and who could say what she might be capable of?

Frustration pulled at me and I lengthened my stride, trying to outdistance it.

All I was finding was more questions. I was going to have to start finding answers. And sooner would be much better than later.

I swallowed the spoonful of clam chowder. "You're nuts. There's nothing wrong with this. It's the best I've ever had."

Kristen frowned mightily and tossed the spoon by which she'd fed me into the nearest kitchen sink. "Why do I even ask? You're the worst taster ever."

"Because I like the food you make?" I looked around for a stool and pulled one up to the restaurant's kitchen island. It looked as if the preopening dinner Kristen had invited me over to eat wasn't going to materialize, not if she was still tweaking tomorrow night's recipes. Ah, well. It wasn't as if we'd go hungry.

"You like anything you don't have to cook." She stirred the chowder, reached for a jar of some spice I couldn't identify, and added a couple of shakes. "That might do it." She grabbed another spoon and tasted. "Ha! Now, *that's* the best clam chowder ever."

"Let me try." I found a clean spoon and reached forward to fill it with the thick, chunky chowder. "Mm," I said. "You're right. That is the best ever." To me it didn't taste any different from the previous spoonful, but why tell that to the cook, especially if there was a chance she might ban me from the crème brûlée that was coming up later?

She ladled two bowls almost to the brim and dragged another stool over to the island. As we sat side by side, companionably slurping up chowdery goodness, I felt warm and cozy and content with life in general. Clam chowder did that to me.

"So, what's going on in your life?" she asked, when the bowls were half-empty.

My contentedness snapped away. "I told you about Adam Deering almost getting hit by that car, right?"

Kristen nodded. "You never told me the whole story, though. You never told me how close you came to getting hit."

"Me?" I blinked at her. "It was aiming for Adam. Anyway, I've been trying to find Seth Wartella. The guy from Chicago."

"Seth who?"

I frowned, midslurp, which was harder than I thought it would be. "I haven't told you about him?"

"Busy, busy, busy." She waved at the kitchen around

us. "Maybe, but if you did it got mixed up with the staff schedule or the produce delivery schedule or that asparagus soup recipe I've been working on."

Or maybe I just hadn't told her, knowing that she was wacky busy with the restaurant opening. But she was relatively calm right now, so I told her about Irene's possible sighting of the man her husband had helped put in prison.

Kristen was frowning. "Why do I know that name?"

"Seth?"

"No, Wartella." She drummed her short fingernails on the stainless steel counter. "Wartella . . ." She grinned. "Got it. Tony Wartella. He's a conservation officer. Didn't you come across him last year?"

"That's right," I said slowly. "I'd forgotten." Last Thanksgiving, I had indeed talked to an Officer Wartella about what might have been a hunting accident. "I wonder . . ."

"If Tony and that Seth are related? You could be right. I think Tony is originally from the Chicago area." Kristen pointed south, in the direction of far-off Illinois. "I can find out, if you want. Tony and his wife are regulars on Tuesday nights."

That was the night she offered a special—buy one dinner, get another half off—something that a lot of locals appreciated. "That would be great," I said, then went on to tell her about not finding any trace of Seth on the Internet, at which she shrugged.

"My mom's not on any social media, either, and the only crime she ever committed was the time she stayed too long in a parking space."

"That's not a crime," I said.

"Tell that to my mom." Kristen scraped up the last of her chowder. "She got a ticket and had to pay a fine, so now whenever she has to fill out a form that asks if she's ever been convicted of a crime, she says yes." She looked over. "You going to finish that?"

I pushed my bowl toward her. "There's one other weird thing." When I told the story of the recent out-of-town Mitchell sighting, she was suitably surprised, but when I told her about stopping to look at the wooden boat and being threatened by a gun-toting senior citizen of the female persuasion, she looked appropriately frightened and indignant on my behalf.

"Why do they let people like that have guns?" she asked.

"I reported it to the sheriff's office," I said. "But she didn't fire the gun, she was on her own property, and I have no proof there was ammunition in it." I shrugged. "But she did scare the daylights out of me."

"What's was her name?"

"Neva Chatham."

"Huh. There are lots of Chatham stories floating around." Kristen scooped out the last of my chowder and spooned it into her mouth. "I wonder how many of them are true. Can't say I know any Chathams personally."

"Don't talk with your mouth full," I said, then started thinking about families. About family resemblances and family traits and how while sometimes if you know one member of a family you know what they're all like. Then again, sometimes members of the same family, even siblings within a year or two of each other, are very different, and not always in a good way.

"What's the matter?" Kristen asked.

"Just thinking," I said, then started to tell her my exact thoughts.

But before I got halfway through, she rolled her eyes, stacked our dishes, and got up. "Sometimes you think too much," she said. "And you can quit with the protest; you know it's true."

"Do not," I muttered.

"Well, you're wrong." She opened the door to the closest refrigerator. "And if you want dessert, you'll admit that you're wrong." Grinning, she pulled out two ramekins of crème brûlée, both already topped with local greenhouse strawberries and sprigs of mint.

Clearly blackmail, but it was blackmail of the most excellent kind.

"You were right," I said mechanically, "and I was wrong." When she continued to hold the ramekins out of reach, I sighed and finished our time-honored litany. "I'm sorry."

"Apology accepted." She slid the desserts down the counter. "So, are you going to try to stop thinking so much?"

"Don't see how that's going to happen." I picked up the spoon that was sliding toward me.

Kristen plopped onto her stool and picked up her own spoon. "Just as well. If you didn't overthink everything, you wouldn't be you, and then where would you be?"

On a count of three, we plunged our spoons through the crackly sugar crust and I knew there was absolutely nowhere else in the world I wanted to be at that moment other that sitting next to my best friend.

*   *   *

It was when I was walking home, post-dessert, that my cell rang with Tucker's ring tone. While we'd been texting almost every day, or nearly, we hadn't actually talked since I couldn't think when.

"Hey," I said, smiling into the phone. "I was just at Kristen's, eating way too much excellent food. What did you have for supper?"

"Leftover pizza, I think. Although that might have been yesterday."

I laughed. "Doesn't your mother feed you?"

"I've been taking extra shifts," he said. "There's a lot to learn here, and the more hours I work, the more I learn."

Which sounded good, but I was suddenly getting a bad feeling about the turn the conversation was taking. I stopped walking and sat on a nearby bench. The sun was down, the streetlights were on, and the sunset's afterglow filled the west part of the sky with a fading golden blush. "So you're working a lot," I said carefully.

"It's the best way to learn."

"Yes, you said that."

The silence between us grew long and thick. I sat there for so long, not talking, that I almost forgot who was on the other end of the phone.

"So," Tucker said, "it looks like I won't be able to make it up there in June."

"Yeah." I suddenly couldn't stand to sit any longer. I got to my feet and started walking. "I had a feeling you were going to say that."

"Minnie, I'd come up if I could."

"Sure. I know." Sort of.

"It's just that I don't want to miss any opportunities. If I'm going to go anywhere and do anything, I need to make the most of this fellowship."

"Sure. I know." Which I'd already said, but Tucker didn't seem to notice my repetition.

"Why don't you come down here?" he asked.

And do what, sit and talk to his parents while I waited for him to come home from the hospital because he couldn't turn down a chance to take an extra shift, even when it was the first time he'd seen his girlfriend in months? No, thanks.

"It's a really busy time for me," I said. "With the book fair and all the summer people coming and vacations starting, it's going to be really hard for me to get away."

"Yeah," he said. "I kind of figured, but I thought I'd ask."

I squinted at the sky's last light and wondered exactly what he'd meant by that. Had he hoped I'd say no? Because that was what it sounded like. "You know I'd come down if I could," I said, echoing his own statement. And again, he either didn't notice the repetition or chose to ignore it.

"Sure."

We made stilted small talk for a little longer, and by the time I got back to the houseboat, my phone was back in my pocket. I opened the door and was greeted by the sight of my cat sitting in the middle of the kitchen floor and staring straight at me.

"Let me guess," I said. "You overheard that entire

conversation and are now ready to offer romantic advice."

He didn't move. Didn't even blink.

"Strike one." I tossed my jacket onto the pilot's seat. "Second guess. You were deeply lonely without me and have been sitting there for hours, pining for my return."

Eddie lowered his head slightly but didn't break eye contact.

"Strike two, huh?" I leaned down to scoop him up. "Third guess. When you woke up from your most recent nap, you realized I still wasn't home and have been sitting there for the last thirty seconds, wondering if your food supply will ever be replenished."

"Mrr!" He nudged the side of my face with his head.

"You are such an Eddie," I said, nudging him back, and as his purr started, the sting of Tucker's phone call faded away almost as if it had never been.

Almost.

Chapter 12

My sleep that night was interrupted by sporadic dreams that featured a book fair attended by a total of zero people, and a wooden boat that had sunk under me the first time I launched it in Janay Lake.

I woke up with Eddie's body snuggled around my neck and his tail tangled up in my hair.

"You know," I told him, "if you stayed down by my feet, I'd sleep a lot better."

He rearranged himself slightly and didn't say anything.

It probably wasn't fair to blame him for my poor sleep, but I hated waking up while I was still tired, and at the time, it seemed entirely reasonable to point fingers at the furry creature who was on my face.

"Off, already, will you?" I gave him a shove.

"Mrr!" He rolled around in a lengthwise somersault and lay there, looking up at me.

I should have apologized right then and there, but I didn't. Instead I flung back the covers and trudged up to the shower without a word to my furry friend. By the time I was dry, he'd retreated to the back of the closet and wouldn't come out, even when I tried to tantalize him with the last of the milk at the bottom of my cereal bowl.

"Come on, pal. I said I'm sorry." I swirled the milk around. "You were right and I was wrong and I'm very, very sorry."

Sadly what had worked with Kristen didn't do anything for Mr. Ed.

"Tell you what. How about I leave the bowl here and you can finish it up on your own schedule?" I put the bowl on the floor and peered into the closet's depths. He was back there behind my boots, but all I could see of him was the furry arch of his spine. "I'll see you tonight, okay? And I am sorry."

He might have said "Mrr," but then again it might have been my imagination. Sighing, I headed up to the library, figuring that my day could only get better. And it did until I went into the break room in answer to Holly's e-mail of *Got something for you. Come and see!*

I grabbed my empty coffee mug and headed out. Holly's chocolate chip cookies were on my list of the top ten best cookies ever, and her peanut butter fudge was better than my mom's, something that I'd never told my mom and never would.

I was in the mood for cookies, so when I walked through the door, my anticipatory smile went flat when I saw there were, in fact, no cookies on the counter. Or fudge. Or brownies or even cupcakes. Instead Holly was sitting at the break table, sorting through a packet of paint samples.

"What's that?" I asked, filling my mug with coffee. I hoped either Holly or Josh had brewed this pot and not Kelsey, who was still trying to convince everyone that coffee thick enough to use as frosting was the best kind.

"They're for Josh," She pushed the long rectangles into half a dozen piles. "You know darn well that he'll just paint every room in his house beige if we don't help him, so what do you think?" She pointed at the small stacks. "Living room. Kitchen and dining. Master bedroom. Bathrooms. Study slash guest room." Frowning, she asked, "Do you think he has three bedrooms?"

I had no idea. "Pink? You really think there's any chance he'll paint even a small bathroom pink?"

"It's not pink." Holly picked up the sample and peered at the tiny writing. "It's strawberry blush."

"It's pink," Josh said.

Holly and I turned. Our coworker was standing behind us, eyeing the wide variety of colors with disfavor.

"Oh, good," Holly said. "You're here. These are the colors you should think about for your living room, and these are—what are you doing?"

He was feeding coin after coin into the soda machine, was what he was doing, and not paying any attention to her at all.

"Come on, Josh," she said, wheedling, "don't you want to look?"

"Not really." He pushed a button and a can rolled down.

"Sure you do."

"Nope."

Don't worry, Holly," I said. "It's not your fault. Most

men don't see the importance of decorating. They like the results, just not the work that goes into it."

Josh gave me a sour look. "Who asked you?"

I wondered if Eddie had somehow been snoring on Josh's head last night, too. "Did you sleep okay?"

He snorted. "What, because I don't want to paint my bathroom pink means there's something wrong with me?"

"No," I flashed back. "It's because there's so obviously something wrong with you that makes us think there's something wrong with you."

"Yeah," Holly said. "You're being really cranky. Are you sick?"

"Oh, for crying out loud," Josh said. "I'm out of here." He stalked away without even bothering to open his soda.

"He can be such a jerk sometimes." Holly looked at her rainbow of colors. "We're just trying to help."

"We?" I echoed. "How did I get dragged into this?"

"Fine." Holly shoved all the paint samples together into a small heap, got up, and tossed them into the wastebasket. "I can't believe no one cares about this. You're both being jerks. Just plain jerks." She stomped out.

I shook my head at them both and did some stomping of my own on the way back to my office. But even before I sat down in my chair, I knew I'd have to do something about the situation to make sure it didn't take a festering turn into a permanent rift. It wasn't likely to, but a little reassurance never hurt.

Thinking fast, I typed an e-mail message to them both. *Sorry I was cranky just now. I didn't get much sleep and I'd like to blame Eddie. Would that be okay?*

After I hit the Send button, I opened up the bookmo-bile's summer stop schedule, but before I could start working on it, I heard the ding of an incoming e-mail.

It was from Holly: *That darn Eddie. I'm okay blaming him if Josh is.*

Ten seconds later, there was another ding. This one was from Josh. *He's a pretty big cat, so yeah, I bet he can take the blame.*

And just as I finished reading that e-mail, a second one came in from Josh. *But it was really the new video game I bought yesterday. I was up half the night figuring it out. Sorry.*

And then came the final one from Holly: *And Wilson has an earache, so I'm sorry, too.*

Smiling, I went back to my spreadsheet, a little sur-prised at how happy their e-mails made me. Reassur-ances, apparently, were a good thing.

By lunchtime, I decided that if I could add another reas-surance or two to my life, it could only be a better thing. My conversation with Kristen the night before about families and siblings had combined with my lack of sleep to trigger a question that needed answering by two dif-ferent people.

My previous research had given me the phone num-bers I needed, and as I walked out the library door, I thumbed on my cell and pushed the proper buttons for calling person number one.

"Good morning, Denver Fire Investigation Unit."

"Hi," I said. "Can I speak to Dennis Gill, please?"

"Is Captain Gill expecting your call?"

I blinked at the title but remained undaunted. "No, but it's about his father's estate." Sort of.

"One moment, please."

The phone went silent. I was just starting to assume that I'd be dumped into voice mail when the silence ended. "This is Dennis Gill. How can I help you?"

I introduced myself the same way I'd done with his older brother, said that I'd been a friend of his father's, was sorry for his loss, and that I was calling because I'd heard a developer was trying to convince them to sell the property.

There was a chance that Mike had told his brothers about my phone call, but it had sounded as if they didn't talk often, so there wasn't much risk I'd get called on it. Besides, I could always say that I'd heard more rumors about the property being sold and just wanted to double-check.

This was all because I'd realized, at three in the morning, that taking the word of a complete stranger about what could be a very lucrative development deal might not have given me an accurate picture of reality.

"Sell Mom and Dad's place?" Dennis asked. "That's the furthest thing from our minds. Yeah, we could probably make a bundle selling it to Stanton, but with Dad gone, we've decided we need to make a real effort to get together. It's too easy to let the years go by, you know?"

I murmured that keeping up the house might be an expensive endeavor, and that property taxes didn't usually go down.

"Sure," Dennis said, "but Dad left behind some decent assets. With some investment luck, the income will pay for everything and maybe even a little more."

"That sounds great." I paused, then said, "I think your dad would have been very pleased to hear all this."

He gusted out a sigh. "I hope so. He was hard to figure out sometimes. Not a big talker, even when Mom was still alive."

I smiled, thinking of Henry's typical communication-by-grunt. "No, but he was a master at getting his point across in one syllable or less. Best ever, if you ask me."

Dennis laughed. "Thanks for calling, Minnie. And let me know if you hear more rumors about the property being sold. I'd like to know where they're coming from."

I promised I would and ended the call. One down, one to go, and I was only halfway to downtown. Plenty of time for another. I thumbed the phone again.

"Northeast Networks, how may I direct your call?"

"Kevin Gill, please."

"One moment."

I got an earful of a techno version of "You Are My Sunshine" and was on the verge of deciding to call back later when the music broke off and a man said, "This is Kevin."

Two minutes later, Kevin Gill was laughing. "Sell Mom and Dad's place? Not a chance. Mike and Dennis and I practically made a blood oath that condos won't go on that property in our lifetimes."

I smiled. "What about your children?"

"You know, we talked about that," he said. "I have a buddy who's an attorney and he says if we really want to lock up the property we should think about adding deed restrictions. We just might do it, too," he added thoughtfully. "And if we tie up Dad's money in a trust, make all the money go to the maintenance and taxes for the place, we can guarantee it'll stay in the family."

I wondered how that might work a few generations down the line, when there might be dozens of Gills, but there are only so many things anyone needed to think about, even me, so I thanked Kevin and let the thought go.

With the second reassurance of the day complete, I was ready for lunch. And since by this time I was all the way downtown and right in front of Shomin's Deli—how serendipitous!—I opened the door.

Inside, the brick-walled, wooden-floored, and tin-ceilinged restaurant was a relatively busy place. Relatively, because with almost half the tables occupied and three people in line, it was very busy for April. In summer, "busy" would mean a line out the door and strangers would be sharing tables, which could sometimes be a lot of fun, but I was fine with the April emptiness.

Of the three people in line in front of the glass display cases, one was a library patron whose name I couldn't remember, one was a minister from Aunt Frances's church, and the third was Felix Stanton. It had taken me a second to recognize him, since he was wearing a tweed blazer over brown pants and dress shoes instead of a canvas coat and hiking boots, but I made the connection before the blank look on my face became too fixed.

I nodded at the first two and said hello to Felix.

"Minnie, right?" he asked. "Good to see you."

I had a quick internal debate. Resolved: that it is best

to share all information at all times. Since the winner of the debate was the part of me who thought that open sharing couldn't possibly be a good thing when a killer might be wandering around, I kept my chats with the Gill brothers to myself.

"How are things going?" I asked. "Any new projects for the summer?"

He smiled affably and rocked back a little on his heels. "Have a number of things on the back burner," he said. "Just working on which one to bring up front first."

"Anything you can talk about?"

"Too early to say." He smiled down at me. "But if you're looking for a nice piece of property, just stop by the office and we'll hook you up with something quality."

At this point in my life, my financial priority was paying off the last of my student loans, not saddling myself with a mortgage, but I smiled at Felix. "I'll keep that mind." Then, before he could turn away, I said, "After I saw you the other day at Henry's place, I ran into a neighbor of Henry's, Cole Duvall."

"And how is Cole?" Felix asked. "I haven't seen him or his wife in some time."

"Well, here's the thing," I said. "Cole said you'd been talking to Henry for months about developing his property, but you told me that you'd only recently approached Henry's sons." In the time it had taken me to speak those two or three phrases, Felix's face had gone bright red. I hoped the man didn't have a heart condition and kept going. "So either Cole has it wrong or I do, and I was just wondering which—"

"Are you saying I'm a liar?" Felix thundered.

The scent of coffee-flavored breath assailed me, but I looked at him calmly and didn't step back. There were many occasions for which I was grateful for being height-efficient, and this was another one. A lifetime of being shorter than everyone over the age of thirteen had inured me to intimidation by size and/or voice.

"No," I said evenly, "I'm just trying to figure out what's going on."

Felix, now at the head of the line, turned away from me and tossed a bill on the counter. He looked back over his shoulder and said fiercely, "Anything that's going on is none of your business, little missy. Just keep yourself to yourself."

He snatched up the cardboard container that the young man at the register had pushed toward him, then stormed out.

"That was weird," I murmured. I'd anticipated either a blank look or a smiling evasion, but to be blasted with vitriol over a simple question was so unexpected that I wondered what was going on inside Mr. Felix Stanton. Not that it was necessarily murder-oriented, but you had to wonder.

"Don't take it personally," a familiar voice said.

I turned and saw that Pam Fazio was standing behind me. "Thanks," I said, laying down the money for my up-coming sandwich. "I appreciate that. I certainly didn't expect to be berated in public by someone I barely know."

"Well," Pam said, opening her wallet, "I've known

him for quite a while and he gets like this every so often." She grinned. "He's being even more Felix-ish than usual, is all."

"Here you go, Minnie," the counter kid said. "One Swiss cheese and olive on sourdough with Thousand Island dressing."

I thanked him and took my sandwich. "So," I asked Pam, "I shouldn't lose any sleep over this?"

She shook her head, tossing her short black hair around. "Nah. He's like that with everyone these days, right, Evan?"

The counter kid rolled his eyes. "You got that right."

I shook off the icky feeling that had crept onto my skin during the unexpected confrontation. Onward and upward—there was something else I needed to do. "I have a quick question for both of you, if you have a second."

"Sure." Pam handed over her money to Evan, who nodded.

"A little while ago," I said, hoping the story I'd manufactured was believable, "there was this guy in the library, and I think he left something behind. A nice leather notebook." This wasn't completely a lie—I had indeed found a notebook. Last summer, but still. "He was short, not much taller than me, with bright red hair."

"Sounds maybe familiar," Evan said, "but I haven't seen anyone like that, not that I can remember."

Pam grinned. "Short, eh? Looking to pick on someone your own size for a change?"

"No one's my size." I sighed dramatically. "I gave up on that a long time ago."

"Well, like my grandma says," Evan said seriously, "you never know what's around the corner."

This was true, and a good thing to remember.

I thanked them both and walked out, thinking hard.

After stopping at a few other downtown businesses, asking after a short red-haired man, and receiving similar answers to Pam and Evan's, I walked back toward the library slowly, so slowly that I figured I could save some time by eating and walking simultaneously. The first bite, however, was so good that I knew I wanted to be mentally present for every chew. I looked around for a place to sit that was in the sun and out of the wind, and found one in a narrow park that ran from downtown to the waterfront.

The sun on my face felt almost warm as I sat, and I mentally crossed fingers and toes, legs and arms, that the weather would be this nice for the book fair, coming to a library near me in one week, two days, and twenty-one hours. Or thereabouts.

But there was nothing I could do about the weather other than worry, and since one of my life goals was to worry as little as possible, I pushed weather thoughts aside and thought about Felix Stanton.

Thought about the chances of Henry being killed because he wouldn't sell his property to Felix for the construction of a condominium project.

Thought about the odds of Felix assuming that Henry's sons would sell the property. Looking at it from Felix's point of view, selling the property only seemed reasonable. Mike, Dennis, and Kevin lived hundreds of miles away and returned to Michigan once a year. Why wouldn't they want to get rid of what would be an encumbrance to them? That property would only be a financial drain; it only made sense to sell.

If Felix had designs on Henry's property, if Henry had refused to consider selling, and if Felix had, in fact, killed Henry to get access to the land, the fact that Henry's sons wanted to hang on to the property had to have been a bitter blow.

Then again, maybe Felix had been telling the truth about not working out a plan for the property until after Henry's death. Which meant one of two things about Henry's neighbor Cole Duvall. Either Cole hadn't remembered correctly about Felix talking to Henry last fall, or Cole had intentionally misled me.

I tried to remember exactly what he'd said, and, three bits of sandwich later, it came to me.

Stanton has been trying to talk Henry into selling since last fall.

Which meant that if Cole was telling the truth, Felix wasn't. Conversely, if Felix was telling the truth, Cole was definitely not.

One of them was lying.

And that raised the big question: why?

I sat there, staring at my sandwich, knowing that a possible answer was "To hide a murder." A sudden wind gust made me grab for my napkin. I looked up at the sun and watched it disappear behind the leading edge of a massive bank of low clouds.

Fifteen seconds ago I'd been happy to sit outside, but

with the wind shifted and the sun gone, inside was suddenly much more appealing.

I tossed the last of my meal into a nearby garbage can and headed back to the safest place in the world, where cold winds never blew, where people were friendly and polite, and where things were interesting but not scary.

The library.

Chapter 13

Thursday, a bookmobile day, was a happy day of children who laughed, adults who smiled, and an Eddie who not only supervised the activity with aplomb, but who willingly participated in any event that seemed to need his assistance. Which, that day, was a toddler who wanted to clutch at the "'itty 'itty" with both hands and an elderly man who said he'd never liked a cat in his life until he'd met the bookmobile cat.

I was a trifle concerned that all the attention might go to his head, but on the way to Chilson, Julia began a recitation of Mr. Mistoffelees from T. S. Eliot's "Old Possum's Book of Practical Cats," which I was pretty sure took the wind out of Eddie's sails, especially when she finished the poem and described the onstage antics of the Mr. Mistoffelees from the *Cats* Broadway musical version.

"Poor Eddie," I said, laughing. "He'll never be the dancer Mr. Mistoffelees has to be."

"Eddie has his own special charm." Julia blew him a

kiss. "Don't you, my fuzzy little friend? We love you just the way you are."

"Mrr," he said agreeably.

"I think he said he loves us, too," Julia said, laughing.

Most likely he was saying that he wanted a treat, that he deserved a treat, and that if he didn't get a treat he was going to sleep on my head that night, but I let Julia keep her anthropomorphic point of view. Why disillusion her? She'd realize soon enough that Eddie, charming though he might be, was just a cat and not a small furry human.

"Mrr," Eddie said again, this time a little louder.

"Are, too, just a cat," I muttered under my breath, quietly enough that Julia wouldn't be able to hear. I flicked a glance over to Eddie, and saw him turn around inside his carrier and present his hind end to my direction.

Mrr to you, too, pal, I thought, then grinned. Who was I to talk about treating Eddie like a human?

After the fine Thursday, it was a little depressing to wake up to a Friday with the dim light of a day that promised little except low, heavy clouds and rain, with the added attraction of some thumping winds.

"What do you think, Eddie?" We were sitting in the houseboat's dining booth. "Looks like the last day of April is going to be decidedly dreary. What are you going to do with your time?"

I set my cereal bowl on the floor, and Eddie jumped down to lick out the last of the milk. When he was finished, he sat and gave his face a swipe with his front paw; then he padded down the stairs and through the short hallway. There was a quiet squish of fabric, and I knew he'd jumped onto the bed.

"Have a nice day," I said as I pulled on my rain boots and raincoat. "Sleep well." When I opened the door to let myself out, I could have sworn I heard the faintest whisper of a sleepy "Mrr."

Smiling, I headed out into the spattering rain. How I could find comfort in knowing that my cat was spending the entire day sleeping on my bed, I didn't know. I only knew it was true, and that I was very, very glad Eddie had chosen to spend his life with me.

A few short hours later, I desperately wanted to join Eddie. To pull the covers up over my head and sleep the rest of the day away. Or even better, to sleep away the next week and two days.

"Did you hear me, Minerva?"

I had, in fact, heard what my boss had just told me over the phone, but I didn't want to believe it. If it had been anyone else, I would have laughed and told him to quit the kidding, that he'd almost scared me with his bad joke, and to try harder next time.

"Yes, Stephen, I heard you." Bizarrely, my voice sounded normal. "But I was hoping . . ."

Stephen snorted. "That I was joking, perhaps? I would have thought you'd know me better than that. No, when I told you that Ross Weaver is having to cancel his appearance at next week's book fair, I was being completely truthful."

"That's what I figured," I said faintly.

"Yes," Stephen said. "Ross has had a family medical emergency involving his mother, and he won't be able to attend the book fair."

"I hope she'll be all right," I murmured.

"What? Yes, yes, she's getting the best of care, and it's likely that she'll be fine, but Ross is canceling all appearances for the time being. I'm sure you understand."

"Of course," I said.

"Well, then." Stephen cleared his throat. "I just wanted you to know the circumstances so you can take appropriate action."

Appropriate action? I held down my laughter, which would undoubtedly end up as slightly hysterical.

"Minerva," Stephen said sternly. "If you have the least desire to take over as director, you'll need to learn to take charge during emergencies of this kind. You'll need to prioritize and to quickly decide which items you can delegate. You'll need to . . . Minnie, are you listening?"

"Absolutely," I said, scribbling another name onto my notepad. "I need to decide what I can delegate."

"Exactly. Now, do you need help with this or can I rely on you?"

I sat up straight, turned to the left, and gave the ceiling a smart salute. You can rely on me, sir! "I'm all set, Stephen."

"Let me know if you need anything," he said, and the phone went silent.

I hung up the phone, looked at my list, then picked it up again. If the book fair had any chance of success, I had to get busy fast.

At the end of the day, the muscles around my jaw were tense from too much talking. I'd called the McCades, I'd called Carolyn Grice, a wealthy woman I'd met last year. I'd called Julia. I'd called the bookstore and the schools and the museum and the chamber of commerce, begging for the name of any author who might be willing to drop everything and come to Chilson.

"*When?*" they'd all asked. "*Well,*" I'd said, "*next Saturday. For the book fair.*" After they realized I was serious, they said they'd try, but the doubt in their tones revealed how unlikely it was that their efforts would be successful.

I thumped my head onto my desk and wondered if I'd have less stress in my life if I switched careers and became an air traffic controller.

I worked late that night, trying to tidy up the Book Fair Fiasco. After calling the newspaper and asking them to print a change-of-plans advertisement, I posted notices about Ross Weaver's cancellation on the library's Web site, on the library's Facebook page, and tweeted the sad news far and wide. Mr. Weaver, if he'd known, would have been pleased at the widespread return concern for his family emergency, and I said I'd pass on all the notes to him. Which I did by bundling them all into one big e-mail and tossing it over to Stephen.

By the time I dragged myself home it was long past dark, and only the knowledge that if I didn't eat something, I might faint dead away on the sidewalk and become an object at which people pointed and murmured vague comments about "How sad, she had so much potential" sent me into Fat Boys Pizza for the sustenance of a sub sandwich. Heavy on the protein, ma'am.

Eddie and I and a fresh copy of Alan Bradley's latest Flavia de Luce mystery went to bed early, and we woke up to a bookmobile day of stiff winds and fast-moving clouds.

When I lifted the cat carrier out of my car for transportation to the bookmobile, a sharp wind gust filled the carrier and twisted me around.

"MrrrRRRrrr!"

"Sorry about that," I said. "It's just that kind of a day."

But it wasn't, not really. Because as soon as Julia came aboard and we were rolling deep into the eastern part of Tonedagana County, the clouds parted and the sun came out.

Julia, though she was a Tony award–winning actress, was not on anyone's list of quality singers. That, however, didn't keep her from singing the song from the musical *Annie*, the one where the little girl is betting her last dollar that the sun will shine the next day.

When she paused for breath, I asked, "Are you sure you want to do that?"

"Do what?"

"This is northwest lower Michigan. Are you sure you want to bet any money, let alone your last dollar, that the weather forecasters are accurate?"

Julia grinned. "Now, Ms. Hamilton, you know perfectly well the song is a metaphor. It's about being optimistic, about looking on the bright side of life. What's so funny?"

I shook my head, trying to get rid of the image from the last scene of Monty Python's *Life of Brian*. "Metaphor, shmetphor. All I care about right now is finding a Ross Weaver replacement. How can the book fair possibly be a success if—" I blinked at the sight in front of me.

"Minnie?" Julia asked. "Are you okay?"

"Um, sure." I gave my eyes a quick rub but was still

seeing what I thought I'd seen. We were approaching Peebles. With a population of less than a thousand, Peebles had a retail district of a block and a half and was primarily known for its outstanding diner-style restaurant.

And right in front of my eyes was Mitchell Koyne, walking into the restaurant next to the same woman I'd seen him with on my trip back from Alpena.

"Do you see that?" I asked Julia, tipping my head Mitchell-ward. "Do you know who that is?"

Julia squinted. "It looks like Bianca Sims. She's a real estate agent. Out of Petoskey, I think. Don't know the gentleman. He's a tall one, isn't he? Do you know him?"

"Oh, yes," I said, grinning inside and out. "I do indeed."

And the last of my mostly self-induced stress about the book fair vanished. How could I ever have thought, even in jest, about changing jobs? Everything would work out, one way or another. Either people would show up or people wouldn't, and all I could do was my best.

Plus, out here on the bookmobile, I came across things like this, seeing Mitchell Koyne, of all people, holding hands with a real-live successful professional woman. How could life get any better?

The second half of the day took us close to the area where I'd followed Mitchell's truck, which meant we were nearing Neva Chatham territory. I told Julia about the incident, and she made sympathetic noises, reassuring me that my reaction to a gun pointed in my general direction hadn't been over-the-top. However, she didn't know anything about the eccentric Ms. Chatham and wasn't sure she knew anyone who did.

"We're in the opposite corner of the county from Chilson," she said, a little apologetically. "I don't know many people over here."

So when the first group of bookmobilers came on board that afternoon, I started asking around, in a sideways sort of way. The first person I asked was a tailored elderly gentleman whom I might have wanted to introduce to my aunt if she hadn't already been seeing Otto.

"Neva Chatham," he said, smoothing his white mustache. "John Chatham's daughter?"

I had no idea, but there couldn't be many people walking around with the first name of Neva. "She lives in an old farmhouse out on Chatham Road."

"That's right," my gentleman said. "John and Marie's daughter. Only child, if I recall correctly." He got a faraway look in his pale blue eyes. "They were good people. Sad, really, what happened."

"Oh?" I asked. "What's that?"

He shook his head, clearing away the memories. "What happens to all of us. We get old, we get sick, and we die." He smiled, taking away the brutishness of his statements. "Don't mind me, I can get a little maudlin in April. It's the weather, you know."

I blinked at him. It was the first of May, and the weather had turned sunny and bright and close to downright warm. But April can hang on inside you, so I knew what he meant.

At the next stop, I asked Mrs. Dugan, a patron I knew to be chatty, about Neva.

Mrs. Dugan sighed and shook her head, her white curls staying in place with steadfast firmness. "I worry about her, I really do. All alone in that big house with no one to talk to. She doesn't even have cable television."

"I heard she was an only child."

She nodded. "That's right. Doted on her father. Not sure she ever left home, especially after he got sick. Then he died and her mother just faded away, if you know what I mean."

"How old was Neva?" I asked.

"When her dad got sick? Goodness, I really don't know. I was just a little girl at the time, so she was probably somewhere in her twenties. And the poor man lingered so." Mrs. Dugan sighed. "Probably lasted twenty-five years. Thinking back on it, he probably had multiple sclerosis. So little they can do about it now, and back then there was nothing."

Which meant Neva was around fifty when her father died. She'd spent the most productive years of her life caretaking her father, then her mother, and never had a life of her own. No husband, no children, and now no grandchildren.

Mrs. Dugan was still talking, so I tuned back in. "How Neva managed to take care of her parents and run that farm I'll never know. The place has been in her family since homestead days, so I doubt there's a mortgage, but the property taxes alone must eat her alive."

Property taxes. Yet another reason to put off buying a house. "It's a working farm?" I asked.

"If you want to call it that." Mrs. Dugan half laughed. "She has a few dairy cows and runs a summer farm stand, selling fruits and vegetables. Raises quite a variety, Neva does, with that greenhouse her granddad made. Gets strawberries before anyone else in the county."

"She does this all by herself?"

Mrs. Dugan shrugged. "Must be. Makes jams and jellies, too. Gets a pretty penny for them, I'll say that for her."

But I was stuck back on the idea that Neva was all alone in her endeavors. "What about her other family, and her friends? What about neighbors? Do they help her? Farming is hard work, and . . ."

Mrs. Dugan was shaking her head. "Help Neva Chatham? I wouldn't risk offering, not if my life depended on it. And honestly I'm not sure she has friends, not to speak of."

There was a tug at my pant leg. I looked down and saw a small child looking up at me. He was maybe four years old with jet-black hair, big brown eyes, and the longest eyelashes I'd ever seen on a human. "Hi," I said. "May I help you?"

He nodded. "Miss Neva is my friend."

"She is?"

Again he nodded. "My mommy takes me to get raspberries. Miss Neva helps me pick the best ones."

I smiled. "You like raspberries?"

He nodded vigorously. "Lots and lots. With cream. And just a little sugar, not too much, Miss Neva says, or you won't taste the berries."

Mrs. Dugan make a *tsk*ing noise and glanced down the aisle to someone who I assumed was the child's mother. "His mother," Mrs. Dugan said, "is perhaps a trifle lackadaisical in her childrearing efforts."

"What's lack-a-daisy?" the child asked.

"Something you'll learn when you grow up," Mrs. Dugan said, patting him on the head.

The kid glared at her, then spun on his heel and went to his mother's side.

"Miss Minnie?"

I turned to see a middle-aged man looking at me. "Excuse me," I said to Mrs. Dugan, and went to help him.

He looked past me, then said in a soft voice, "I heard what Mrs. Nosy-Toes over there was saying and I wanted to make sure you got the whole story about Neva."

"Okay," I said, quietly and cautiously.

"No one," he whispered, "but no one, has been inside the Chatham house in twenty years, not since her mother died."

I blinked at him. "That can't be right."

"Ask around," he said. "No one has been allowed past the porch since her mother's coffin left the house. More than a little weird, don't you think?" He tapped his temple, shook his head, and went back to perusing the bookmobile's small selection of travel books.

So, according to the adults, Neva Chatham was an eccentric recluse who shouldn't be allowed near children. According to the child, Neva was a friend. What I needed to do was talk to the boy's mother and get another adult point of view.

But when I turned around, they were both gone.

"You have reached the Carters' landline. Please leave a message at the tone." *Beep.*

"Hi, Rachel," I said. "This is Minnie Hamilton from the

bookmobile." I'd asked Mrs. Dugan the name of the young woman with the little boy and she'd told me all about Rachel and her husband and Rachel's mother and father. She would have gone on, I'd been sure, to share decades-old gossip about Rachel's grandparents, but I'd cut in as politely as I could and thanked her for the information.

But this was the second time I was leaving a message and I was starting to wonder if I was ever going to hear back. I left a brief message, gave my number, and asked her to call, then hung up.

"Well," I said, "what do you think?"

Eddie, who was sitting on the houseboat's dashboard, turned his head ever so slightly in my direction. He might have been responding to my question, but he also might have been watching the seagulls wheeling over the blue waters of Janay Lake.

It was late on Sunday morning, a beautiful day in early May, and I had yet to decide what to do with myself. Eddie and I had stayed in bed for a decadently long time, him snoring, me reading a lovely long mystery by Charles Todd and wishing for a restaurant that delivered breakfast.

But eventually I'd crawled out from under the covers into a bright blue day, showered, and walked up to the Round Table, where I'd indulged myself with their new offering of sour cream blueberry pancakes with a side of bacon brushed with maple syrup. The food was remarkably tasty, and the only problem was now I didn't feel like doing anything.

"Vacation mode," I told Eddie. "That's the problem with going out to breakfast. It makes me feel as if I'm on vacation. Now I don't want to do anything except play. Which is tempting, but there are things I should be doing."

Eddie turned his head and, this time, looked directly at me.

"Not you," I assured him quickly. "I'd never expect you to do anything. Honest. It's me who should do something productive with my day. Since I have thumbs and all that." I waggled said appendages at Eddie.

He stared at me with unblinking eyes. "Mrr!" he said sharply, and returned to his seagull contemplation.

Smiling, I slid into a comfortable slouch on the booth's bench and peered at the stack of books I'd piled up during the week. Eventually I'd get up and do some laundry. Go for a walk. Go see Kristen. Something. But for now I was content to sit and read.

I was three chapters into *All the Light We Cannot See* by Anthony Doerr when my cell phone, which I'd put on the table, beeped with the incoming text tone. Since I was a happy little reading camper, I wasn't sure I felt like responding to whoever was on the other end, but since you never knew when an emergency might turn up, I twisted my head around to look at the screen.

Tucker.

I pulled the phone toward me and tapped at the screen to view his text.

Hey, guess what? Been invited by boss to go to his condo on Lake Tahoe!

Multiple emotions flared at once. Pleasure, that Tucker got along so well with his boss that he'd be invited to a vacation home. Annoyance, that I obviously wasn't part of the invitation. And puzzlement, because while I was sure Lake Tahoe was beautiful, why would you bother traveling so far to a lake when there were plenty in Michigan?

"Sitting on top of one right now," I said to Eddie while I looked out at the wind riffling the tops of Janay Lake's waves. And beyond the dunes, the mass of Lake Michigan lay just to the west. Clear water, clear skies, and not a single expressway within fifty miles. Maybe it wasn't Lake Tahoe, but it was right here, right where my job and my life were.

I tapped out a message: *Sounds like fun. When are you going?*

I'd returned to my book and was half a dozen pages into the next chapter when Tucker's next text came in.

Same week in July I was going north. Sorry, but I can't pass up the opportunity. I'm sure U understand.

Oh, I understood all right.

I started thumbing a message full of fury and bitterness and scorn and hurt. Halfway through, my mother's voice tapped me on my mental shoulder. *Minnie, are you sure you want to do that?*

"Absolutely," I muttered, and kept tapping.

Minnie, she said, drawing out the vowels. *How absolutely sure are you?*

I cleared the text, tossed the phone to the table, and got up. I needed to move, to do something physical, and to not think for a few minutes.

Two hours later, every window on the houseboat was sparkling clean, inside and out. I stood outside on the front deck, hands on my hips, studying my efforts. "What do you think, Eddie?"

"Mrr," he said.

"You're right." Cheerfully I patted his furry head. "I'm pretty sure they've never been so clean." I went inside and picked up the phone, ready now to do what needed to be done, what couldn't — or at least shouldn't — be done via a text message.

I entered his cell number and, when he answered, started talking before he even got in a greeting. "Hey, Tucker. It's Minnie. I think it's time we call this relationship quits."

Chapter 14

Kristen took one look at me across the crowded kitchen and grabbed the closest bottle of wine. "I don't know what's wrong, but I'm sure it will be better with a hefty dose of Merlot."

I plopped myself on a tall stool and eyed the stemmed glass she was filling. "Alcohol does not cure problems."

Without a word, she whisked away the glass and the wine bottle. "How about a big bowl of chocolate ice cream?"

"Can I have chocolate syrup?" My voice was plaintive.

"And whipped cream—the real stuff, not the kind you use—and chocolate sprinkles and a cherry on top."

I sighed. "You are the best friend ever."

"Of course I am." Kristen nodded to Harvey, her sous-chef, and he went to work on what Kristen had ordered for me. For a couple of years, I'd thought that Harvey was in love with Kristen, but he seemed unfazed by her attachment to Scruffy.

"So, what's up?" she asked. "Family issues? Are your parents okay?"

I'd already told her about the book fair cancellation, so there wasn't much use in pretending that was what had drawn me to her restaurant hours ahead of the time I usually showed up on Sundays. "It's Tucker," I said, and her face went quiet.

Around us, the kitchen staff kept on doing kitcheny things. Misty, the head chef I'd greeted on my way in, kept slicing big bits of meat into smaller bits. The two seasonal hires, a middle-aged woman and a young man, both of whom I had yet to meet, continued to chop whatever it was they were chopping. Harvey placed a perfectly presented bowl of ice cream and a spoon in front of me and wafted away.

"So . . . ?" Kristen asked.

I picked up my spoon. Not so very long ago, when I was washing windows, I'd been sure I was making the correct decision. So how was it that now I was waffling? I picked up the spoon and shoved a far too big bite of sugary goodness into my mouth.

"Broke up with him," I said through the ice cream. Speaking with my mouth full was a transgression my mother would never have tolerated, and one I did try to avoid ninety-nine point nine percent of the time, but somehow telling Kristen I'd ended a semi-long-term relationship with my mouth stuffed full of her food made it easier.

She muttered something I didn't quite catch. "What was that?"

Kristen grinned, showing her teeth, white against the

tan she'd accumulated in Key West. "I said it's about time. You're far too good for him and he didn't deserve you. No, don't go all sympathetic and say your schedule was just as wacky as his and half of the problems were your fault, because I won't believe any of it."

A small smile tickled one side of my face. "You won't?"

"Not a chance. How many times did you make plans with him and then cancel? Zero, I bet, yes? Yes. And how many times did he make plans with you and then cancel? No, don't start using your fingers and toes to count, because I'm sure you don't have enough digits."

"It wasn't just that," I said, shoveling in another bite.

"No, it was also because he thought his job was the one that counted. And that attitude was turning into whatever he wanted was what counted, whether or not it had to do with his job."

I blinked at her. She was right and I'd never seen it. "Why didn't you ever say anything?"

"Because I am the best friend ever." She thumped herself on the chest.

Once again, she was right. If she'd told me what she really thought about Tucker, I would have gone all defensive and stuck to him just to prove her wrong. It was a part of my personality I didn't care for, and someday I'd try harder to do something about it.

"So now you can go out with Ash Wolverson," Kristen said. "You want me to call him, or will you?"

"Give me a couple of days, okay?" The idea didn't sound horrible; matter of fact, it sounded quite good, but I knew that jumping out of one relationship and into another wasn't the best idea. I pushed my bowl toward her a couple of inches. "Want some? I hear it's the best in town."

"Do I get my own spoon?" she asked.

"You can have mine," I said, handing it over, "if you don't mind sharing."

She gave me a light elbow in the ribs. "I can share if you can share."

I nodded and started to feel a little better. I would probably shed a few tears in the night, but between Kristen's friendship and Eddie's purrs, I had the feeling that I'd be smiling again soon.

"Hey, Minnie!"

My right foot had been poised to step onto the dock that led to my houseboat. Rafe's call, however, startled me enough that I tripped on the small break between concrete sidewalk and wooden dock. I stumbled forward a few steps and saved myself from falling into the drink by grabbing a piling.

"Hey, Stumble Toes, you all right over there? Got a favor to ask you."

I blew out a breath. There was no good reason for me to be annoyed at him—he probably hadn't intended to surprise me—but I was still on edge about Tucker and men in general and my irritation level was close to the surface. "Yeah, I'm fine," I said, walking back toward his house. When I got close, I asked, "What's up?"

"Got a question." He was on his front porch, waving something at me, but in the evening's dusk, I couldn't see what it was. "It's a girl thing."

"And I'm the only girl you know?" I asked, climbing

up the front steps. Last summer they'd been old and weathered. Now they were solid and sturdy and freshly painted a bluish shade of gray.

"Nah." He grinned. "You're just the handiest one. Look at these and tell me what to do." He held out a small rectangular stack of cardboard pieces at me.

I put my hands behind my back. "Nothing doing. No way am I going to help you choose what color to paint your house."

"Not the whole house," he said, fanning the samples out into a rainbow of colors. "The outside is easy. It's the inside that's hard."

I squinted at him. "And you think I can help? I haven't chosen a room color since I was eight and painted my bedroom dark green because I'd just read *The Children of Green Knowe* and wanted my room to match the cover of the book."

Rafe looked at the paint samples. "Yeah? How did that turn out? I mean, that's probably the stupidest reason I ever heard to pick a room color, but dark green might be okay, somewhere."

My annoyance rushed back. "If you think I'm so stupid, why are you asking me anything? If you want decorating advice, talk to Holly Terpening. She's all over paint colors." I stomped down from the porch and was off into the night's gloom before he could say another word.

My sleep that night was accompanied by a few tears, but by the time I woke up, I was mostly ashamed at how I'd treated Rafe. He hadn't deserved to be on the receiving end of my little hissy fit, and I needed to tell him so.

"Would a phone call do?" I asked Eddie as I washed out our cereal bowl.

He was back to sitting on the dashboard, but he turned his head a millimeter when I asked the question.

"To apologize to Rafe," I explained. "Can I just call? Or better yet, send him a text?"

Eddie heaved a heavy sigh and jumped to the floor. He padded the length of the kitchen, down the stairs, and into the bedroom, where he jumped up onto the bed he'd vacated five minutes before.

"Fine," I said to the sink. "I'll go over there at lunch." Somehow I'd ended up with a cat who held me to the same moral code that my mother did. "Not fair," I muttered, but then started smiling inside, because maybe it was, in fact, eminently fair.

The thought kept me amused all morning, which was good, because it was a day that needed all the amusement it could get. Recalcitrant computer programs, a water leak in the book return, and not a single response to my frantic calls for a new author to headline the book fair didn't make for a happy Minnie.

I pushed out the door at lunchtime and sucked in a breath of fresh air. It felt so good that I pulled in two more, and then had to stop myself before I hyperventilated. Refreshed, I headed up the hill to the middle school and to Rafe's office, where I knew he would be at his desk, eating a bologna sandwich with mustard and mayonnaise on white bread.

"When's the last time you had anything different for lunch?" I flopped into his guest chair. "Kindergarten?"

He gave me an affronted look. "I'll have you know

that just last year I ate a turkey sandwich. Right here at this very desk."

"Well, that's good. I wouldn't want you to get into a rut."

"I prefer to think of it as a very deep comfort zone." He took a bite of sandwich so big that it pouched out his right cheek enough to make him look like a squirrel feeding on a windfall of nuts.

For the millionth time, I wondered how Rafe managed to run a middle school so successfully. "Well, I wanted to stop by and apologize for last night."

"Huh?" He swallowed hugely, then asked, "What are you talking about?"

I really should have known better. Some guys were sensitive to the moods of women, but most were not. Rafe fell deep into that second category. "I was a little cranky about the paint colors. If you really want help, I'll do what I can."

He squinted at me. "Cranky? You? How did that happen? Wait, I know. You lost your spot in a book and had to start over again."

And to think I'd wasted my lunch hour coming over here. I started to stand, but froze in place when I saw his wall calendar.

"What?" he asked, his mouth once again full of sandwich.

"Your calendar." I sat back down. "It's wooden boats."

"Yeah, so? It was a Christmas present. I like woodies. I'm not wacko about them like some people, but they're pretty cool."

Wacko. Like some people. Exactly. I looked at the calendar. Looked at him. Looked at the calendar again. "How do you feel," I asked slowly, "about doing me a favor?"

A few minutes later, I'd explained what I wanted and Rafe was looking at me with an odd expression on his face. "Can I ask why you want me to do this?"

"Sure," I said, and sat there, smiling.

He rolled his eyes. "So I can ask, but you're not going to tell me why you want me to do this tremendous favor for you that will take up so much of my valuable time and pull me away from my many duties as a responsible and supportive school principal."

"Exactly." I beamed at him. What I wanted was to figure out was if Neva Chatham had brandished her gun at me because of trespassing, or because she was being protective of her boat. If it was the boat, maybe she was unhinged enough to have killed Henry and tried to kill Adam. "And quit with the whining. It's a simple phone call and won't take you more than five minutes."

He heaved out an Eddie-quality sigh, pulled a tattered phone book from his desk drawer, and flipped though the flimsy pages. After giving a grunt when he found the correct entry, he picked up the phone and dialed.

"Good afternoon," he said jovially. "Is this Neva Chatham? Hi, Neva, my name is Rafe Niswander. I live in Chilson—what's that? Yes, Dave's my cousin." He squinted at me. "Well, sorry about that. He's got a pretty good reputation for the plumbing work he does and—" He waited for her to finish. "Well, again, I'm sorry about that. I'll be sure to mention it next time I see him."

His eyebrows went up. "Sorry, ma'am, I can't say for sure when that will be, but—" Again he waited. "Yes, ma'am. I will quote you exactly, you can count on it. Now, the reason I called is a friend of mine happened past your house a while back and saw a wooden boat out front. I'm a huge wooden boat fan"—he rolled his eyes at me—"and I was just wondering if your boat was for sale. I'd be—"

Even from halfway across the room, I could hear Neva's voice coming through the receiver.

"You leave that boat alone! I have a shotgun, young man, and I know how to use it, so keep your distance or I'll be after you next."

Rafe hung up the phone and looked at me. "I don't think she's interested in selling." Then his straight face broke up and he started laughing. "Did you hear that? 'I have a shotgun and I know how to use it.'" He slapped his paper-filled desk with the flat of his hand. "Where's a pen? I need to write that down. Hey, what's the matter?"

"I am so sorry," I said. "She knows who you are, and she can probably figure out where you live."

"What?" Rafe stared at me, then started laughing again. "You think she's going to come after me? The woman must be seventy-five years old and might weigh a hundred pounds, dripping wet. What's she going to do, have a heart attack on me?"

I stood and gave him my Librarian Look. "She is obviously unbalanced. Who knows what she might do? I am very sorry I asked you to call her, and please be careful."

Rafe snorted. "Right. Okay, I promise to look both

ways before crossing the street, although since it's only the first week of May I really don't need to look even one way, but if it would make you feel better . . ."

"It would." I apologized again, got another eye roll, and headed back to the library with Neva's words ringing in my ears.

I walked down the hill, thinking about the phone call I'd persuaded Rafe to make and about what Neva had said.

"I'll be after you next."

I pulled my cell phone out of my coat pocket and stopped in the middle of the sidewalk to push the appropriate buttons. Some people could practically do data entry with their phones while walking, but every time I tried to do that I started feeling as if I were on the teacup ride at Disney World and wishing for an emergency stop button.

"Adam?" I asked. "It's Minnie. Got a question for you. When you and Henry stopped to look at Neva Chatham's boat, did you take a close look at it?" I'd asked him earlier about it, and he'd said Henry had looked closely at the boat, but that he hadn't. Now I wanted to know exactly what that meant.

"Got close enough to see that it was too big a project for me," Adam said.

"Sure, but how close was that?"

There was a pause. "I didn't crawl around on the ground, if that's what you mean. What are you getting at?"

"Well . . ." I wasn't exactly sure how to say what I was thinking—excellent preparation, Minnie!—so I didn't say anything for a moment. Adam, however, was happy to fill the conversational gap.

"But if I had the skills, I'd pick up that boat in a heartbeat. Did you see what it was? It's a 1934 Hacker, triple cockpit. Hardly any of those are left and it's a crime it's in such rough shape. This baby is twenty feet long, and I looked it up, it has a six-foot, seven-inch beam. Too small for the big lake, but it'd be perfect for Janay."

"It would?" I asked vaguely.

"Nothing better. Now, it'll probably need a new engine, but if it were me, I'd put in a Chevy MerCruiser, a two-hundred-and-sixty-horse. It'd probably top out around thirty-five miles an hour, and that's a nice speed for a twenty-footer."

He started to go on about the kind of varnish he'd use when I interrupted. "I think Neva might have been the one who almost ran you over."

Dead silence. "You . . . what?"

I repeated what I'd said. "Are you laughing?" I asked suspiciously.

"A little," he said, sputtering. "Thanks for your concern, Minnie, but I'm pretty sure I could handle Neva Chatham. I mean, do you really think that frail little old lady could have cut down the tree that hit Henry? She's not even five foot tall!"

"Size doesn't matter," I said, "when it comes to murder."

Adam was quiet for a moment. "You're right," he said, sighing. "And I suppose it could have been her driving that car, easy enough. It's just so weird, to think someone I've actually met might have tried to kill me."

There were oodles of statistics out there that informed us that the vast majority of murders are committed by someone who knows their victim very well indeed, but I didn't say anything. Adam probably knew it anyway.

I felt basically useless. "Take care of yourself," I said.

"Sure," he said. "You, too."

The phone went silent, but I continued to stand there for some time, just thinking.

If size didn't matter when it came to murder, what did?

What was I missing?

Chapter 15

Thanks to being suddenly short-staffed because of illness and my continued and fruitless phone calls in pursuit of another big-name author, my lunch hour was reduced to the time it took to eat the sandwich I'd made that morning and the time it took to make a few phone calls to more downtown businesses, telling my tale of the man who might have left a nice leather notebook at the library, a man who was short and had bright red hair.

I heard the same thing that everyone else had said, that though the man sounded like someone familiar, no one had seen anyone like that, not that they could remember.

In the evening, I went downtown and asked a few more questions about a red-haired man, but heard nothing that would confirm the presence of Seth Wartella. The closest I got was the owner of the jewelry store, who squinted at the ceiling. "Red hair? A while back there was a guy in here, looking for a present for his wife, but that was around Valentine's Day. And he was tall, not short."

Just because I couldn't find anyone who remembered seeing Seth didn't mean that he hadn't been in Chilson, but I'd run out of time Monday for asking around, and Tuesday would also be out because it was a bookmobile day.

"But this is our favorite kind of day, isn't it, Eddie?" I nudged my feline friend, who was sitting on the carpeted step. It ran the length of the bookmobile on both sides, making a handy seat and an even handier step for those on the bookmobile who needed an extra few inches to reach the top shelf. This included me and almost all the children under the age of seven and a few of our elderly patrons who'd started doing the shrinking thing.

Eddie and I were sitting on the step, doing our combined best to encourage a number of small children to come on over to the picture book section. We were parked at a new stop, which had been squeezed in because how could I turn down a request from a day care provider who said she wanted, more than anything, to show kids how wonderful books could be?

The only problem was, the kids seemed more interested in climbing up and down and up and down the bookmobile steps than in books.

"Emily," coaxed the beleaguered day care lady. "Don't you want to see the books? Yesterday, you couldn't wait for the bookmobile. And here's the bookmobile kitty. Remember? There's a kitty just over there."

"His name is Eddie," I said. "And he'd love to meet you."

Emily didn't seem interested, but one of her companions did. "Where's the kitty?" he asked, abandoning the stairs and looking all around. "I want to see the kitty cat."

"Right here." I put Eddie on my lap and gently arranged him into a lying-down position. "He's purring," I said as the kid came closer. "Do you hear it?"

The boy dropped to his knees and slapped his head against the furry body. "He's noisy!" he exclaimed.

You have no idea, I thought. "That's because he likes you," I said.

"Emily, Emily!" The boy jumped to his feet. "The bookmobile kitty likes me!"

There was a small stampede of children, headed by the apparent ringleader, Emily, and it was coming straight toward Eddie and me. Eddie had already tolerated much that day: a slam-hard-on-the-brakes stop to avoid hitting a deer, a shrieking baby at the first stop, a complete lack of treats because I'd forgotten to refill the canister, and this was apparently the tipping point.

He took one look at the oncoming horde and launched himself out of my lap.

"Ah . . ." I gritted my teeth at the pain and made a mental note to clip his back claws that night. And to file them round.

"Where did the kitty go?" Emily said plaintively. "I want to hear the bookmobile kitty go purr, purr, purr."

I smiled at her and the rest of her cohorts. "He just needs a minute to himself. When he's ready, I'll bring him back and each of you can pet him, one at a time."

Emily, with her lower lip stuck out in an adorable sort of way, gave the topic serious thought. "I guess that's okay."

With the group subdued, at least for now, I showed them the picture books and pulled out a copy of *Mike Mulligan and His Steam Shovel*. I handed it to the day care lady. "Always a crowd pleaser," I said.

She laughed and sat herself on the step. "Who wants to listen to a story?"

The kids crowded around and I headed to the front of the bookmobile to check on Mr. Ed's whereabouts.

"Hey," I said quietly. "Eddie. Where are you?"

His black-and-white head popped up from underneath the driver's seat.

"They're not coming after you," I told him. "Come on out. I promise I won't let them— Hey, what are—"

Eddie jumped up to the seat, clambered over the steering wheel in a completely graceless manner that no self-respecting cat would be caught dead doing, landed on the dashboard, and shoved his face up against the windshield.

"Wonderful," I muttered. My arms weren't quite long enough to clean the glass, so now I'd be looking at Eddie nose prints until I could get someone else to do the washing. "Come down, will you? There's nothing out there except a straight mile of road, a bunch of trees, and maybe a squirrel or two. You might want to play with the squirrels, but I'm sure they don't want to play with you, so turn around and come join the party, okay?"

My monologue was doing nothing to distract Eddie from his inspection of the windshield. "Mrrrr," he said.

"Mrr to you, too." I sat in the driver's seat and reached forward, but Eddie was having nothing to do with me.

Without visibly moving, he edged six inches away and said, "Mrrrr!"

"Right. You said that before. Now, if you'd just—"

"Mrr!"

I winced. "Quit howling," I whispered. "You're going to scare the kids and I know you don't want to do that, so—"

"Mrrr!"

Just as Eddie's howls pierced my eardrums, a battered pickup truck rattled past. On the side was a magnetic sign that read BOB'S BUSINESS; WE DO THE CHORES YOUR HUSBAND WILL NEVER GET AROUND TO.

I smirked at the sign and, since Eddie was studying the truck intently, used the opportunity to lean forward and snatch him off the dashboard. I gave him a good snuggle and in seconds he was purring. "Now, what was that all about?" I asked. "Didn't you like the noise that truck made?" Because it had been loud. "I bet that's what was bothering you, wasn't it?"

Eddie made an annoyed kind of chirp and squirmed off my lap. As he marched down the aisle toward Mike Mulligan, a new thought popped into my brain.

Did Henry's neighbor, Cole Duvall, have a guy who did chores for him? Because I couldn't think of anyone better to talk to about Duvall than his caretaker. A caretaker would have opinions about Duvall's character, would know when Duvall had been north, and would know his habits and hobbies. And maybe, just maybe, the caretaker would be able to give me that magic piece of information that would make the entire puzzle fit together.

I tucked the idea in the back of my head for later follow-up and went to join the story.

The evening was close to warm, and after a dinner of grilled cheese and salad—no, Mom, I don't eat out every night—I went to sit in the front deck's sunshine and make some phone calls. Half an hour later, not even the brilliant sun sparkling off the water was making me feel any better.

I tossed my cell onto the table and looked over at Eddie, who was lounging on the chaise like a lion over-looking his pride.

"If you were a true friend," I said, "you'd be a little more help. I mean, don't tell me you don't know any bestselling authors who would jump at an opportunity to visit a small town in northern lower Michigan."

Eddie rolled onto his side, one front leg stretched out long, the other curled up against his chest. I had no idea what that meant in cat language, but no matter what he was saying, it wasn't helpful.

"Not even one name?" I asked. "It doesn't have to be a *New York Times* bestselling author. Any old kind of bestselling author will do. *People* magazine. *USA Today*. *Detroit News*. The *Traverse Record-Eagle*. Anything."

Eddie yawned, showing small, pointed teeth. Then he sat up, blinked once, and began studying a duck flotilla that was looking for dinner handouts.

"Again," I said, "that isn't much help."

"Mrr."

"If you were that sorry, you'd find some way to lend me a hand."

My cat stood, jumped into the air, and landed on my chaise. He butted my sweatpants-clad shin with the top of his head, then flopped next to me and began to purr.

I petted his fur smooth. "You are okay," I said, "no matter what Aunt Frances says." Of course, my aunt loved Eddie dearly, but Eddie didn't need to know that, not for sure. I let the peace of a cat comfort me for a few minutes, then picked up the phone again.

And, after another half an hour and another dozen phone calls, I struck out a second time.

"Can you believe that?" I asked. "No one knows if the Duvalls have a caretaker." Not my aunt, not Kristen, not Rafe, not Holly, and not any of the other people I'd called. The Duvalls were newcomers, sure, but usually word got around about who was taking care of whose cottage.

It had been an evening of frustrations, and a need to get up and move around stirred in me. I'd have gone out for a run, but I hadn't bought new running shoes in a couple of years and everyone knew you shouldn't start a running program on old shoes. I might have taken my bike out for a ride, but I knew for a fact that the tires were flat and I had a feeling my hand pump was still at my aunt's house. And there was no way I was going for a swim—the water in Janay Lake wouldn't reach even sixty degrees for weeks.

"I could go for a walk," I said, petting Eddie. "There's more than an hour until it gets dark. Want to come along?"

His reverberating snore was answer enough.

It was past dark when I returned. My walk had taken me past the boardinghouse, where I'd stopped in to talk to

Aunt Frances, past the Three Seasons, where I'd popped in to say hello to Kristen and her crew, and I'd paused to shake my head at Rafe, who was on his roof brushing Black Jack onto his chimney's flashing.

"Do you realize," I called up to him, "that it's too dark to see what you're doing?"

"Minnie, is that you? You know I can't hear when it's dark out."

"I said, I hope I don't have to take you to the hospital for falling off the ladder when you can't see the rungs for climbing down."

"When you hear a thud, come running."

There were many things I didn't understand about Rafe Niswander; his penchant for working so hard on his house was just one more. I called a good-bye and walked the last few yards to the marina, but when I made the final turn toward my dock, I stopped short in surprise.

When I'd headed out for my walk, the berth to the right of my adorable little houseboat was empty. Now it was filled with a sleek cruiser half again as wide as my boat and almost twice as long. Chris had said I'd be getting a new neighbor, but I hadn't thought it would be so soon.

I eyed the boat's insignia. Well, at least it was a Crown, which meant it was designed and built right here in Chilson. And it wasn't nearly the size of the boat that had berthed in that slip the last few years. What remained to be seen was if the new folks would turn out to be friends, like my left-hand neighbors Louisa and Ted Axford, or if they would turn out to be more like what Gunnar Olson had been. I didn't even know which to hope for, since my cut-rate slip fee more or less depended on the new guy being a jerk.

"Nice night, isn't it?"

I spun around and looked up at a fortyish man. In the light cast by the marina lights, I could see that he was wearing shorts, running shoes, and a Wayne State University sweatshirt that had seen better days. He also had untidy brown hair, an easy smile, and was high on the one-to-ten scale of hotness. Not a ten, I wouldn't award that to anyone who wasn't an angel descended from heaven, but certainly a solid eight.

"Hi," I said. "Minnie Hamilton. That's mine." I gestured at my slip and steeled myself for the inevitable smirk.

He introduced himself as Eric Apney, then nodded at my summer home. "Nice," he said. "I've always had a thing for houseboats. Yours looks handcrafted. Did you do it yourself?"

Aunt Frances could have done it in a winter, but my woodworking skills were more in the paint-what-Aunt-Frances-made category. Still, I was pleased that my new neighbor had assumed I was that capable and mentally slid him into the Friend side of the aisle. I told him I'd purchased it from a local couple who'd since moved to Florida.

"Where are you from?" I asked.

"Grand Rapids. My family has summered in the area for more than fifty years and I love it up here. I don't want to take care of another house, but you don't have to snowplow a boat's driveway." He grinned.

Smiling back, I asked, "And your wife? Has she spent much time in Chilson?"

"No wife," he said. "Divorced years ago, and never got around to marrying again."

We chatted a little more, then went our separate ways. But as I got myself ready for bed, which consisted mostly in brushing my teeth and moving Eddie to the side of the bed instead of the exact middle, I kept thinking one thing: Hmm. It was too soon after my breakup with Tucker to think about dating, but still . . . hmm.

Just as I was sliding between the sheets, maneuvering myself around Eddie, who'd edged back toward the center, my cell phone rang.

I picked it up off the small chest of drawers that served as my nightstand and looked at the screen. "No idea who this is," I said to Eddie. "Looks like a corporate name. And I don't even recognize the area code. What do you think, should I answer?" I was starting to put the phone back down when Eddie picked up his head and stared at me.

"Okay, fine," I grumbled. "But if it's a telemarketer, you don't get any treats for a week." I thumbed on the call. "Hello?"

"Minnie, my dearest, my beloved, my most treasured of all bookmobile librarians, how are you this evening?"

Grinning, I sat up and pulled my knees to my chest. "Trock, my most favorite of all the celebrity chefs I have ever met in my life, I am just wonderful. How are you?" I'd met Trock Farrand, host of *Trock's Troubles*, last summer and was still reeling from the force of his personality.

"I am," Trock said cheerfully, "in the depths of despair."

"You are?"

"I am. And it's all your fault, dear one."

"Oh?" I reached out to pet Eddie, who began a low rumbling purr. "How's that?"

"Because I heard through the grapevine—a very twisted one, mind you—that you are in difficulties and that you did not call me for assistance."

I frowned. "What difficulty? I haven't been in the kitchen for a week." Which wasn't exactly true, but it was the point that mattered when conversing with Trock, not the details.

"Your library's book fair, my sweet. That last-minute cancellation from the erudite Ross Weaver."

"You know Ross Weaver?" Maybe everyone did, except me.

"But of course." He chuckled, and I could almost see the big man's round face all puffed up with laughter. "It's New York, Minnie dear. The biggest small town in the world. Besides, we share a publisher."

"A . . . publisher?"

"Dear, dear girl. Didn't you know I was coming out with a cookbook? Yes, I resisted the lure of publication for years, so much work, you see, but I was finally convinced to assemble a collection of my favorite recipes. Delectable, every single one, and the pictures are exquisite."

"Sounds nice," I said.

Trock *tsk*ed at me. "You are not getting the point, my curly-haired young friend. My cookbook was released this week. And I will fly to your tiny little airport on Friday so I can appear at your book fair on the a.m. of Saturday."

My mouth got stuck half-open. The only noises that came out of me were odd squeaky ones that made Eddie pick his head all the way up off the comforter and look around.

"Is that an acceptable solution to your difficulty, Ms. Hamilton?" Trock asked.

I sniffed. "That's . . . that's . . ." *Sniff.* "That's wonderful. You're wonderful. But I can't let you. It's too much. It's too far to fly for a little book fair. I can't let you spend that kind of money."

"Ha." He scoffed. "My son tells me I'm made of money. And if money can't help me do a favor for a friend, what good is it?"

Sniff. "None, I guess. Trock, you're—"

"Indebted to you for many reasons," he said gruffly. "And stop blubbering. It's unlike you, and far, far worse, it's making me uncomfortable."

Which made me laugh. I gave him the details of the event, asked how many books he could bring, asked if he had anything special he wanted us to provide, thanked him again, and ended the call. Then I jumped out of bed.

"Mrr?" asked a sleepy Eddie.

"Sorry, pal," I said, grabbing my laptop from the other bed and turning it on. There were Facebook posts to make and a press release to write and e-mails to send and an emergency flyer to convince Pam to create.

"This is going to be great," I murmured. Trock hardly ever made public appearances in Chilson; it was his vacation home and he didn't like to tape there unless the show's schedule demanded it. To have him volunteer to attend the book fair—in the off-season, no less—made it even more of a special event.

The book fair was a go. "It's clear sailing from here on out," I told Eddie. "Nothing else could possibly go wrong."

I really should have known better.

Chapter 16

The next morning I woke up to sunshine.

"Which is the best way to start the day," I said to my unmoving feline friend. But his inactive state was understandable because slightly over half of his body was lying inside the sunshine and nothing short of an irresistible force was going to get him to relocate.

And since I had the morning off, nothing short of an immovable object was going to keep me from heading off into the wild blue yonder and checking out the timing on a couple of new bookmobile routes.

So as soon as I'd showered, dressed, and breakfasted, I was out the door and into my car, stopping only to get my standard provisions of a can of diet soda and a bag of popcorn.

I timed the possible routes while driving at bookmobile speed, and considering the parking options at three new homebound patrons. "It'll work," I said, nodding to myself. How I'd manage to squeeze the new routes into the current schedule was a different question, but it wasn't one I was going to worry about on this gorgeous spring day full of open skies and sun and trees that were growing leaves as fast as I could watch.

But on my way back toward town, while driving over forested hill and lake-filled dale, my mind circled back to Henry and Adam.

How, I wondered, could I find out if Felix was being truthful when he said he hadn't been on Henry's property before Henry was killed? Who would be able to tell me? Was there anyone who might be able to—

A small mental lightning bolt zinged my brain all the way awake. "Duh," I said out loud, and took the next left. Five minutes later, I was puttering up Irene and Adam's driveway.

Irene opened the door. "Good morning! Is it a bookmobile day?" She peered outside.

"I was driving around, planning some new routes. I have a question for Adam, that's all. Will he let me come inside if I don't have any books?" I spread out my empty hands, palms up.

"No," he called.

Irene laughed and opened the door wide. "Don't listen to him. He's only cranky because the doctor just told him he can't start working again until the full two months is over."

Which explained why Irene was here and not at work—she'd taken Adam to the doctor. "It'll be here before you know it," I told him. "And then you'll be complaining that you have too much work to do."

But the worried glance Irene gave her husband made me rethink my casual statement. Adam was self-employed. If he couldn't get his clients' work done on time, they'd go elsewhere, perhaps never to return.

There was nothing I could do about that, though, so I perched on the edge of the couch and said, "Adam, I was wondering. Did you see anyone at all near Henry's property? Not necessarily the day he died, but any time you were out there. A neighbor, a friend of Henry's who stopped by, a door-to-door salesman, anyone?"

"Do you mean guys only?" Adam asked. "Because I don't remember seeing anyone other than that redhead."

"What redhead?" He'd never mentioned her. "When did you see her?"

"Day before Henry died. So, the first Saturday in April."

"Was she a neighbor of Henry's?"

Adam shrugged. "Henry said he'd never seen her before, but he also said a couple of houses on the lake had sold over the winter, so who knows?"

"What was she doing?"

"Not much." He laughed. "Not the way she was dressed. Wearing those stupid little boots that aren't really boots at all but heels that go past the ankle. No hat, no gloves, jeans tight as paint, and a short jacket that wasn't long enough to keep her waist warm, let alone her rear end."

Irene and I shared a glance. "Sounds as if you got a close look," Irene said. "She was pretty, too, I bet."

"Not my type," Adam said, shaking his head. "Seriously high maintenance. And definitely not the kind of girl who'd be able to take down a tree, let alone a huge one in a certain direction at a certain time."

I wanted to speak up in defense of womanhood, to say that you never knew what people were capable of, that it didn't do to underestimate anyone, but Adam was getting that "I need a nap" look, so I thanked him and got up to leave.

"I'll walk you out," Irene said.

Outside, clouds were sliding over the sun, so instead of a comfortable chat in the sunshine, we stood next to my car, shivering in a rising wind.

Irene hunched her shoulders and rubbed her upper arms. "There's something I need to tell you. I know I'm probably being stupid and please don't tell anyone because it's probably not true, but I have to tell someone, and you know all about this, so I thought you'd be the one to tell."

"Okay," I said, not smiling, because in spite of her run-on sentence she seemed deadly serious. "Tell."

She blew out a breath. "I think there might have been another attempt on Adam's life."

"Here's where I figured we'd put the big guy," Gordon said.

Gordon, whose last name I hadn't figured out, was the owner of the company who was supplying the tents for Saturday's book fair. Tent rental had originally been my boss's idea, and I'd objected to the expense at first, saying that it was a small fair, that we could hold it inside the library, but he'd told me to use my imagination. This had, of course, irritated me no end, since I was the one with the imagination, not him, so I'd stood there in his office and closed my eyes, trying to see what he was seeing.

"Ah," he said with patronizing satisfaction. "You're picturing it, aren't you?"

I was, and it was wonderful. In my head, the library grounds had turned into something between a circus and a medieval fair. White tents with high peaks, colored streamers, vendors hawking their wares, and people milling about everywhere.

"You're right," I'd said, opening my eyes. "The tents alone will attract interest."

"Hmm?" Stephen's attention had already returned to his computer. "Oh, the tents. Yes. See to it, Minnie, will you?"

And so I did. And I was. Which was why I was walking around the library lawn with Gordon, making last-minute placement decisions that I hoped would turn out okay, because a significant percentage of my brain was still thinking about what Irene had said that morning.

"We were at the hospital," she'd told me, hugging herself against the wind. "They're doing all that construction, putting on that big addition, remember? I'd wanted to drop Adam off at the door, but he wouldn't let me, said he was perfectly capable of walking across the parking lot."

"Sounds like him," I'd said, smiling.

Irene hadn't smiled back. "The problem is, with the construction, the sidewalks are all torn up and they want you to walk all the way around that annex building to get to the front door and I could see that Adam was getting tired, so I made him cut across the grass."

I'd felt my brow furrowing in the effort to picture

what she was talking about. "Doesn't that mean you were walking through the construction area?"

She'd nodded. "It was shorter by at least a hundred yards—you could see a path where a lot of people had gone that way. And there was no one working there, so I didn't have a problem doing it. When we left the building, we walked back the same way and"—she'd hugged herself even tighter—"and this huge pile of bricks fell on the grass right next to Adam. It almost hit him."

"Right over there."

The male voice brought me back to the here and now. I blinked, and there I was, standing on the library lawn, working out the future location of tents. "I'm sorry," I said. "What was that? My mind was wandering."

Gordon nodded, a sideways sort of smile on his face. "I bet. You probably have a thousand things to do between now and Saturday morning."

Actually things were pretty much set, but it was nice of him to be so understanding. "Thanks. Tomorrow I'll be out on the bookmobile, so it's today and Friday to finish up."

"You run the bookmobile?" His face lit up. "I've seen it around, but I didn't realize that was you."

I beamed. He had a sympathetic personality and he liked the bookmobile. If he hadn't been a little too old for me and, if the ring on his finger was any indication, already married, I'd have thrown myself into his arms. "We've been on the road for almost a year and I get requests for new stops almost every week."

"We lived downstate when I was a kid," he said, "and

there was a bookmobile stop practically at my front door. I grew up thinking it stopped there just for me." He grinned. "Funny the things you think when you're a kid."

"I'm not sure that ends when you grow up," I said.

He laughed. "So, is driving the bookmobile as much fun as it looks like? Please don't say it's not. You'll ruin my last illusion."

"Not a chance," I said firmly. "We even have a bookmobile cat."

"Eddie." He nodded. "I've heard of him."

My cat, bookmobile ambassador to the world. I made a mental note not to tell him. Catlike, he already had an inflated view of his own importance.

"Which means you knew Henry Gill," Gordon said.

As non sequiturs went, this was an excellent one. And a little creepy. "How do you know that?"

"Got a cousin Bob who does property management. Used to be in real estate. Well, I guess he still has his license, but he doesn't use it much anymore." Gordon shrugged. "Anyway, he takes care of some summer places over near Henry's, and with Henry being the only year-round guy out there, they'd talk once in a while."

My guess was that Bob had done most of the talking.

Gordon smiled. "Henry told Bob about the bookmobile and its cat and the nice ladies who helped him find books."

Sudden tears pricked at my eyes. "So annoying," I said, "him being nice behind our backs like that."

"That was Henry all over," Gordon said, nodding.

A small, but very bright, lightbulb belatedly clicked on in my head. "So, your cousin Bob," I said. "Does he take care of Cole Duvall's property? He's on Rock Lake, practically right next to Henry."

"Sounds right," Gordon said. "Big guy, married into money?" He laughed. "Wish I'd done that. This working-for-a-living stuff is getting old. But if you're looking for a property manager, give Bob a call. He's okay, even if he is one of my blood relatives." He said he'd get me his cousin's phone number, and we moved on to locating the next tent.

On the outside, I was calm and professional and focused. On the inside, however, I was mentally high-fiving it with serendipity.

Inside the library's break room, however, there was no high-fiving, no fist bumps, and it didn't look as if serendipity had a chance of gaining a foothold any time soon.

I looked from Holly to Josh and back to Holly, then at the wall clock. There was only five minutes until our self-mandated mutual break time was over. If I was going to smooth over whatever was going on, I had to leap straight into the fray, no time even for a short bout of recaffein-ation.

After one longing glance at the coffeepot, I said, "What's wrong? No, wait, let me guess. Stephen's going to eliminate the library's children's section because the kids are too noisy." As an opener, I'd had better, but it was better than nothing.

Holly sniffed. "He won't tell me his new address."

I glanced over at Josh and he shrugged and took an-other sip from the coffee mug he was clutching. He'd given me the address a couple of weeks ago and I'd driven past once, just to see. Though it was an older house, it had a reasonably new roof and the windows had been replaced. Not very big, but Josh was a single guy and it should do him just fine.

"I bet he's told you," Holly said, narrowing her eyes. "He has, hasn't he?"

Josh glared at me. It was a clear warning to keep the location to myself.

Now what was I supposed to do? There was only one course of action that could take this little scene in a positive direction. Immediate diversion.

"Remember I told you that a car almost ran over Adam Deering?" They nodded. Reluctantly, but they nodded. "Well, his wife, Irene, says she thinks someone tried to kill him a second time."

"What?" Holly looked shocked. "That's horrible! Did she tell the police?"

"Hang on," Josh said. "If she's only thinking it, she must not be sure. What happened, exactly?"

I wasn't sure, either, which was one of the reasons I wanted to talk this over. I passed on what Irene had said, telling them about the construction, the long walk, and about the bricks that had come so close to crashing down on his head, bricks that might have hurt him badly, or even killed him.

"What do you think?" I asked. "Accident or intentional?"

"Intentional," Holly said.

"Accident," Josh said at the same time.

Which was just what I'd figured they'd say. I glanced

up at the clock. "One minute left. You each have thirty seconds to make your case. Holly, you first."

"Had to be on purpose," she said. "If there was no construction going on in that spot, no workers would have been up there. Bricks don't fall down by themselves. Someone had to push them over."

Josh made a beeping noise. "Time's up. And you're wrong. Bricks can fall over if a pallet isn't balanced right. All it takes is a gust of wind in the right direction. And it was windy this morning. Plus, how would someone know Adam was going to be walking there? You think some guy is following him around, looking for a chance to make an accident happen?" He snorted. "You've been watching too much bad TV."

Holly pointed at the clock. "And you've gone way over your time limit. That means I win and you lose."

"Minnie makes the call." Josh knocked back the last of his coffee, made a sour face, and looked at me. "Who's right?"

But I didn't know.

That night, Eddie and I were eating our dinners of cat food (Eddie) and take-out Chinese (me) when my cell phone rang.

"Could you get that?" I asked. "You're closest."

Since Eddie didn't even look away from the bowl of cat food he was eating, I got up myself and got the phone out of my backpack. "Hello?"

"Minnie, it's Gordon with the tents. Say, I have my cousin's number if you want it."

"Thanks," I said, grabbing a pen and paper out of a kitchen drawer and writing down the numbers. Maybe Gordon didn't have a last name. Like Sting. "Any potential tent problems?"

"Smooth sailing," he said. "We'll have them all set up by midafternoon tomorrow."

I thanked him again and, as soon as I ended the call, punched in the phone number for his cousin. When he answered, I introduced myself, told him how I got the number, and asked if he took care of the Duvalls' property.

I planned to start with the easy questions, then slide into the probing character questions. Not that I could ask outright if he thought Duvall could have committed murder, but I was sure I'd figure out something. Of course, it wasn't as if I had any real reason to suspect Duvall, other than that one potential lie, but my initial reaction when I'd met him had been one of fear. And though maybe I shouldn't let that single episode guide my current actions, I couldn't ignore how I'd felt, either.

"Sure," he said, sounding a lot like his cousin Gordon. Part of me wondered if Bob had a last name, but the rest of me was trying to focus on the topic at hand. "Nice lady, pays right away, usually gives me plenty of lead time for opening up the place."

"Usually?" I asked.

"Well, not her so much as her husband. Cole, his name is. Nice enough, I guess, but asks a little too much, if you know what I mean. I can't always jump on what he needs, depending on what else is going on. Sometimes it takes a day or two to get over there. If he calls when he's on his way up, well, the place probably isn't going to get to seventy-two degrees when he walks in the door."

"Was this recently?"

"A week or two ago. Maybe three."

Or four? "Is there any way you can pin it down?" I asked.

"Well, I guess. I'd have to look it up, at home." There was a question in his voice, as in why on earth did I want to know?

It was a very good question. And I wished I had a good answer for him. Then inspiration struck. "You know Adam Deering, who was out there the day Henry Gill died? Adam thinks Cole might have helped him call 911 and he wants to thank him. But he doesn't want to thank the wrong guy." It was mostly a lie, but it wasn't a lie of malice, so with any luck it wouldn't count against me.

"Okay, sure," Bob said. "When I get home, I'll look it up and give you a ring."

I thanked him and thumbed off the phone. "Progress, Eddie. We're making definite progress."

"Mrr."

During the phone call, Eddie had finished his dinner, stretched, yawned, and was now sitting next to the front door, looking at the handle. "Mrr," he said again.

"You sure you want out?" I asked. "The wind is picking up and you know you don't like that."

"Mrr." He put his head half an inch from the doorframe. "Mrr."

"You are the weirdest cat ever. Sometimes you seem

more like a dog than a cat." I opened the door. "Don't say I never did anything for you, okay?"

"I never would."

I jumped a little, then saw my new neighbor, Eric Apney, standing on the dock between our boats and smiling at me. My very good-looking new neighbor. "Hello," I said. "But I was actually talking to my cat."

"Does he talk back?" Eric asked, watching Eddie jump from one chaise to the other.

"All the time."

Eddie looked back at us. "Mrr," he said, and settled down on the chaise where I usually sat.

"I see what you mean," Eric said, nodding. "Do I need his permission to ask you out?"

"He'd probably like you to." I felt a wide smile building up inside me. "It's not necessary, though."

"I know we only met the once," Eric said, "but I'm new up here, hardly know a soul, and I like your cat and your boat, so what do you think about dinner and maybe a movie?"

Though my initial impulse was to blurt out an immediate yes, I hesitated. This was not the time to say I'd just been through a breakup, but there were questions that had to be asked. "You're not allergic to cats?"

"Not allergic to anything, as far as I know."

"And you're not committed to anyone?"

"Well, my mom and dad, but that's probably not what you're talking about."

Friendly, liked cats, had a good relationship with his parents, and had a sense of humor. Things were looking up for Minnie in the romance department. I smiled at him.

"What do you do for a living?" I asked, then laughed. "Let me rephrase that. Just tell me you're not a doctor. I'm not sure I care what you do, as long as you're not a doctor."

"You're kidding, right?"

All the fun went out of me. "You're a doctor," I said flatly.

"Cardiac surgeon." He frowned. "Is that a problem?"

I sighed. Of all the professions in all the world, why had he picked that one? Even so, I was tempted. He was on vacation when he was up here. He wouldn't be on call, couldn't be yanked into the hospital at a moment's notice. Why not go out for dinner? What could it hurt?

A cell phone trilled. Eric reached into his pocket. "Sorry, that's the hospital's ring tone. I have to take this."

Then again, there were a lot of reasons not to go out with him.

I sent him a polite smile, waved good-bye, and, followed by Eddie, headed back inside.

A few minutes later, I was feeling trapped on my own houseboat. Eddie, apparently exhausted by his short stint in the great outdoors, had flopped himself onto the dining booth's seat and was curled into a flattish ball.

I, however, had the itch to get outside and do something in the last couple hours of daylight. The only problem was that Eric the surgeon was still standing on the dock, talking away on his cell phone. He was staring at the lake with a serious expression, and if my experience with Tucker was worth anything, he would either be on the phone for a long time or soon be taking a quick trip downstate.

Not that there was any real reason that I couldn't have walked out of my own boat, past him, and out into the wilds of Chilson, but I'd just created a socially awkward situation and would have liked to wait a day or two before talking to him again.

Of course, if he was still on the phone, I wouldn't have to talk to him at all.

I pulled on a light jacket, grabbed my backpack, patted the snoring Eddie on the head, and went out the front door. Eric's back was toward me—more serendipity!—and I escaped off the boat and down the dock without having to make eye contact.

But once I'd reached the sidewalk, I realized I had no destination in mind. The temperature had dropped and the wind had come up, so going for a walk or a bike ride wasn't appealing. It was a school night for Aunt Frances. She was teaching a night class in wood turning right that second, and the texts I'd received from Kristen that day had been fraught with restaurant staffing woes, which meant she'd be too busy to talk. I thought about going over to bug Rafe, but I could see his house from here and I didn't see any signs of light or life.

I could have driven over to talk to Irene and Adam, but I didn't want to have to see the disappointment in their faces when I told them I hadn't learned anything new.

Which led me to a conclusion I should have reached far earlier—I needed to learn something new. And suddenly I knew exactly what to do.

I knocked on the door of the large lakeside home. It looked like a front door, but on lake houses it was hard to know for sure. Because if you had a house on a lake, surely you'd make the prettiest side of the house face the water, and wouldn't that be the front? Then again, shouldn't the front door be the door where people first entered the house? It was a conundrum, and once again I patted myself on the back for not having the financial resources to live on a lake. Just think of all the problems I'd avoided.

The door was opened by a middle-aged woman and I mentally breathed a sigh of relief. At least I wouldn't have to explain myself to Cole Duvall.

"Hello," the woman said. "Can I help you?" She wasn't tall, exactly, but appeared tall at first glance because she was solidly built from head to toe. Her brown hair was pulled back into a soft bun and her face, while not one of beauty, was full of a kindly intelligence.

"Hi," I said. "Sorry to bother you, but are you Mrs. Duvall?" When she nodded, I introduced myself. "I was a friend of Henry Gill's and—"

"That poor man." Her face crumpled into sadness. "Oh, bugger. I'm going to start crying." She pushed the door open. "Come on in and keep me from bawling my eyes out. I just go to pieces every time I think about it."

By the time we were settled on wicker furniture in a glassed-in porch, I'd learned Mrs. Duvall's name was Larabeth, that she was Cole's second wife, and that he was her first husband. "I was just too busy for years working on the stores. Somehow I got to forty before I once thought about getting married. When I looked around, there was Cole," she said, smiling.

I also learned that Cole hadn't wanted children—"He

and his first wife had a boy and a girl and he said he didn't want to do that all over again"—and finally that Larabeth was the sole heir to the Dwyer grocery store chain.

"Really?" I almost squeaked. "I love those stores!"

And I did. Dwyer was the name of an extremely successful regional chain of specialty food stores. What made the Dwyer stores different was that each one was customized for its location, carrying not only local produce, but as many local items as possible, from wine to cheese to pasta. And though the main decor of all the stores was similar, each store had personalized wall murals that captured the local flavor. "Are you going to open one in Chilson?"

Larabeth sighed. "Don't I wish? The town isn't big enough to support one of our stores, not without taking too much business away from what's already in place."

A businesswoman with a conscience? I was so busy putting her into my mental Friend category that my slide into the next phase of the conversation was awkward. "Yes, it's very sad that Henry's gone," I said, "and that's partly why I'm here. Did you know that there was someone else out with Henry that day?"

"I hadn't heard that." She frowned. "Was he hurt, too?"

"Not directly." I explained about Adam and the heart attack and about the fictional man who'd called 911 on Adam's cell phone and helped direct the EMT crew to Adam. The story was getting better every time I told it, and I was sorry it wasn't true.

"Anyway, Adam never learned the name of the man who helped him and I said I'd try to find out. I don't suppose it was your husband, was it? Adam would love to thank him."

Larabeth was shaking her head. "Couldn't have been. Cole flew out West skiing that weekend." She sighed. "I would have liked to go with him, but there was a grand reopening at the Lansing store and I never miss those."

We chatted awhile longer, during which she became an ever firmer friend by smiling when I told her that I drove the bookmobile, and when the sun started dropping into the water, I headed home, thanking her for her time.

All the way back to Chilson, I thought about times and dates, about marriages and money.

But I also thought about wooden boats.

Chapter 17

The next morning I did my best to play catch-up on the tasks that had gone undone while I was out the day before, so it was nearly noon before I remembered to act upon my brilliant middle-of-the night idea. I reached for the phone, hoping it wasn't too late.

"Is this Pam Fazio?" I asked. "The world-famous graphic designer?"

"Shh," she hushed. "Didn't I tell you to keep that a deep, dark secret?"

"Haven't told a soul," I said. "And if you want, I'll make a pinky swear on it at lunch. Round Table in half an hour? I'll buy, because I want to ask you something."

"Not Shomin's Deli?" she asked.

"I haven't seen Sabrina in a while," I said. "Don't want her to get too lonely."

Pam laughed and said she'd see me soon.

And half an hour later, I was sitting at one of the diner's back tables when Pam came in. I waved her over and she made the trek across the room, fake-panting as she dropped into a chair. "Whew! Wasn't sure I was going to make it all the way." She drew her hand across a brow that wasn't the least bit damp. "If this is your way of getting me to exercise, it's not going to work, because I'll need dessert to get me back to the store."

"I'd prefer," I said quietly, "that this conversation not be overheard."

"Oh-ho!" Pam, suddenly perky, sat up and plopped her elbows on the table. "An excellent opener. What's the topic of the hour?"

"Felix Stanton," I said.

Pam's perkiness slid away. "Felix. Ah. Well."

"And do you girls need menus today?" Sabrina put down glasses of ice water and took out her pad. "I didn't think so. Ham sandwich with a side salad and raspberry vinaigrette for you," she said, nodding at Pam, "and a burger with everything but and an order of fries for the bookmobile lady. Anything other than water? Right. I'll put this up and you'll have your food in a jiffy."

She walked over to where her husband, Bill, was sitting while tapping away at his computer, planted a kiss on the top of his head, and headed off to the kitchen.

I turned back to Pam. "When we were at Shomin's last week and Felix was being all cranky, you said you'd known him for a while. That he gets like that every so often." I fiddled with one of the straws Sabrina had left. "But you've only been in Chilson a year and Felix . . . well, I guess I don't know if he's a native, but he's had that real estate and development business for years." I tipped my head questioningly.

Pam grinned. "Should have figured you'd pick up on

that." She ripped open her straw and jammed it into her ice water. "Felix and I grew up together, down in Ohio. It's because of him that I heard of Chilson in the first place. His parents came up here every summer when he was a kid, and as soon as he was old enough to be on his own, he moved north."

It was a familiar story. A lot like mine, actually. "So the two of you are friends," I said.

"We have a lot of history—no, not that kind of history," she said, rolling her eyes at my smirk. "We were next-door neighbors from kindergarten through high school. He was another brother, practically. Just one that didn't live in the same house."

"A lot of shared history, then," I said, "and a lot of shared loyalty."

"Not so much of that second one." She looked at the ceiling for a moment, then back at me. "Felix isn't the kind of guy who inspires loyalty, somehow. I like him, even love him in a distant cousin sort of way, but . . . well, let's just say that if I wanted some help moving across town, he's not who I'd call."

I knew what she meant. "So, if I asked why you said he was being even more Felix-ish than usual, would you tell me?"

She shrugged. "I thought it was common knowledge."

Apparently not common enough. "What is?"

Pam looked around, but no one was sitting within two tables of us. "You know that new big mixed-use building on the waterfront? Retail shops on the first floor, professional offices on the second floor, residential units on top?"

"Sure." I also knew it was more than half-empty. "Are you saying . . . ?"

She nodded. "It's Felix's pet project and he's overextended to the max. He keeps telling me all he needs is one good anchor store to make it work, but every time he gets close to signing someone, they back out." She sighed. "I'm getting worried about him, to tell you the truth. If he doesn't get a big success soon, I'm not sure what he's going to do."

Our lunches arrived and the talk turned to other things, but all the while, part of my brain was chewing over what Pam had told me and thinking pretty much one thing: *hmm.*

Deep in thought, I walked back into the library and I was still so deep in thought that I didn't notice how the personal space between Holly and Josh was playing out until I'd almost walked past the main desk.

At that point, however, I clued in to the fact that something was wrong, came to a slow stop, and then backed up. Holly was at the desk, being perfectly friendly as she checked out books to an elderly man. Josh was nearby, working on the library's most hated printer.

There they were, less than three feet apart, and Holly had managed to turn herself so that her back was to the printer. This couldn't have been an easy thing to do, because the printer was placed next to the computer where she was working. I watched the scene for a moment, wondering what was going on and hoping Holly didn't end up with a stiff neck by the end of the day.

Josh looked up, rolled his eyes and mouthed a single word: *House.*

This could only mean that Josh still wasn't giving Holly the address of his new place and that Holly was getting well and truly miffed. Which was understandable, because the three of us shared all of our major life events and most of the minor ones. Why Josh was making this a point of contention, I didn't know, but I hoped it wouldn't cause lasting damage to our happy trio.

My concern must have shown on my face, because Josh—after making sure that Holly wasn't watching—grinned at me, then winked.

I sighed and continued on to my office. Sometimes it was best not to know exactly what was going on.

Late the next afternoon, it had been prearranged that I drop Julia off at her sister's house. Why, exactly, I was doing so I hadn't understood from the beginning, but it had something to do with a birthday and soup and family traditions, and who was I to stand in the way of traditions? Besides, since the final stop of the day was barely two miles from the sister's house, it wasn't a problem.

"I'll see you," Julia said, standing at the top of the stairs and pointing at me down her long arm, "on Saturday. To be completely honest, I hadn't planned on coming, but missing an opportunity to buy Trock Farrand's cookbook from the man himself would be ludicrous."

She exited stage right, and shut the door as she departed.

"Go figure," I told Eddie. "Turns out that some cook hawking a book about getting dishes dirty is a bigger draw than one of the bestselling thriller writers of the decade."

"Mrr."

"Well, sure," I said, putting the bookmobile in drive and sailing away, "Trock's a great guy and I suppose you do end up with something to eat before having to do the dishes, but at the end, isn't food just fuel?"

"Mrr!"

"Well, I guess we'll just have to agree to disagree."

"Mrr," he said.

But Eddie's point of view was understandable. Last summer, Trock and Eddie had become fast friends and the cat treats the famed chef had concocted were the hit of my cat's day.

"Is the way to a cat's heart through his stomach?" I asked.

Eddie, however, was too busy licking his front paw and swiping the top of his head with it to answer the question.

"Just as well," I said. "You should never ask a question for which you aren't ready to hear the answer."

That little aphorism had been one of my dad's many phrases of wisdom, and it had been one that I hadn't understood until the time I asked a high school boyfriend who he liked better, Miss Marple or Hercule Poirot. He'd said he wasn't sure who they were, unless they were the new teachers, and our relationship drifted apart soon afterward.

"And that was just as well, too," I told Eddie. "If that had lasted, I might have gone with him when he moved out West after college, and then I wouldn't have the bookmobile and I certainly wouldn't have found you."

This loving statement also didn't get any response

from Eddie, which was slightly disappointing, but I soldiered on.

"What do you think?" I asked. "About Henry and Adam, I mean. I still have no idea what really happened, and honestly don't know how to go about finding out. But Irene's getting to be a real mess and Adam's not far behind, so I need to . . . Eddie, what are you doing?"

My cat was rubbing his face against the wire door of his carrier. This not only made a very odd noise, but it also made his little kitty lips pull back so that I saw way too much of his gums.

"And very healthy gums they are," I said, "at least according to your doctor. But if you want the truth, they're not your most attractive feature."

"Mrr!"

Once again, we decided to agree to disagree, and I went back to thinking out loud. "What I really need to do is find out more about Neva. You know, the shotgun-toting senior citizen? From all accounts, she hardly ever leaves the house, so I'll have to go to her and . . ."

My outward musings tailed off, because if I took a single back-road shortcut, we were only a handful of miles from Chatham Road and Ms. Chatham herself.

"No time like the present," I said bravely, trying not to quail at the thought of confronting a woman who'd brandished a gun at me the one and only time we met. But the sheriff's office didn't seem to think she was threatening, and besides, I was in the bookmobile, which many people were convinced had a magical power to create happiness in everyone who came near.

I planned out what I was going to say to Neva as I

drove carefully down the bumpy Chatham Road and parked the bookmobile out of sight of her house.

"There you go." I released Eddie from his carrier. "I shouldn't be long, but if I am, do you remember how to call 911? Oh, wait." I sighed heavily. "You don't have a phone, and even if you did you don't have the thumb power to make the call. Poor Eddie," I said, patting him on the head.

He put his ears back and squinted at me with a dire expression. I gave him one more pat, slid my phone into my pocket, and headed down the stairs.

I opened the door, but before I could turn around and shut it, a black-and-white blur shot past me. "Eddie!" I cried. "You get back here!"

Ignoring me, he zoomed across the road and onto Neva Chatham's property.

There was really no point in calling him—he was a cat, after all—so I locked the bookmobile and hopped into a jog, muttering a monologue as I went.

"Why can't he stay on the bookmobile like a normal cat? Because normal cats have no interest in bookmo-biles, that's why. Normal cats don't talk to you as if they understood what you said. Normal cats don't—huh."

I'd passed through a line of trees and was on the edge of a wide-open field. Neva's garden, I supposed, but there was no sign of my runaway cat. I looked around and down, trying to find his kitty footprints.

"Ha!" I'd spotted the Eddie trail. It headed south, straight toward a trio of greenhouses. "I'll get you, my pretty." Jogging again, I followed the tracks, which, Eddie-like, didn't go in a straight line, but zigged and zagged.

"Cat, if you give me motion sickness," I panted, "you're not getting treats for hours, do you hear me, hours, and—"

I stopped running and talking, because off in distance I'd heard a voice. A female voice. An elderly female voice.

Neva.

From a standstill, I leaped into a flat-out run. Through the far half of the garden, past two greenhouses, and around the end of the third, all the while following Eddie's tracks, all the while hoping that Neva didn't have her gun, that she wasn't . . . that she wasn't . . .

I came around the corner of the last greenhouse and skidded to a stop. Neva was sitting cross-legged on the ground, with Eddie on her lap, petting him and talking to him as if she'd known him for years.

"You are a shedder, aren't you, my dear?" She shook her hand free of Eddie hair and I watched it twist away in the breeze. "But you're well groomed and wherever you came from, I'm sure someone is looking for you."

"Um," I said. "I'm afraid he's mine."

Neva looked up and squinted at me. "I know you. No, don't say, I'll remember." She continued to pet Eddie as she squinted. "Ha! I got it. You were looking at my dad's boat. Scared you off but good, didn't I?" She grinned, and once again I wondered about her mental stability.

"That's right," I said. "But this time I came in the Chilson Library's bookmobile."

Neva's grin dropped away and I tensed. Maybe she had a thing against libraries. Or bookmobiles. Or librarians. Or Chilson. Maybe that gun was behind her and she was going to pull it out and—

The elderly woman placed Eddie on the grass and

sprang to her feet twice as fast as I could have managed. She charged toward me, and I was stuck in place so tight that I might have been glued. There was nowhere to run, nowhere to hide. I'd have to defend myself as best I could and—

Neva was holding out her hand. "I have to apologize," she said.

"You do?"

"I do." She clasped my hand between hers and pumped up and down. "There was no excuse for going after you like that. I'd tell you about how that afternoon I'd had to write a big fat check to my accountant and how that made me cranky as all get-out, but that doesn't excuse me, so I apologize."

"Apology accepted," I said, starting to smile. I was also starting to see why the sheriff's office hadn't considered Neva a threat.

"Come on in." She released my hand and started striding to her house. "I have to show you something. Better grab that cat of yours." Neva opened the back door and ushered Eddie and me inside. "Here you go. What do you say about a drink? Tea? Water? Something stronger?" She winked.

I opted for water and looked around the kitchen as she opened the door of a Hoosier cabinet and took out two jelly jars. One of the bookmobile folks had said that Neva lived in her parents' house, and I was suddenly sure it had been her grandparents' house, too. Either that or no owner had ever changed a thing since the day the house was hatched.

There was a large porcelain sink underneath a set of

two double-hung windows. There were wooden counter-tops. Open shelves and the Hoosier cabinet instead of cabinets. A single ceiling light fixture. Plaster walls that showed trowel marks. Pegs next to the back door that held jackets. A round wooden table so scarred I could hardly tell what kind of wood it had been made from.

The entire room was squeaky clean and smelled of sunshine and outdoors. It also reminded of my aunt's boardinghouse kitchen, which tempted me to put Neva on the side of Good.

"Have a seat," she said, putting the glasses on the table and pulling out a chair. "Him, too," she added, nodding at Eddie.

My show-off cat jumped up and sat in the middle of the chair's seat, looking at Neva as if she might give him a treat.

"You," she said, "are a cat among cats, but I do not feed pets at the table."

He inched forward so his chin was almost on the edge of the said surface.

Neva laughed and fuzzed up the fur on his head. "Like I said, no treats at the table. You'll get yours later, mister." She looked over at me. "What did you say his name was?"

I introduced Eddie and myself and said I already knew her name.

"Just bet you do." She chuckled. "Probably talked to Kit Richardson, didn't you, after that day? She's a good sheriff, that girl."

I'd never thought of the tough, take-no-prisoners sheriff in terms of gender, let alone a term like "girl," but I gave a vague nod.

"Anyway," Neva said, "I need to tell you about my dad's boat. It was his dad's before him and when Granddad got too old to take it out, it sat in the barn for years. Dad wouldn't dream of working on Granddad's boat without permission, so it sat and sat." She sighed.

"That's not good for a wooden boat, is it?"

"True words." She nodded. "Granddad lived till he was ninety-three, and Dad didn't want to start on the boat right after he died, if you see what I mean, and then Dad got sick." She petted Eddie absently. "Then it was Mom's boat and then it was mine, and I don't have the know-how to fix it up or the money to pay someone else to do it for me."

Eddie started purring and she kept petting. "But I can't let it go," she said. "Not that boat. Not now, not ever." Her voice was soft, but determined, and I believed every word.

Neva gave Eddie one last pet. "I should get a cat," she murmured. "Been too long."

"Mrr," Eddie said.

The three of us chatted a little while longer, and then Eddie and I returned to the bookmobile.

I wanted to like Neva, wanted to very much. Okay, I did like her. But I still wondered about her temper. It could obviously run high, and if Henry had stoked it high enough, could she have been angry enough to kill him if she thought he was after her father's boat?

"What do you think, pal?" I asked.

But for once, Eddie didn't have a single thing to say.

"Sorry about bugging you," I said, recording my third voice mail for Bob, Gordon's cousin, "but I'm still trying to find out the weekend in April that Cole Duvall was up here." I paused, then said, "It's very important, and I need to find out as soon as possible."

I tried to think of something to say that might get him to call back quickly but couldn't come up with anything other than shrieking at him like a harridan. And though that might move him to action, it likely wouldn't be the action I wanted, so I just said thanks and hung up my cell phone.

"Are we taking bets?" Julia leaned forward to unlatch Eddie's door. "Fly and be free, little one."

"Bets on what?" I tossed the phone onto the console and flipped the driver's seat around in preparation for the bookmobile stop.

"Whether your plaintive bleat will encourage Bob to call you back."

I debated getting out the five-dollar bill that I always had in my wallet for bets with Rafe, but decided to let it stay there. "No bet. We wouldn't be able to get a definitive answer."

Julia smiled one of her stage smiles, the sultry temptress version. "Do you really think so?" she asked in a low, husky voice.

"It's not me you have to convince," I said, laughing.

"Good morning, ladies," a voice said.

We turned around and saw a man coming up the stairs. "Good morning," Julia said.

I would have said the same thing, but I was busy being puzzled. Though I was pretty sure I'd never seen this middle-aged man before, something about him seemed very familiar.

"Minnie?" he asked, looking from one of us to the other.

I held up my hand. "That would be me. And you are?"

"Bob," he said. "Gordon's my cousin."

Light dawned with a sudden, illuminating flash. "You're Bob!" Which was a stupid thing to say, but it wasn't the first time I'd said something stupid to a stranger and I was sure it wasn't going to be the last. "I've been calling you."

He nodded. "Yeah. I've seen your bookmobile out here before, so I figured I'd just stop and talk to you instead of calling."

That would have made perfect sense to another man, I was sure. "So you pinned down the date Cole was here in April?"

"Hey, there's that cat I heard about. Here, kitty, kitty." Bob crouched down and rubbed his fingertips. Eddie, the ham, came trotting over. "You're a friendly little cuss, aren't you?" He chucked Eddie under the chin. "Got a good purr machine there."

Eddie bumped his head against Bob's knee hard enough that the resulting crack echoed around the bookmobile.

"When was Cole Duvall here?" I asked a little louder.

"What's that?" Bob looked up. "Oh, right. Duvall came north that first weekend in April."

He went on about what he'd done for Cole, how he'd had to haul in logs for the fireplace, how he'd scraped ice off the driveway, and how he'd even been asked to go for groceries.

I tried to listen politely, but all I could think was one thing.

Cole Duvall had been here the weekend Henry died.

Chapter 18

I woke up the next morning, which was Friday morning, which was also the day before the book fair, knowing that my day was going to be packed full of things that had to get done. It was unlikely I'd have time to stop for lunch, so I slapped together my typical bookmobile lunch of a peanut butter and jelly sandwich and a little baggie of potato chips.

Eddie, lying on the back of the dining booth, watched this preparation with great interest.

"It's not a bookmobile day," I told him, trying to stuff the plastic bag of potato chips to that perfect limit: full enough so the chips didn't slide around, but not so full as to have the chips break from internal pressure. "I'm going to the library and you're staying here."

"Mrr."

I shrugged. "Okay, don't believe me. But you're not going anywhere. Not today and not tomorrow, either."

"Mrr."

"I've told you why," I said. "Tomorrow's not a book-mobile day because it's the book fair."

"Mrr."

"No, you can't go to the book fair. It's not for cats and"—I tried to head off any pending argument—"while I know that any place a cat wants to be is a proper place for cats, please trust me when I say that you won't enjoy a book fair. Too much noise, too many people, too many feet that might accidentally step on your tail. It's not a good place for Eddies."

"Mrr."

This kind of conversation could go on all day, so I shoved my lunch into my backpack and kissed the top of Eddie's head. "See you later, pal. Be good."

"Mrr."

The morning zoomed by. Then lunchtime went roaring past and I remembered to eat my sandwich and chips only when the emptiness in my middle told me it was past time to fill 'er up or bear the consequences.

Since I tended to get either light-headed or cranky when I was really hungry, and sadly, sometimes both, I wolfed down my lunch between the last few phone calls I needed to make.

All went well until I called Pam Fazio. "Hey, Pam, it's Minnie. Do you—"

"Pickle!"

"Bread and butter or dill?" I asked.

She laughed. "Don't deserve either. I was going to bring up those cookbooks, but I haven't had a minute to get away. You wouldn't believe how busy we've been."

Pam, upon hearing that the famed Trock Farrand was appearing at the book fair, had not only volunteered to redo the book fair flyer for use in every e-publication I could come up with, but she'd also volunteered to lend the library a number of antique cookbooks for a tie-in display.

"Tell you what," I said, thinking fast. I'd walked to work, but Pam's store was only a few blocks away. It wouldn't be too much of a chore to take the library's handcart for a short jaunt. "If you can get them in a box in the next half hour, I'll come and take them away."

"You will? That would be wonderful!"

"I should have done this in the first place," I said. "You're the one doing us the favor."

"Silly Minnie!" She laughed. "See you in half an hour. And thank you!"

I didn't understand why she was thanking me, but shrugged and went back to the phone calls.

In slightly less than half an hour, I was trundling down the sidewalk, trying to determine whether it was easier to push or to pull the ancient handcart, when I looked up and saw a sign I'd walked past hundreds of times before but had never had any reason to bring into my frame of reference.

Northern Development.

Hmm. I tucked the handcart next to the office's window box and went in the front door.

An extremely blond young woman was sitting behind a desk. "Hi," she said.

She couldn't have been thirty—might not have been twenty-five—and from what I could see of her above the desk, she was taking to heart the idea of dressing for the job you'd like to have. Assuming that she wanted to be a real estate developer, that is. Her blazer was trim and tailored, her hair was neat and tidy, the only jewelry she wore was a simple gold chain, and I didn't see a single tattoo.

"I'm Janine, Felix's new assistant," she said, smiling. "What can I do for you?"

"Hi." I smiled in return but didn't give my name. "I have some friends who inherited some property and they're not quite sure what they're going to do with it." Which wasn't exactly true, but surely Henry's sons hadn't planned out everything. "I was walking past, so I thought I'd ask a few questions about development."

"You've come to the right place." She nodded. "Have a seat and ask away."

I sat on the edge of one of the two chairs in front of her desk. "I suppose timing is the first thing. How long does it take to develop a property?"

Janine nodded again. "Great question. The only thing is, it depends." Her expression was one of sympathy and understanding. If she kept on in real estate, she was bound to make a fortune. "Depends on the property, on what you want to do with it, on the existing infrastructure, on the market, and on dozens of other things."

"Let's use a for instance, then," I said. "Are you familiar with Henry Gill's property?"

Her smile dipped a little. "Actually yes, I am. Why do you ask?"

Uh-oh. "My friends say the property they inherited is a lot like that one." So similar, as a matter of fact, that you'd think they were the same. "How long do you think it might take to, well . . ." I ducked my head in faux embarrassment. "Not to be crass, but how long do you think it might take to get money out of it."

"Oh, I see." Janine was back to nodding. "Well, again, it depends. If you want to turn it over fast, your friends could sell it to a developer. You might not realize the highest possible profits, but it would be cash in hand and no risk."

My new acquaintance Janine was not only personable, but extremely bright. "Could my friends develop it themselves?"

"Sure. But it takes time and money and a lot of decision making. They'd be hiring a surveyor, a civil engineer, a contractor." She ticked off the expensive professions on long, slender fingers. "They'd have to talk to utility companies and to attorneys and then there are the tax issues."

"It sounds complicated," I said faintly.

"But fun, too." Janine grinned. "I can't wait until Felix starts up another big project. To be a part of something like that?" Her grin became wide. "It'll be great."

"So Felix is looking for something big?" I asked.

"Developers are always looking for the next big thing," she said. "Take the Gill property. After Mr. Gill died, Felix was talking to the heirs of the estate, but they're not interested in selling. There's always another property around the corner, though. You never know what's going to walk in the door."

I laughed. "Sorry I wasn't bringing you the next big

thing. But I wish you luck in finding it." And somehow I was sure she would.

Once outside and wheeling the handcart away, I reflected on what I'd learned, which was that Janine didn't seem to know that Felix's finances were precarious, and that she also didn't appear to have any knowledge of Felix talking to Henry last fall about selling.

Then again, maybe Janine was just very good at not letting people see what she didn't want them to see.

I continued down the street. Two doors away from Pam's store, a dark green truck passed me, the image of a gold shield on its door, and even through the truck's closed windows, I could see the bright red of the driver's hair. The truck slowed. Its turn signal blinked on, and the truck made a left turn into the Round Table's parking lot.

As I stood there, watching, a tall man stepped out from behind the wheel, stretched even taller, and walked into the diner.

I slapped my pocket for my cell phone and pulled it out. "Irene? Could you take a break and come downtown for a minute? . . . I know, but this is important."

Irene and I walked into the restaurant's lobby. "Over there," I murmured. It was an unnecessary comment, because the dining area was empty except for an elderly couple at a table and the red-haired guy sitting in a booth by himself.

"Is that who you saw?" I asked. "The guy you thought was Seth Wartella?"

"Um . . ." She stared at him hard. "I . . . don't know."

"Hang on," I said, and walked up to him. "Hi," I said.

"Tony, right? I'm Minnie Hamilton. We talked late last year, in the winter."

He smiled, which made his ears seem to stick out even farther, and stood, forcing me to look up, his height being six foot. "Sure. You're the bookmobile lady, right? Nice to put a face to the name." He held out a hand and we shook. "How are things going in library land?"

We chatted for a moment, and then I said, "Nice meeting you."

"Likewise." He smiled and slid back into the booth, and I walked away.

Irene had her hand on the door and led me outside to the fresh air before I could say a word.

"He was the one I saw," she said, hugging herself. "He's wearing the same clothes in that weird green color. But he's not Seth. This guy is way too tall. And he looks a lot more, oh, I don't know, outdoorsy somehow."

"That's because he's a conservation officer," I said. "COs enforce hunting and fishing regulations." They also protected the state's natural resources, were often first responders to natural disasters and emergencies, and did general law enforcement. Which was all stuff I'd learned last winter. I might have been born and raised in suburbia, but I was learning.

"Oh." Irene glanced back at the restaurant. "I thought he was a security guard or something."

I smiled. "In Chilson? We don't do security here."

But the response to that was obvious to both of us: maybe we should.

*   *   *

After I parked the cookbooks in my office, I headed out to the lawn with Gordon to look at the tents. We were almost done when a movement at the edge of my vision caught my eye. I turned and saw Kelsey, one of our part-time clerks, pointing in my direction.

Gordon noted that my attention had wandered from our discussion of how to flag the tent pegs and guy ropes so that people wouldn't walk into them. "Problem?" he asked.

"Not sure." I watched as a large woman barreled across the lawn toward me. Her arms were pumping, her hair was flying all around her head, and there wasn't a single obvious ounce of that kind intelligence that had been so obvious when I'd met her two days ago.

"Are we all set?" I asked, easing away from Gordon. Because whatever Larabeth had to say to me, I was guessing no one else needed to hear it. "I'll be back later, to see how things are going." And then, before he could say anything and just before Larabeth got close enough to start talking—or yelling, as the case might be—I stepped away from Gordon and all the people who were milling about.

"I need to talk to you!" Larabeth shouted, making me wince; she was so close that I could have heard her if she'd whispered.

"Sure. How about over here?" I gestured for her to follow me. We went around the corner of the library into a shaded and secluded nook where, now that it was warm, flowering plants were starting to leap out of the ground. Soon there would be an abundance of lilies and all sorts of other pretty flowers I couldn't name. Even now, with only a few leaves sprouting from the shrubs, it was a soothing place and I hoped that it would calm Larabeth.

"Let's sit." I took one end of a teak bench and nodded for her to join me.

"Can't," she said through gritted teeth. "Too mad." She strode back and forth, arms still pumping, her hands in fists, her face bright red.

"At me?" I asked.

"What?" She whirled around to face me and it was then that I noticed that it wasn't just her face that was red. "Of course not you," she said, smearing at her reddened eyes with her knuckles. "I'm only here because I need to find out for sure and you're the only one I can talk to. You don't know me, so it's okay, you'll tell me the truth, you don't have any reason to lie, and besides, you're a librarian."

How the librarian occupation followed with the rest of her rambling sentence, I wasn't sure, but it was nice to think that my profession was considered a trustworthy one. "What's the matter?" I asked.

"It's . . . it's . . ." A tear trickled down her cheek. She turned away, muttering, "I'll be right back," and strode off.

I sat back and looked up at the sky. Clouds were moving in, but it was still a lovely day. The birds were singing, the grass was growing green, and the book fair was going to happen regardless of whether I ran around like a madwoman these next few hours trying to make sure everything was perfect. So why not take a few minutes to enjoy the day? Why not breathe in the smell of damp dirt and clean air and—

"All right." Larabeth sat down hard on the other end

of the bench. "I'm better now. And all I really have is one question for you. I can see that you're busy and I'm sorry to take up your time. Normally I would have called first, but I had to get out of the house and next thing I knew, I was on my way here."

She was almost to the rambling stage again, so I jumped in when she stopped for breath. "You have a question?"

"When you stopped by the other day . . ." Her hands gripped each other. "The other day," she said carefully, "when you stopped by you asked . . ."

I had a sudden, sick feeling that I knew where she was going. "I asked if your husband had been up North the first weekend in April."

Larabeth gave a sharp nod. "That's right. And I told you . . ."

I waited, but when she didn't say anything, I gave her her own answer. "You told me that Cole had been out West skiing."

"And that's what he'd told me," she said stonily. "That it was going to be the last good skiing weekend, so he and his buddies were going to fly out to Colorado, to Vail, and do nothing but ski and sit in the hot tub. That maybe this would be the time he'd try telemarking, that he wished I could go, but he was glad I understood. Understood!" She snorted. "Took me long enough, but I understand, all right. The rat was up here the whole time."

She turned and looked straight at me. "That's the question I have for you. He was up here, wasn't he?"

Over the years, I'd developed the ability to not tell people everything I knew, but I was a horrible straight-out liar. "Yes," I said. "He was."

She nodded, thumping her fists on her thighs. "For months I've tried to hide from this. Late nights, long weekends out of town, big batches of money gone. He's having an affair and this is the proof. There was no reason for him to lie about going to Vail if he'd been coming up here for anything else other than cheating on me."

I remembered what Adam had said, that he'd seen a redheaded woman that weekend, but kept quiet. That was secondhand information and I didn't need to add fuel to Larabeth's fire; she was stoking it along all by herself quite nicely.

"I'm sorry," I said. "I had no idea that my question would lead to this."

"Don't be sorry." She banged her fists on her legs one more time and stood up. "I should thank you."

"For what?"

She flashed a wide smile that reminded me of how Kristen could sometimes look. Sharklike. Predatory. Dangerous.

"Thanks again, Minnie," she said. "I'll see you later."

I watched her stride purposefully across the lawn, then stood up slowly. Larabeth had been so focused on her husband and her hurt that she hadn't realized the potential significance of her husband's April weekend at their cottage.

But I did.

I pulled my cell phone from my pocket and dialed the sheriff's office. From memory. It startled me that the number was stuck in my head, but I decided not to think about that fun fact.

"Tonedagana County Sheriff's Office."

Not for the first time, I thought that while it was nice that the region's founders had chosen a Native American name for the county, it would have been even nicer if they'd been able to come up with one that was shorter than five syllables.

"Hi," I said. "Is Detective Inwood available?"

"One moment, please."

I was treated to a bout of silence, during which I wondered whatever happened to the ubiquitous hold music that everyone used to enjoy complaining about so much. I'd decided to believe it had been a victory of good taste over poor when the detective himself came on the line.

"Inwood."

"Good afternoon, Detective, this is Minnie Hamilton."

"Ah, Ms. Hamilton. Please tell me that you are calling to brighten my day."

Though I was talking to a sheriff's detective, I was also watching two of Gordon's many minions tie bright pink strips of plastic to the tent stakes and guy ropes. The pinkness fluttered prettily in the wind. "That should do it," I murmured, now sure that no one paying the slightest amount of attention to where they were going would walk into a tripping hazard.

"Excuse me?" Detective Inwood asked.

"Sorry," I said. "I was talking out loud, but I do have some information of interest for you."

He exhaled loudly. "Please say this isn't going to turn into more work for me."

Probably. If I was right, almost certainly. I told him everything I'd learned the last few days, about Irene's likely mistake about Seth's presence in the area, about Felix's shaky financial status, and that Cole Duvall had been at his cottage the weekend Henry died.

I hesitated, then added the critical part: Larabeth's certainty that her husband was having an affair. Spreading gossip went against everything my mother had ever taught me, but this was information that could be critical to an investigation.

After I said all that, I waited for a response. When I didn't get one after roughly a year, I asked, "Detective? Are you still there?"

"Hang on," he said. "I'm writing . . . okay, got it." There was a creak and I imagined him leaning back in his chair. "Good leads, Ms. Hamilton. You sure you don't want to join the department?"

"Not a chance. I think I might be scared of Sheriff Richardson."

He made a noise that might have been a tired laugh. "We all are. Now, I have to tell you that we're still understaffed. It might be a couple of days before I have time to track down Duvall and talk to him."

"Sure," I said. "I understand. Besides, I don't see how a day or two could make any difference."

At the ripe old age of thirty-three, you'd really think I'd know better than to say things like that.

"Gordon," I said, "you are amazing."

He grinned. "Can I quote you to my wife?"

"Give me her phone number and I'll tell her myself."

The two of us were standing on the sidewalk that ran in front of the library, surveying the assemblage of canvas. Gordon has masterfully set up the tents of varying sizes to entice the fairgoers further up and further in by placing the smallest one closest to the main street and decorating it to the hilt with streamers and a huge sign that proclaimed to one and all that this was the "First Annual Chilson District Library Book Fair." The tents grew larger and larger as you walked through, inexorably drawn to the largest tent of all, where Trock would be in all his glory.

The visual spectacle alone was enough to draw in anyone who happened near the library. All day, cars had been slowing down long enough to see what was going on, and many had stopped to ask. I was hopeful that word would spread to anyone who hadn't seen the last-minute notice in the paper or the social media blitz we'd been pushing the last few days.

"Well," Gordon said, "since I can't think of anything else to do, I guess I'll head home. I'll be here at daybreak to make sure everything's still good."

"Why wouldn't it be?" I asked, and glanced at him.

He wasn't looking, as I'd supposed, at his expensive tents. Instead he was studying the sky. "Weather," he said. "There's something coming in."

These days, I rarely paid attention to the forecast. Driving the bookmobile across the county had shown me that the weather in Tonedagana County could change dramatically from one side to the other and the best I could do was to be prepared at all times for three seasons of weather, if not four.

"Rain?" I asked.

He sniffed at the air and shrugged. "Let's hope."

I was going to ask him what he meant, but he headed off before I could frame the words.

At home, I asked Eddie about it. "What do you think he meant? Better rain than . . . what? Snow?" The thought was painful, but a May snowfall wasn't unheard of. "Hail?" I hoped not. Gordon had insurance, but the hassles would be hard for him and his business.

"Mrr."

Eddie jumped up onto my lap. I was sitting at the houseboat's dining booth, watching the sky. I had no idea what Gordon had been watching, but all I was seeing was the sun setting over the ridge of land that separated Janay Lake from the waters of Lake Michigan. The sun was a soft glow above the dark ridge of treetops and—

"Wait a minute," I said, going very quiet and very still. "That's not trees. That's clouds."

As I watched, the line of black clouds rushed past the sun, turning the evening's soft glow to darkness in a matter of seconds.

"Oh, jeez . . ."

I dumped Eddie onto the floor and ran outside. "Eric!" I shouted. "Eric, are you in there?" I didn't wait for an answer, but rushed about my small foredeck, picking up seat cushions and feeling a little like Dorothy when the tornado was headed straight for Auntie Em and Uncle Henry's farmhouse. "Eric!"

"Hey, Minnie," he said, poking his head outside the side door of his boat. "What's up? Need a doctor?" He grinned.

I pointed westward. "Storm's coming. Better batten down your hatches."

He laughed. "I'm not sure I have any. Or that I'd know what one would look like if—" A gust of wind tore his words away, sending them east at about thirty miles an hour. "Good Lord," he said, or at least that was what I imagined him saying, because I couldn't hear a thing he said over the noise of the wind and waves.

"Will you be okay?" he shouted, pointing at my boat, which suddenly seemed very tiny.

Clutching my cushions to my chest, I nodded. My boat had seen decades of storms, including the famed summer storm of 1968. Of course, I'd never been on board during a big one, but it was too late to do anything about that now.

Crack!

Eric and I both jumped as lightning struck Janay Lake. Electricity sizzled in the air, and I didn't even reach a count of three before the thunder boomed.

"Inside!" Eric shouted.

But I was already halfway through the door. I didn't need some surgeon to tell me to stay inside during a wind-driven lightning storm.

"Mrr!"

I dropped the cushions on the floor and picked up my cat. "Sorry, pal, but I'm afraid it's going to be a wild night. Thunder and lightning and wind and—"

Crash!

Somewhere outside, a tree thumped to the ground. I hoped it wasn't the big maple outside Rafe's house. With the wind, that tree could easily have fallen straight onto the front porch.

The houseboat rocked back and forth and up and

down. I sat at the dining bench, told myself that we were tied up firmly to the dock at four corners, and snuggled Eddie close. He didn't purr, but he didn't pull away, either.

We stayed like that, waiting for the storm to pass. The electricity went out thirty minutes later and I carried an unprotesting cat to bed.

Soon enough Eddie was purring, and then snoring, but I lay awake for hours, listening to the wind and the lightning and the thunder.

Chapter 19

I fell asleep at some point during the night, but when morning finally came, I felt as if I hadn't slept at all. Fatigue filled my eyes, and my arms felt twice their normal weight.

Of course, that could have been because I was lying on my side and Eddie was flopped across both of my arms.

I kissed the top of his fuzzy head and slid out from underneath him. "Thanks for staying with me," I whispered. The night had been grueling, but at least I'd had the comfort of a cat to keep the worst of my fears at bay.

Now, however, I had to face those fears.

Fear number one, that there'd no electricity and I'd have to go to the book fair unshowered and grungy, was happily untrue. The bathroom light went on, I had hot water, and in a few minutes I was dressed and blotting as much dampness as I could out of the curly mess that was my hair.

I trotted up the stairs to the kitchen and steeled myself to look outside and face fear number two.

"Oh, wow . . . ," I whispered.

The world was a mess. Branches had been ripped from trees and tossed headlong. Leaves were strewn everywhere. Garbage cans, lawn furniture, bright plastic children's toys, and tarps had been blown hither and yon, reminding me somehow of a game I'd played as a kid when everyone took off their shoes and put them in a pile.

I tossed down a bowl of cereal, grabbed my backpack, and hurried outside.

Eric was on his boat's deck, sweeping it free of rain and leaf debris. "Made it through the night, I see." He paused in his sweeping to smile at me. No hard feelings for turning him down, apparently, which was nice. "Did you get much sleep?" he asked.

"Not much," I said, stepping onto the dock. "And there's a book fair at the library today. Trock Farrand's signing his new book."

"If I buy a copy, do I have to learn how to cook?" Eric asked.

I grinned and waved as I started a fast walk toward downtown. But there was one quick stop I had to make before heading to the library.

Rafe was standing in front of his house, hands on his hips, surveying the damage.

I walked up and stood next to him. "Well," I said. "It could have been worse." Because while a massive branch had ripped off the maple tree in front of his house, the branch had mostly missed the porch, and most of the tree was still standing.

Rafe nodded. "Yeah, and I was just thinking the other day that I should have done that trim a different way."

"Well, there you go." I almost asked him if he was

going to come to the book fair, but I doubted he'd be able to tear himself away from his new project. I said good-bye, he grunted a reply, and I hurried off.

The closer I got to downtown, however, the more worried I got. Each block I walked showed increasing amounts of destruction, and by the time I reached the heart of the retail district, I realized there was no electricity. No signs were lit, no shop windows glowed, no welcoming anything anywhere.

This wasn't good. At all.

Without thinking about it, my fast walk turned into a slow jog. My brain's worrying cells, the ones I tried to keep quiet and inactive, flared bright and strong and, try as I might, I couldn't force them back into hibernation.

So I ran.

I ran through the far end of downtown, up the short hill, and left two blocks, feet flying, arms pumping, backpack thumping, breathing hard and fast, my lungs burning with the unaccustomed exercise.

There were no signs of electricity two blocks away from the library . . . no electricity one block away . . . leaves and tree branches everywhere, loose shingles in front yards, lawn furniture a tangled mess . . . and then I reached the library.

Panting and wheezing, I came to a dead stop. I stared at fear number three and it stared straight back.

The book fair tents, Gordon's tents, were a flattened mess. Not a single one remained standing. A tree had fallen across the largest, and its two peaks, formerly graceful and sweeping and reminiscent of castles and fairy tales, were on the ground, their magic gone.

I took one step toward the disaster, then stopped. There was nothing I could do. Nothing anyone could do. Tent poles were snapped, stakes were yanked out of the ground, canvas was ripped. Even if all the equipment had been intact, it had taken a full day to set everything up, and we didn't have that kind of time. What we had— what I had—was two and a half hours.

My knees went a little jellylike. I wanted desperately to sit down or, even better, to go find a quiet dark corner and some chocolate chip cookie dough, and not come out until it was gone.

Instead I took a deep breath, pulled out my phone, and starting making calls.

Half an hour and a lot of fast talking later, I took my cell phone away from my ear and hoped that none of those urban legends about heavy cell phone use causing cancer had any truth to them.

I put my phone in my backpack and stood there for a moment, thinking and not thinking at the same time, which should have been impossible but clearly wasn't, since it was happening to me. For every thought I had, there was an equal and opposite reaction of blankness in my brain. If I thought about the vast number of people who needed to be contacted in the next two hours, the next thing that went into my head was a large bubble of nothingness. Self-defense, probably, but it wasn't helping me get things done.

"Move," I muttered to myself. Whenever I was stuck on a problem, it always helped me to get up and move around, and this was a problem of serious magnitude.

I'd found a new venue for the fair, I'd started a phone tree to notify all the vendors about the new location, and I'd even convinced a local printer to slap together some temporary signs. When he'd said he didn't have any electricity to print anything, I pushed away my panic and asked him to summon his creative abilities and see what he could do by hand.

"You mean with real paint?" he'd asked. "And brushes?"

Wildly I'd wondered if anyone still made poster paint. "Absolutely with real paint," I'd said. "In any color you want, as long as people can read it."

He'd made an interested noise and said he'd come up with something. "I'm not going to promise it'll be pretty," he cautioned.

I'd reassured him that communication was the only thing that mattered, thanked him profusely, and had gone on to the next call, which was to the current president of the Friends of the Library. I'd told Denise where to take the food and beverages they'd planned to sell for a nominal fee at the event. "There's no electricity," I'd told her, "so you might need to track down coolers and ice and whatever else you need to keep things cold or warm. It's a mess down here, a huge mess, and—"

"Minnie," she'd said calmly, "don't worry about a thing. We'll be there."

I'd gulped down a grateful sob. Denise and I didn't see eye to eye on . . . well, almost everything, and it was reassuring to know that she would rise to the occasion. I'd thanked her, then ended the call. Which was when I'd started staring at the untidy world, trying to think what needed doing next, and told myself I needed to start moving.

So I leaned over and started picking up sticks and branches and leaves from the sidewalk. It was a pointless task, since the crew that did our regular lawn and landscaping maintenance would do the job properly in a day or three, but it felt good to do something.

"Minnie?"

I looked up. Ash Wolverson was standing not ten feet away. He was wearing a hooded sweatshirt and shorts and I was suddenly quite sure that I'd never seen him wearing shorts before, because I would have remembered that his legs, on a one-to-ten scale, were at least a nine-point-five.

"Are you going to cancel?" he asked. "The fair, I mean?"

"Not a chance," I said. "New location, but the show will go on." The sticks in my hand suddenly felt heavy and I decided not to explain what I was doing. It would take too long and there was no way I would look good at the end of the story. New subject, then.

"Have you talked to Detective Inwood?" I asked. "I called him yesterday with some information and he said he'd be talking to you."

But Ash was shaking his head. "I had a couple of days off. I'll be in the office tomorrow, though."

"Oh." I tore my gaze away from his muscular legs. "Well, that's good," I said vaguely.

"Do you need some help?" Ash gestured at the vast mess surrounding us.

"Thanks, but we have a grounds crew. I'm sure they'll get to us as soon as they can."

Ash glanced at the sticks in my hands. My face grew warm and I knew I was about to start babbling. "It's just—"

"See you later, Minnie," he said, turning away.

"Wait!"

He stopped, then came halfway back, but he didn't say anything.

"So," I said, "the other day, when you . . . well, back then, things were different."

"Things?" he asked.

In a perfect world, I would have thought about what I'd say before blurting out everything that was in my head. "I'm not seeing that doctor anymore," I said. "In reality, I haven't for weeks. Months, even. It just took this long to make it official."

"Oh." Ash put his hands in the front pocket of his sweatshirt. "Sorry to hear that."

"No, no," I said. "It's good. Things weren't working out and—" And there was no way Ash wanted to hear any of those details. "So I was wondering if . . ."

"If what?" Ash asked.

I wanted to stamp my foot. Why was he making this so hard? Then I detected a small smile twitching up one side of his face. "You know," I said.

"Nope." He grinned. "I'm just a dumb cop. You're going to have to spell it for me."

Of all the things Ash was not, dumb was at the top of the list. But I'd already turned him down twice when he asked me out, so it was only fair that I make the move.

"Would you like to go to dinner?" I asked, my heart suddenly beating loud, my breaths coming fast. "With me? Sometime?"

His grin eased into a kind and exceedingly attractive smile. "Anytime," he said.

Just then, Gordon's truck came to a screeching halt in the parking lot. He leaped out and rushed to his tents. "Oh, man," he said, looking at the damage. "Minnie, I am so sorry. I can get some of my guys here. We can maybe get some of these back up, but . . ." He shook his head. "I am so sorry."

Later we would hear that the storm had pushed one-hundred-mile-an-hour winds through a narrow swath of the county. Straight-line winds, they called them, that could create damage on par with a minor tornado. In some ways we'd been lucky, because the worst of the winds had hit outside town on state forestry land.

I smiled at him. "Not your fault. I've found a new place to hold the fair. Not ideal, but it'll work."

"Is there anything I can do?" Gordon asked. "Anyone you want me to call?"

And suddenly I remembered the one person I should have talked to long ago. "Stephen," I said, and started laughing. "I really should tell my boss about this."

A few fast hours later, I took a long look at all the activity going on about me and sucked in a huge sigh of relief. In spite of everything that Mother Nature had tossed at us, the book fair had not been canceled. It was actually turning out to be what you might call a success.

"Hey, Minnie." Josh was walking toward me, carrying a box of books. "Where do you want these?"

I stood on my tiptoes to peek at the contents. More cookbooks. I pointed toward the long line of people who were waiting for their chance to get a signed copy of Trock's first-ever publication. "Over there. Thanks."

"Miss Librarian?" A small child stood in front of me, looking up with big unblinking eyes. "Is there anywhere I can get a book about horsies?"

"You bet," I said. "See that table over there, the one with a red tablecloth? They have some wonderful books about horses and barns and . . ." I'd never gone through a horse phase, and the appropriate terms weren't coming to mind. ". . . And saddles and boots."

The child ran off, followed by a smiling father, who thanked me.

It seemed that the entire huge room was filled with smiling people, a fact that was stunning, yet somehow not surprising, given how things were turning out.

My first frantic phone call that morning had been to Rafe. Most Saturday mornings he'd have still been in bed at eight o'clock, but since I'd seen him outside his house already, I knew he was awake.

"I need a favor," I'd asked.

"Okay."

"A really big one."

"Can it wait? Because I don't know if you remember, but I have a tree on my house."

"It's only part of a tree and it's your porch and I need to borrow the middle school's gym."

There'd been a pause.

"I'll help with your tree later," I'd said quickly. "But the tents are smashed and I need a new place to hold the fair. There's not enough room in the library."

"And there's no electricity at the school," Rafe had said. "The maintenance guy already called me."

I'd been ready for that teensy little problem. "I have

a plan. All I need is permission and someone to unlock the door."

"Minnie," he'd said slowly, "I don't—"

"I'll get down on my knees," I'd said, grunting a little as I'd done so. "I'm risking grass stains on my khakis to do this, because if you don't let me use your gym, we'll have to cancel the fair. There's no other place in town."

I'd known I was asking a lot. Rafe was the middle school's principal, but he worked for the school board and they made the calls on the big decisions.

There'd been a longer pause, but this time I didn't interrupt.

"I'll call you back," he'd finally said, and I'd walked around in small circles on the sidewalk until he did.

"Thank you," I'd whispered when he gave me the thumbs-up. "You're all right for a . . ." But I hadn't come up with an appropriate insult, not that time.

"Yeah, yeah," he'd said. "I know."

Happily he'd hung up before I got too sentimental, and now that the fair was in full swing, I was ready to trade verbal abuse with my friend. Of course, he didn't deserve any abuse at all, since he not only secured permission from the school board's president for me to use the gym, but also forwarded to the parents of the school's students the text blast I'd sent to the Friends of the Library, asking everyone to bring battery-powered camping lanterns.

Emergencies can bring out the best in people, and I couldn't begin to count the lanterns that were lighting the gym, giving it a cozy glow that was encouraging conversation. One father had even hauled over a small generator, and Trock's table was so well lit it was like a beacon in the night. Plus, many of the folks who'd brought in lanterns had stayed to wander around the displays, and, wonder of wonders, they were purchasing books, too.

The signs my printer friend had pushed into the ground at the library had, I'd been told, been so amusing that even people who hadn't planned on attending the fair had shown up, and Pam Fazio had called to tell me that the downtown merchants, far from being annoyed that the fair was pulling people away from their stores, were pleased at the influx of fair-bound tourists, and had been pleased for days.

"It's your fault."

I turned. Trock Farrand was standing there, glowering at me. "What is?"

"This." He flung his arms out at the people, the books, the fairyland of lights, the general air of cheerfulness and goodwill. "I am charmed, Miss Hamilton, simply charmed by this entire event. I am inclined to write another book so I can attend next year, and writing a cookbook is a tremendous amount of work, and, therefore, my upcoming busy schedule is completely your fault."

I didn't believe a word of it, but I had the perfect response. "It was my boss's idea."

"And who did all the work?" Trock asked, raising one bushy eyebrow. "Yes, I thought so. Ideas are cheap, my sweet bookmobile librarian. Turning them into reality is the key. Now. Here is a gift for you." He handed over a copy of his cookbook.

I blinked at him. "For me?"

"My dear," he said sorrowfully, "I know you think

cooking is for other people, but surely even you could think of a use for this."

"Oh. Thanks." It was a big book. Maybe it would work as an industrial-sized paperweight. "But you don't have to give me a copy. I'm happy to buy one." Sort of.

"No, no." He took the book out of my hands and flipped through the pages. "Here," he said, handing the open book back to me. "Since I'm certain you would never even glance through the outstanding recipes for months, I have to present this to you personally." He patted me on the head—something I wouldn't stand from anyone else in the world—and steamed back to his adoring fans.

I looked down at the cookbook and didn't know whether to laugh or cry, because right there in front of me was a recipe titled "Eddie's Salmon Snacks: Treats for Cats of a Discerning Nature."

"Hey, Eddie!" I poked my head inside the houseboat's door. Most days, Eddie was there, waiting for me. Early on in our relationship I'd thought he was waiting for me, anxious about my absence and worried that I'd never return, but I eventually realized he was waiting for me to open the door so he could get outside.

This time, however, he wasn't at the ready. Sleeping, no doubt.

I came all the way inside and slid my backpack off my shoulder. "Wake up, Eddie. I have something to show you." Because not only had Trock named his cat treat recipe after Eddie, but he'd also included a photo of said feline and signed the page with his name and "Thanks for the inspiration, Mr. Edward. You are a king among cats."

While I wasn't sure I wanted to read the inscription to Eddie, I had to do it at least once, and I might as well get it over with.

"Eddie? Where are you?"

Even on a houseboat smaller than any apartment in which I'd ever lived, it was possible for a cat to find hiding places that took me ages to find.

I checked in the closet.

No Eddie.

Looked in the bathroom cupboards.

No cat.

Stretched high to see the top of the kitchen cabinets.

Nothing but dust.

I even got down on my hands and knees and looked underneath everything there was to look under, but still didn't find him.

"Well." I got to my feet and put my hands on my hips. Where the heck was he? He'd been sleeping when I left that morning, so he couldn't have slipped outside. Then again . . .

I tried to remember if the door had been locked when I came home. Surely I'd locked it when I left, but the morning had been rushed and anxious and I couldn't remember, one way or another.

"Eddie? Game's over, okay? You win. I lose. Let's get some dinner."

But there was no pad-pad-pad of Eddie feet coming my way and I was starting to feel a flutter of panic. Maybe I'd left the door unlocked. Maybe I'd left it unlatched. Maybe he'd pushed the door open with his little Eddie nose and slid outside. He wasn't the most graceful cat in the world; maybe he'd fallen in the water and—

No. I wouldn't think that. He was here somewhere. Or outside somewhere. Maybe Eric had seen him. Maybe Eric had adopted him and was cooking Salmon Snacks for him. Maybe Eddie would never want to come home and—

My cell phone rang, making the noise it made when a new number was calling.

I scrabbled through my backpack and looked at the phone. Unknown caller with a downstate area code. Odd. "This is Minnie Hamilton."

"And this is Cole Duvall."

"Oh." I blinked, not having any idea what to say to a man I'd told police might be a killer. "Um, hello."

"I have your cat," he said in a low voice.

My eyes flew open wide and I turned around, looking frantically for a trace of the best feline friend anyone could have. "There's no way. You can't. There's—"

"If you want him back, meet me at my cottage in an hour."

I protested, I shouted, and I yelled, but he was gone.

Chapter 20

"**E**ddie!" I tore around the houseboat, looking everywhere I'd already looked. "Eddie?" After all, maybe Duvall was just messing with me. Maybe he really hadn't taken Eddie, maybe he was just trying to get me out to his cottage and—

The beep of my phone interrupted my anxious thoughts. Since the thing was still in my hand, it was a relatively loud beep and, reflexively, I glanced at the screen. There was an incoming text message and there was a photo attached. I opened the image and immediately sat down. Hard.

It was a picture of Eddie. An Eddie crouched in the far corner of a cardboard box, his mouth frozen open in what I could see was a loud "Mrr!"

"I am so sorry," I whispered to his picture. Eddie hated being shut up in dark boxes. My early attempts at using a picnic basket for a cat carrier had not ended well. "Don't worry. I'll get you out of there."

Only . . . how?

Ash had given me his cell number that morning,

which seemed long ago and far away now, but when I called the number, I was instructed to leave a voice mail. I stumbled over what to say—was catnapping a crime?— and ended up just asking him to call me as soon as he could.

I started to call 911, then stopped as I imagined the conversation. "Yes, ma'am, let me get this straight. Your . . . cat has been . . . kidnapped?"

Duvall had given me an hour. No way would I be able to explain everything and get a police presence out to Duvall's cottage in less than . . . well, I didn't know how long it might take, but it was bound to be more than an hour. Maybe Duvall would make good on his time limit and maybe he wouldn't. I wasn't about to take any kind of a chance, not with Eddie.

A sob came up out of my throat. From where I was sitting, on the narrow stairs down to the bedroom, the noise sounded a lot like a whimper.

"Stop that," I said out loud.

That made me feel a little better, so I stood and tried it again. "Stop that. You need to figure out what to do."

But what?

I paced around the kitchen, trying to come up with a plan, but all I did was get dizzy. Time ticked away and I knew I had to get going if I was going to meet Duvall's deadline. There was no choice about that—he had Eddie and I had to get Eddie back, no matter what the risk might be.

And, after all, maybe Duvall just wanted to talk. Maybe he'd only taken Eddie to make sure I'd take him seriously. There was no way Duvall could know that I suspected him of killing Henry and trying to kill Adam, so how could I be at risk? Well, okay, his wife could have told him what I'd said about knowing his whereabouts the first weekend of April, but when Larabeth stopped by the library, it hadn't sounded as if she was about to have any long conversations with him. And though it was extremely unlikely, it was possible that he'd been following his wife and had overheard our conversation.

So actually, there were lots of ways I could be at risk. I pushed them all out of my head. What mattered was Eddie.

I slid my phone into my backpack, grabbed my car keys, scrawled a quick message on the kitchen whiteboard, and hurried to rescue my cat.

It was almost dark by the time I reached the road where Henry had lived. Halfway there, I had called 911, and though the conversation had started out much as I'd anticipated, once I'd explained the whole story, the dispatcher had assured me that deputies would arrive on the scene within half an hour. She'd told me sternly to stay away from the scene, saying that the officers would do everything they could to ensure my cat's safety.

The dispatcher talked, and I listened; then I talked, and talked some more. Eventually I was transferred to someone else, but I kept glancing at the clock on my car's dashboard, wondering whether I'd make it in time, wondering what Cole Duvall would do if I was two minutes late, hoping that the few moments I'd taken in the car to breathe deep, think ahead, and plan a little hadn't jeopardized my . . . hadn't made Duvall . . . wouldn't end . . .

"Stop that," I said.

"Excuse me?" said the voice on the other end of the phone.

My car's headlights caught the reflective flash of the numbers on Duvall's mailbox. I reached out and turned the headlights off. While I wasn't sure sneaking up on him would help, knowing that I had the ability to control at least this little thing gave me half an ounce of confidence.

"Time for me to go," I said, turning off the phone in the middle of an instruction to stay away from Mr. Duvall.

Coasting through the trees, I eased down the slope toward the cottage. Toward the water. Closer in, I could see that the only lights on at the house were exterior ones, small shin-high lights that would undoubtedly lead me around to the dock.

A hundred yards away, I did a three-point turn and parked off the side of the driveway and behind a cluster of shrubs, putting the car's front bumper in the heading-out direction, just in case we needed to make a fast exit.

I slipped out of the car, shutting the door so quietly I barely heard it myself. Soundlessly I made my way to the front door and peeked inside through the tall, narrow side windows. Nothing in there but darkness and vague furniture shapes. I tried to open the door, but it was locked.

My faint hopes of finding Eddie alone inside a closet or a bathroom, grabbing him under my arm, and running off to freedom faded almost before they'd had a chance to grow.

Now what, smarty-pants?

I slid my cell phone out of my pocket and checked the time. Nine o'clock straight up. My hour was over. I couldn't wait any longer.

Pulling in a deep breath for courage, I walked around the side of the house. The horizon on the west side of Rock Lake was still pale with the sunset's afterglow, and I could see the silhouette of a man sitting on a bench at the end of a long dock.

Cole Duvall.

Still moving quietly, I walked down the stone steps, keeping an eye on Duvall. Now that my eyes had adjusted to the darkness, I could see that he was sitting casually, one arm laid across the back of the bench, one ankle over the opposite knee. He was also lifting his other arm, every so often, in a motion that could only mean he was drinking something.

Around and about me, the spring flowers were blooming and the summer ones were starting to poke out of the ground, but it was still too early for the summer lawn games to be out and available. No sense in putting out a croquet set when there was still a chance of snow. I looked hard for a set of lawn darts, but since I'd never played that game as a kid, it was probably just as well that the Duvalls didn't have any around. I'd be just as likely to stab myself in the leg as to do any real damage to my enemy.

Because Duvall was my enemy. I couldn't let myself forget that. Getting Eddie back, safe and sound, was the priority of the night, but taking care of Duvall was a close second.

I made sure my cell phone was secure in my pocket and stepped onto the dock.

The moment my foot hit the wooden boards, Duvall turned. "You're here," he said. "Took you long enough."

I told myself not to antagonize the man. What I wanted was my cat. That was what mattered right now. Sticking up for myself against a bully could wait another day. Not two, because that would grind in my stomach like bad beets, but I could stand twenty-four hours.

"Where's Eddie?" I moved up the dock slowly. Duvall didn't seem to have any weapons, but since he was more than a foot taller than I was, and, at a guess, more than a hundred pounds heavier, he didn't really need anything more than his own bulk. The self-defense classes I'd taken last year had been useful, but they were designed to help me escape a man's grip, not to walk right up into the mouth of the lion and demand things that would anger him.

"Right here." Duvall's foot bumped what I could now see was a cardboard box.

From inside I heard a "Mrr," and that faint bleat pushed red into my thoughts and emotions and actions. I took one fast, hot step forward, then pulled back.

No. Rushing headlong into a physical confrontation with Duvall would not help anything. *Keep calm, keep him talking, and keep thinking.*

So instead of the classic "What do you want?" question that I so desperately wanted to ask, I said, "Nice spot you have here."

Duvall stared at me. "What?"

I kept on with my slow walk toward the end of the dock and said, "How long have you had this place?"

"None of your business," Duvall said.

So much for opening pleasantries. I tried to widen my focus to include the empty boat lift that was on my left and anything it might offer me. The bench where Duvall was sitting was on an assemblage of dock sections that made up an L-shaped area. I searched for a weapon—a boat hook, an anchor, a rope, anything—but the only things I saw were the bench, Duvall, and Eddie's box.

"Mrr," the box said, and scarlet rage fell down upon me like a net.

"What do you want?" I asked, my teeth tight together.

"I want you to undo what you did." Duvall snorted an unattractive laugh.

An Undo button for life. Now, that would be useful. I stopped about fifteen feet away from Duvall, well out of his reach. "It would help if you told me what you're talking about."

"Don't play dumb with me," he snapped. "You know perfectly well."

Well, no, I didn't. Not for sure. But I could guess. "Larabeth came to her conclusions on her own," I said. "All she wanted from me were confirmations."

"And you did what, just handed them to her?"

He snorted again and I got the feeling that snorting was a habit of his. A few years of that and it would be no surprise that his wife wanted to divorce him. Though it wasn't until I'd started poking around that Larabeth had started putting the pieces together, she was a smart woman and would have figured out on her own that Cole was cheating on her. Maybe I'd jump-started the process, but if it saved her from having to listen to that condescending snort even once, I couldn't say I was sorry.

Of course, he still had my cat. And I still needed to know—desperately needed to know—if he'd killed Henry and tried to kill Adam.

Duvall turned on the bench and faced me full-on. "Make this go away," he said, "and I'll give you back your cat. Although why you'd want this thing is beyond me." He gave the box a shove with his foot, pushing it a few inches closer to the edge of the dock and eliciting another "Mrr!" from inside. "All he does is whine, whine, whine."

He'd taken on a tone close enough to Eddie's voice that made me think that my cat had said more than usual on the trip out here. Which brought me to another question.

"How did you know that I had a cat?"

Duvall snorted. "Everybody knows about the bookmobile cat. You can't talk about the bookmobile lady and not hear about her freaking cat. 'Oh, he's so cute,'" he said in a high-pitched voice that didn't sound like any woman I'd ever heard in my life. "'Eddie is just the nicest cat there is.'" He dropped the fake voice. "Even if there was such a thing as a nice cat, this one wouldn't be it, not the way he complains about everything."

No cat liked to be grabbed and stuck in a box, but if Duvall didn't know that by now, there was no hope for him.

"How did you know where I lived?" I asked.

"Where do you think you live, Chicago? You live in Chilson, for crying out loud. All I had to do was walk downtown and ask about the bookmobile lady with the cat. Everybody I talked to was so happy to talk about you, about your houseboat and your aunt with the boardinghouse." He snorted. "Only up here would there still be such a thing as a boardinghouse. Doesn't she know they stopped existing fifty years ago?"

Again, I pushed away the anger threatening to take over my brain, pushing away worry about Aunt Frances, pushing away worry about Eddie and whatever might happen in the next few minutes.

"Why did you lie to me?" I asked. "Up by Henry's sugar shack. You said Felix Stanton had tried to talk Henry into selling last fall."

"Really?" Duvall asked, sarcasm oozing from every letter of the word. "You can't even figure that out? It was obvious you were poking into things that were none of your business. It was dead easy to give you a shove in the wrong direction and get you off my back."

It was obvious to me that his ploy hadn't worked at all, but whatever. I put my hands in my pockets and felt the reassuring bulk of my cell phone. I'd set it to record, and hoped its recording qualities were good enough to work through my pants. Speaking of phones . . . "How did you get my cell number?"

Duvall laughed and took a long swig out of what I could now see was a beer bottle. "You should really tell your library staff to be more careful," he said, swiping his mouth with the back of his hand. "People like me might be calling and saying they're an uncle who happens to be in town but doesn't have your phone number."

He was probably right; I should tell them to be more careful. Then again, did I really want to take away their willingness to help? Where did you draw the line? Where did you decide to take a stand?

"I can't make your problems go away," I said calmly. "And anything you do to me or my cat will only make things worse." Especially my cat. I balled my hands into hard fists, enduring the pain of my fingernails digging into my skin. "Talk to your wife. Apologize. Tell her you'll never do it again. If you're sincere, it should all work out."

"Don't be stupid," he said shortly. "She'll never believe that I won't have another affair. I promised after the last one to never do it again. She said she'd give me one last chance, and this was it."

"Ah." When I'd talked to Larabeth, that wasn't the story she'd given me, but I could understand rearranging reality a little to save her pride.

Duvall upended the beer bottle into his mouth, emptying it of every last bit of alcohol. When he was done, he said, "Last night, after I drove all the way up here, she told me to pack my stuff and get out before she called someone else to do it for me. Then she took off."

"Where did she go?" I asked.

"How would I know? That woman is too jealous for her own good. If she hadn't been like this, I never would have cheated on her in the first place."

I squinted at him, once again wondering how people could hold two opposing viewpoints in their heads at the same time and not blow up. I also wondered at a man who, after years of marriage, couldn't make a guess as to where his wife had fled after an argument.

Then fear stabbed at me. What if he'd killed her?

Duvall flung the empty beer bottle into the water. Flagrant littering: another reason to put him in jail. "She called this morning," he said. "I tried to talk with her, tried to reason with her, but she wasn't having any of it, said that after she'd talked to you everything became clear." He stared at me. "So now I want you to take it back. I want to stay married to Larabeth. She's the best meal ticket I'll ever get and she's so busy running those stores that I hardly have to see her. All I have to do is get you to convince her I wasn't up here that weekend with my friend."

While I was relieved at Larabeth's continued life, I was appalled at her husband. "You married her to get a free ride?"

He laughed. "Little Miss Naive, aren't you? You'd think I'd marry a woman who looks like that for any other reason? I mean, honestly, look at me."

I did look at him, and in the last vestiges of the day's light, I didn't see what he expected me to see, which was a handsome man in his mid-forties, a man full of confidence and appeal. What I saw was a grasping and desperate man who would stop at nothing to keep the life of luxury to which he'd grown accustomed.

"You killed Henry," I said, in as strong a voice as I could, which wasn't very, but still. "You were up there that weekend with your girlfriend, and Henry saw her with you. You knew Henry well enough to know he'd never lie for you, so you figured a way to make Henry's death look like an accident."

Though the sun had dropped behind the tree line, the rising half-moon was sending out enough light that I could see shapes, if not colors.

"What of it?" Duvall toed Eddie's box, sending it another inch toward the edge of the dock.

"And you saw Adam try to get Henry out from under the tree, didn't you?"

Duvall chuckled. "Yeah, figured that guy was toast, the way he fell to the ground, grabbing at his chest. Pissed me off something royal when I found out he was still alive, let me tell you."

"How did you know that Adam had seen your girlfriend?"

"Didn't." Duvall shrugged. "But I couldn't take that chance. I hoped that heart thing would kill him off, but no, he got better and came home to a wife that hovered over him like a nutcase." He snorted. "Took me a while to figure out a way to get at him." He glared at me. "And you had to go and mess that up, too."

"He's my friend," I said quietly. "I help my friends."

"That's great for them," Duvall said, his voice hardening. "But who helps you when you need it? What happens then? Do they come running, lending a hand when you need it?"

Actually they did. And had done so that very day. It would have been hard to count all the friends who had gathered around when I called that morning when I was panicked for the book fair.

Trock had been a trouper, the library staff had hardly blinked an eye, Rafe had come through like a champ, Kristen had handed out the emergency fliers Pam printed up until her restaurant opened, my downtown friends had willingly helped direct people to the school, and there was

Ash and my aunt Frances and her friend Otto and the marina folks and—

"Yeah, I thought so," Duvall said. "You can't count on anyone these days." He stood, towering over me, his bulk blotting out the moonlight. "Just like I won't be able to count on you."

Of course he couldn't. Why on earth would he think he should be able to? I barely knew him and didn't care for what I did know. In addition to making no sense, the man was a jerk of the first order, and I wondered how he'd managed to fool Larabeth long enough to convince her to marry him.

Duvall's foot slid to the side and I suddenly realized what he was about to do.

"No!" I shouted, and lunged forward, flinging myself onto the cardboard box, the flimsy, wouldn't-hold-water box, the box that held my furry friend, my confidant, my pal.

My hands snatched the box out of Duvall's reach just before the rest of my body hit the dock. I *oof*ed out a painful grunt and twisted my body away, rolling as far as I could as fast as I could, trying to escape his powerful kick.

Still rolling, I scrabbled to open the box. It was taped shut, but I yanked away the sticky stuff and pulled open the flaps.

As soon as I did, Eddie, howling and scratching and hissing, launched himself out of his small prison. His paws barely hit the dock as he bounded away from me and onto the Duvall's empty boat lift. He galloped along the narrow metal beams, clawed his way up the vertical padded posts, and leaped up onto the metal of the canopy's framework.

I held my breath, because that framework was made of metal tubes and wasn't anything any normal cat would typically be happy perching upon, but Eddie was no normal cat and this was definitely not a normal situation.

"What's with him?" Duvall asked.

"He's scared," I said, and so was I. Because it was now obvious to me that Duvall had given up on having me clear things up for him with Larabeth. He'd passed the moment when I might have convinced him to work on his marriage. He might have passed it before I even arrived. And the moment I thought about that, I knew it was true.

Duvall had never intended to let me go. Even if I'd sworn to keep quiet, he would never have allowed me to go home, free to call Larabeth and tell her what her husband had just done to me. He'd brought me here to kill me and I'd walked right into his manipulative trap. Too Stupid To Live, they called this. TSTL.

"Stupid," I whispered to myself. Because now what was I going to do? Duvall was far too big for me to fight and I hadn't heard the least hint of police sirens.

I could try to run, but unless I got a huge head start, he'd catch up to me before I got off the dock. I could scream, but it was too early in the year for anyone to be around, and the only weapon I had was . . . well, nothing.

I studied the boat lift, thinking to emulate my cat, but I didn't see how I could climb what Eddie had climbed. Besides, Duvall could just step onto the horizontal bits, reach up, and yank me down. In the end, he might leave Eddie alone.

Then again, I didn't want to leave Eddie an orphan. Aunt Frances would take him, but Otto already had a cat and the one time we'd tried to encourage their friendship had not gone well. Kristen's apartment was above the restaurant and she wouldn't want that much cat hair floating about. Holly had a young dog, and Josh wasn't a cat guy. I toyed with the idea of Rafe and Eddie, but wasn't sure Rafe would remember to feed and water him on a regular basis. During the school year, sure, but what about during the summer when Rafe went for three months without a haircut because his secretary wasn't there to remind him? So Rafe was out, and I didn't know Ash well enough to say, not yet anyway.

The dock creaked. Duvall was moving closer to me. I cleared my mind of the panic-induced cobweb of thoughts it had drifted into and inched backward.

"What are you doing?" I asked loudly.

"Nothing," he said. "Not just yet anyway."

"Well, what are you going to do?" Brave Minnie, facing down her foe with courage and a fierce determination to battle her way free. If only her voice hadn't sounded so squeaky.

"I'm not going to do anything."

His voice was calm and pleasant, and now that he was close to me—far too close—I could see that he was smiling. The smile creeped me out more than anything else had yet and I whirled away, starting to run, wanting to run, trying my hardest to run, but not being able to because a huge meaty hand had clamped onto my upper arm, the weight behind it keeping me from going anywhere.

"No," he said, "I'm not going to do a thing. But you, you're going to have an accident. It's going to be very sad. All your little bookmobile and library friends will boo-hoo when they hear."

I tried to yank free of his grip. "No one will believe it. I'm not accident-prone."

He snorted. "So what? You'll be dead. Besides, no one will be able to tell. You're going to drown, that's all. Happens every year. Someone falls in the water, doesn't realize how fast hypothermia works, and blub-blub-blub, down they go." He chuckled, and that was when I really started to hate him. Killing me was one thing, but he didn't have to be so jolly about it.

"I can swim, you know." I gave my arm a quick twist, hoping to break his grip. Though it didn't work, I kept trying. I thought about trying to hit him, to scratch at him, to kick him, but was wary of the danger that his other hand—his other fist—presented. One good hit and I'd be down and incapacitated.

"Of course you can," he said, dragging me toward the end of the dock. "You'd have to be an idiot to live on a houseboat and not be able to swim." He stopped. "Hang on. You know how to swim, so you're not an idiot, but you have to be pretty stupid, coming out here all on your own. Kind of makes you wonder what the difference is between stupidity and idiocy, doesn't it?"

He made a *huh* sort of noise, and we started moving again, me dragging my feet, him with his hand so tight around my upper arm that I knew I'd be bruised up something horrible the next day, assuming there was a next day. Close to despair, I glanced at the lake's shoreline, but there was no sign of life, no sign of anyone who might help me.

"Anyway," he was saying, "this lake here? It's deep and it's cold. Did you know the last of the ice came off just two weeks ago? No, I didn't think so. I checked the water temperature tonight and it's only thirty-nine degrees. Brr!" He shivered. "That means you can be in the water about twenty minutes before you go unconscious. Now, twenty minutes may seem like plenty of time for you to find a way out of the water, but not if I give you a nice whack over the head before you go in."

He pulled a rock from his pocket and held it high.

With sudden and absolute certainty, I knew that there was only one chance for me to get out of this, and that this was it.

I sagged down, forcing him to adjust his stance. He had to release me, at least a little, to rearrange his grip on my arm, and when he did, I took my chance.

With all my strength and all my weight and all my might, I shoved at him, pushing him toward the water. Though he grunted as he flailed his rock-laden arm, trying to keep his balance, he didn't release me. But his grip did lessen.

I twisted hard and fast and, at the same time, stomped on his instep. I didn't know if he let go or if I broke free and I didn't care. His hand came off my arm and I did the only thing I could.

I dove off the end of the dock.

And the last thing I heard before the shockingly cold water closed over my head was "Mrr!"

Chapter 21

The water was more than cold. And it was more than water, it was a physical presence that wanted to crush me with its power. I couldn't even think that I was wet, couldn't remember to swim, could barely remember not to open my mouth.

But I wanted to. I wanted to shriek at the top of my lungs, announcing to anyone and everyone within a mile radius that I was in water that was too cold for human survival. How fish managed to live in this environment, I did not know, and I made a personal vow to brush up on my basic biology when I got back to the library.

If I ever did.

I tried to swim underwater, out and away from Duvall, but the fleece sweatshirt that had been keeping my upper half warm was now saturated and making every move of my arms sluggish. My legs, clad in jeans, weren't doing much better, and my feet, which I assumed were still at the end of my legs, wore running shoes that weren't doing anything to help my speed in the water.

I gave one last underwater stroke and let myself rise to the surface, hoping I was out of reach of Duvall and his rock. My head popped up into the air, and although I tried to stay quiet and hidden, my breaths were loud, panting, and full of a kind of pain that I'd never before experienced.

Cold. I was so cold. Twenty seconds ago, I'd been comfortably warm. Now I was so cold it felt as if the top of my head were about to blow off. There was no way this water was thirty-nine degrees. I was surprised it wasn't still ice. Panting, I let my feet drift down, trying to see if I could touch bottom.

"How's that water?" Duvall asked cheerfully. "By the way, it's plenty deep out there. My boat has a deep draft, so the dock is extra long. Off where you just dove, it's probably six feet deep. You're what, not even five feet tall?" He chuckled. "Way over your head."

I was, too, five feet tall. No more, but certainly no less, and I added the error, intentional or not, to Duvall's growing list of crimes.

"Now, I might not have had time to give you a nice smack on the head with my rock," Duvall said, "but you know what? All I have to do is wait. You can't swim any faster than I can walk, so there's no way you'll be able to get to shore without me getting there first. And you'd never make it to the other side of the lake. It's too far. So I can wait. Twenty minutes isn't all that long."

I heard a creak and knew he'd sat back down on the bench.

"Probably less than twenty, really," he said. "You're so small that the cold will get to you faster." He laughed.

"You shouldn't have had so much coffee when you were a kid. Stunts your growth, you know."

Making fun of short people was beyond the pale and this, too, went on his list.

I was treading water, a silent endeavor, but my short puffy breaths had to be giving away my location. My one chance, which had been diving away from Duvall before he could crack my head open, wasn't turning out to be much of an opportunity. Not exactly out of the frying pan and into the fire—a fire would be welcome at this point—but the analogy was close.

There had to be a way out of this, but I couldn't think what. My hands were already numb, so even if my cell phone was operable underwater, I doubted my fingers would be able to do anything more than point, quaking with cold, in the general direction of the screen.

I scanned the shoreline, looking for something, anything, that might help. Of course, since it was almost full dark, I couldn't see what was ten feet away from me. Clouds had drifted across the face of the moon, and what little light it had been giving out was now gone.

"Getting cold?" Duvall called out.

Come on in and find out, I muttered, but only in my head, because I was starting to get an idea in my cold-fuddled and shivering brain. Though it might not turn out to be a very good idea, I had to do something, and do it fast, because I could already feel the early effects of hypothermia slicking away my strength.

I sucked in a long, shallow breath and sank below the water's surface. Once again, my head felt as if it were going to explode, but I told myself to quit being such a sissy and get on with it. Because if I was completely submerged, Duvall wouldn't be able to see me and wouldn't be able to hear me. All I had to do was swim far enough away that, when I got to shore, he wouldn't notice when I inched out of the water.

My arms pulled, my legs kicked. The darkness was an almost palpable thing, threatening me, jeering at me, taunting me. I longed to open my eyes, but if I did I'd lose my contact lenses, and anyway, opening my eyes wouldn't help me see.

Because it was dark.

The blackness of a northern night was something I hadn't understood before moving here permanently. In cities, there is no real dark. Streetlights, the lights on buildings, lights on signs, lights on buildings, there is light all the time. Up here, though, there was nothing except nature. Even in summer, when the county's population tripled, you could still see the wide dusty white of the Milky Way, strewing its stars in a path across the sky.

Arms pulled, legs kicked.

My lungs burned, yearning to breathe.

Pull. Kick. Pull. Kick.

Pull . . .

Then, when I couldn't go any farther, I let myself rise to the surface. I wanted, oh how I wanted, to noisily gulp in air, but I forced myself to take it in slowly. Silently. I kept my mouth wide-open for fear of Duvall hearing my teeth chatter together, and felt for the lake's floor with my feet.

"Where are you?" he asked sharply.

His voice was off to my right, closer than I'd hoped, but far enough away that I felt a little bit safer.

"Come on," he said, "I know you're out there. What game are you playing?"

Survival.

My stretching toes brushed the bottom of the lake, bumpy from the small rocks that had been deposited long ago by a passing glacier. So the water here was a little taller than I was. I sucked in a long, quiet breath, aimed myself, and went deep.

Kick. Pull. Kick. Pull.

I was taking a steep angle toward shore, trying to travel as far along the lake's edge as I could while still getting into shallow water. If either my engineer father or engineer brother had been handy, he could easily have figured out my rate of travel and the maximum time I could swim between breaths, and plotted the best possible course for me to take.

Kick. Pull. Kick.

Of course, neither one was around, and to be honest, I would have preferred a law enforcement officer to either of my closest male relatives. I loved them dearly, but I wasn't sure how either one would perform in this kind of situation.

Pull. Kick.

Then again, who was I to talk? I wasn't performing very well myself. My lungs were, again, burning with the urge for air, but I wanted to get farther away, way farther away.

Carefully, slowly, I rose, breaking the smooth surface so quietly that the only thing that made any noise was my hair, dripping water off its curly ends.

"Hey!" Duvall called.

I froze, and never had the phrase seemed so appropriate. Reaching down, I could tell that my fingers were brushing rocks, but there was no sensation of feeling. Same with my toes—though I could feel them smacking something, it was a feeling of numbing dullness.

How long had I been in the water now? Five minutes? Six?

"You've been in there ten minutes," Duvall said. "Bet you're losing feeling in your toes, huh? And your fingers, that's probably long gone. Fingers are the first to go."

And he'd know this how, exactly? Somehow I was sure he hadn't researched the topic properly. At most he'd used the computer and the top return on his search engine. Certainly he hadn't looked up any scientific journals. That was what a librarian would have done—librarians do it correctly.

With the useless appendages I used to call my toes, I pushed myself forward.

"Twelve minutes," he called. "You know what I'm going to do when I get to twenty? I'm going to walk up to the cottage and make myself a hot toddy. Steaming hot. It'll practically scald me when I take the first sip, but there's nothing like a hot toddy when you take a chill."

Since I didn't care much for strong spirits, this particular taunt didn't bother me a bit. Now, if he'd mentioned hot chocolate, that would have been different.

I was walking myself along the lake floor with my hands now. I could stand and be thigh-deep in water, but I'd make too much noise climbing out. I had to get as shallow as I could before attempting my final escape.

"Sixteen minutes," Duvall said. "Bet you're cold as the

dickens now, aren't you?" His voice sounded different. I slowed almost to a stop, then realized he was talking in the opposite direction. It was pitch-dark and he couldn't possibly see me. As long as I got out of the water and stayed out of his grasp, I'd be safe.

But now my body had started to shiver. These weren't the normal shivers that everyone gets on occasion, the shivers from eating ice cream too fast or the shivers from sitting in a cold car before it got warm. No, these were the shivers that meant Minnie's impending doom. Large, quaking things that rippled the water out from around me. Huge teeth-chattering shivers I couldn't control.

I had to get out of that water.

Moving faster than I dared, but not as fast as I would have liked, I forced my lumpy hands to propel me onward and upward. One step, two, three . . .

"And bingo, here we are at twenty minutes!" Duvall shouted jovially. "Ready to come in?"

Absolutely.

It was dark and I couldn't see diddly and Duvall was still too close, but I had to get to shore. Maybe Duvall's twenty minutes was a figment of his manipulative tendencies and maybe it wasn't; either way my body was starting to shut down.

I inched toward shore.

"Where the hell are you?" Duvall called.

Way over here, I was tempted to call, just to hear his reaction, but even if I could have safely done so, I wasn't sure I'd be able to get out the words. My face was so cold that I wasn't sure my mouth would work well enough to speak intelligibly.

"Bet she already drowned," he muttered.

Not a chance, buster.

"Well," he said. The bench creaked under his weight and I pictured him standing. "There's only one thing left to do, then. What do you think about that, you mangy little ball of fur?"

My feet were set wide, since I was trying to get as much stability as possible, and I stood slowly, slowly, easing myself up out of the water, inching up, letting the water slick away, trying to keep it from dripping, keeping my movements silent and hidden and invisible.

The dock creaked under Duvall's weight. I pictured him walking up the length of it, climbing the stairs to the cottage, and the door slamming shut behind him.

And as soon as that door shut, I'd tiptoe to the dock, get Eddie, and sneak away into the dark. We'd get into my car, drive away fast, crank up the heat as far as it would go, and zoom to the sheriff's department, where, with luck, the cell phone's audio recordings I'd made while I talked to Duvall would be recoverable.

"Come here," Duvall said. "I know you're up there. Get down already."

"Mrrrr-rrrr."

I stopped dead.

"Here, kitty, kitty," Duvall crooned. "Don't you want to take a bath? A cold bath, but you won't notice that after a few minutes. Here, kitty, kitty."

All the cold I'd been feeling was pushed aside by sheer fury, and the fuzziness my brain had been sinking into sharpened into hard thought. Still moving slowly, still moving silently, I changed my plan. Instead of moving away from Duvall, as soon as I got out of the water, I would head straight toward him.

"Why are you being like this, cat?" Duvall asked. There was a metallic clang. He was climbing onto the boat lift, trying to get at Eddie.

Urgency shouted inside me, yelling at me to move, screaming at me to run. But I couldn't. Not yet. I couldn't let Duvall know I was still alive and kicking, not out there in that frigid water, succumbing to the effects of hypothermia.

I inched into shallower and shallower water, hoping the clouds would stay in front of the moon long enough for me to get to land. My feet, numb now, rolled left and right as they stepped on rocks. I wondered how many times someone could sprain an ankle, then decided that was something I didn't need to know.

"Get down here!" Duvall yelled.

"Mrrr!" Eddie yelled back.

If my face had been working properly, I might have smiled.

"Same to you," Duvall said. "Tell you what. You stay right there and I'll come and get you. I can't have you being around here when her body is found. You're too noticeable. But if you drown, too, well, who's to say what really happened?"

I was out of the water now and on the lake's rocky shoreline. Fast as I could make my body move, I clambered up the stubby bluff and onto . . . someone's front yard, probably, but there was still no light to see by. Running in the dark would send me straight into a tree, a fire pit, or a fence, so I had to creep along, waving my hands in front of me.

From the dock, I heard Duvall, still trying to entice Eddie into his reach. "Come here, you flea-ridden mouse brain. You're useless and pointless and the world will be better off without you, so come here and—ouch!"

This time I did smile. Eddie had given him full warning; I'd heard both his growl and the hiss that always came right before a paw swipe, claws extended.

"I'll get you for that," Duvall said in a low voice, "you crappy little cat. More trouble than you're worth. And . . . ah. Gotcha."

Trees and fire pits and fences didn't matter any more. I jumped into a trot, then a run. I had to get to Eddie before . . . before anything happened. The heavy weight of my wet clothes dragged at me, trying to sap my speed, sucking at my strength, but that couldn't matter now.

"Stop wriggling," Duvall said, accompanied by metallic creaks as he climbed off the boat lift. "This won't take long. Soon you'll be together with your mistress and won't that be nice for both of you?"

I was running full force, arms pumping, legs pistoning.

"That's a good kitty," Duvall said almost jovially as the dock creaked underneath him. "We're almost there."

The thick clouds that had been in front of the moon blew past, and the lakeshore was gently illuminated. It should have been a scene of great beauty, but all I could see was a great hulk of man on the end of a dock, about to toss my cat out into deep and frigid water.

"Leave him alone!" I shouted, and ran toward the steps to the dock.

Duvall whirled and cursed.

Suddenly bright lights glared all around us. "Mr. Duvall," blared a voice through a bullhorn, "this is the police. Please put your hands up."

But Duvall didn't. I could tell that he was intent on sending my cat into the water and nothing anyone said was going to stop him. He turned around and I could see that he held a spitting and struggling Eddie with one outstretched hand.

I hurtled down the steps and reached the dock.

"Mr. Duvall," the bullhorn said. "Put your hands up."

Mr. Duvall did not. He kept walking, out to the very end of his dock.

I pounded down the wooden slats. "Put him down!"

"I'll put him down all right," Duvall said. "Right in the—"

"MRR!" Eddie flung himself around and latched his claws straight into the back of Duvall's hand.

"Ah!" Duvall yelled and dropped Eddie. "You miserable cat, I'll—"

But that was all he got out before I caromed into him with all my weight. Shoulder first, head down, elbow tight to my body, I thumped him and I thumped him good.

Duvall, still yelling, flailed about with his arms, trying to recover, but I'd caught him off guard and off balance and he fell into the water with a great splash.

I scooped Eddie off the dock and snuggled him close. "Are you all right, pal? He didn't hurt you, did he?"

Feet hurried toward me. I turned and saw multiple

officers rushing toward me. Sheriff Kit Richardson led the way, followed by Detective Inwood, followed by Ash, followed by two other deputies.

The sheriff stood at the dock's end, flashlight in hand, and took in the situation. "Wolverson, make sure he gets out of there fast. That water's cold." She glanced at me. "Ms. Hamilton, you need a hospital. No arguments. Your lips and fingers are blue. A deputy will take you. Now."

The command was sharp and crisp and I did not dare disobey. But . . .

Sheriff Richardson smiled. "If he'll let me," she said, "I'll take care of Eddie until you get home. From what I can tell, he's the hero of the hour."

"What d-do you s-say, Ed-die?" I asked through chattering teeth as a deputy put an emergency blanket around my shoulders.

"Mrr," he said, and bumped my chin with the top of his head.

Chapter 22

Sunday afternoon, Kristen thundered out a laundry list of unnecessary orders to her staff, gave them a good long glare, and ended with "I'll be back in a couple of hours. Don't burn the place to the ground when I'm gone, okay?"

Each and every one of the white-coated staff members rolled their eyes, right in front of their boss. "We'll be fine," the head chef said as she stirred something in a huge pot. "Go have some fun before you forget how."

Kristen sniffed loudly, turned to me, winked, and together we headed into the sunshine, destination: the party at Josh's house.

"Ash Wolverson, huh?" she asked as we walked along. Her elbow caught me in the middle of my upper arm. "He's pretty hot. What are you going to do on your date?"

"Go to a different town," I said promptly. "Or maybe Canada. It's not far, really, and it's a nice drive across the bridge."

I'd been joking, but it wasn't a bad idea. No one would know either of us in Canada, which held great appeal, because I'd had many a romantic meal hijacked by friends who'd wanted to stop and chat. And then there'd been the memorable occasion when I took a date to Kristen's restaurant and she played waitress for us.

"With Trock in town for the book fair," I said, "why isn't Scruffy hanging around you like a lost puppy dog?"

"They're behind on the TV show," she said. "Flew back to New York this morning. I barely saw him at all."

"But he'll be back for the summer, right?" Kristen and Scruffy made a wonderful couple. I didn't like to think of them apart for too long a stretch.

"Memorial weekend," she said, happiness clear in her voice. "Then on through to Labor Day."

I sent an elbow her way, which smacked into the top of her hip. "Should be a good summer, then."

"Only if you finish telling me what happened to you last night."

"How much did I tell you?"

It had been Kristen who'd picked me up from the hospital, where I'd been delivered, so to speak. Ash had driven my car to the houseboat, and after the emergency room doctor said my body temperature was at a safe level, I used the hospital's phone to summon my best friend. My cell phone was in the hands of Detective Inwood, who would be taking it to their computer forensics guy, who would do his best to recover my audio recordings of Duvall's threats to me and his acknowledgment of what he'd done to Henry and Adam.

Kristen had been full of questions last night, but I'd

fallen asleep within two blocks and had barely woken when she gently pulled me out of her car, walked me to my houseboat, and dribbled me into bed.

"For clarity's sake," Kristen said now, "let's say you didn't tell me anything."

This was sensible, because whatever I'd told her last night couldn't have been very coherent. "Well," I said, "it all started when Cole Duvall called me after the book fair and said that he had Eddie."

Kristen made a T with her hands for a time-out. "Sidebar. How is Mr. Ed?"

"He's fine. Kit Richardson brought him home this morning. I think he likes her better than he likes me."

"Hang on," Kristen said. "You're talking about the sheriff?"

"Well, yeah. Is there any other Kit Richardson in Chilson?"

She shivered. "You let her take Eddie? You sure she didn't eat him and bring a substitute in his place?"

"What? No, of course not. What's the matter with you? She's perfectly nice."

"I doubt that word has ever been associated with Sheriff Richardson," Kristen muttered, then looked around to see if anyone had heard her.

"You're an idiot," I said.

"And you're what, smart?" She made a rude noise. "Going off to meet a guy you suspected of murdering Henry Gill and trying to run over Adam Deering isn't what I'd call stellar brainwork."

"It wasn't as bad as you make it sound," I said. "Matter of fact, I—"

"Say," Kristen interrupted. "Isn't that your aunt? And Otto?"

I clutched at her arm. "Don't tell her anything about last night. I'll talk to her later."

But Aunt Frances was headed straight in my direction. "Minerva Joy Hamilton," she called, "I need to talk to you."

"Okay," Kristen said, grinning. "I won't tell her a thing."

"What were you thinking?" my aunt scolded as she enveloped me in a huge hug, smushing my face against her shoulder. "Going off like that without a word to anyone, walking straight into danger . . . For heaven's sake, I thought you knew better!"

"I do," I said in a muffled way.

"What? Speak up, child." She held me away from her. "You don't look the worse for wear, but what on earth possessed you to do something so stupid?"

I knew an eye roll would get me another scolding, so I kept it internal. I also wanted to know how she'd known about last night—I certainly hadn't told her—but Chilson was a small town and I should have called her earlier to let her know I was okay.

"Can we sit down?" I asked. Then, without waiting for an answer, I ushered all three of them to a nearby bench and sat them all down in a row, Otto in the middle. I stood in front of the trio and started my lecture.

"No interruptions, please," I said, clasping my hands behind my back and rocking back a little on my heels. They agreed and I started to enjoy myself. "Last night, I got home late because of the book fair. Soon afterward,

I got a phone call from Cole Duvall, saying he had Eddie and that I had to be at the Duvall's cottage in an hour to get him back."

Kristen, Aunt Frances, and Otto all nodded. This part they already knew.

"I'm going to be completely truthful here," I said. "I panicked. Freaked out, actually. I didn't know what to do and I was scared."

"Why didn't—" Aunt Frances started, but Kristen shushed her to silence.

"Thank you," I said. "I called Deputy Ash Wolverson"—this was for Otto's benefit, because my aunt and Kristen were well aware of what Ash did for a living—"but had to leave a voice mail message." Last night's fear came back full and strong. I shook it away and went on.

"I knew it would take more than half an hour to drive to Duvall's place and I'd already used up almost fifteen minutes of the hour by calling Ash and making sure Duvall wasn't playing some cruel joke and that Eddie wasn't still on the houseboat somewhere. So I got in the car."

Kristen started to say something but stopped when both Aunt Frances and Otto glared at her.

"Halfway there," I went on, "I pulled over. I had a few extra minutes, so I used them to think."

And I had, after I'd pounded the steering wheel in frustration until my fists hurt. I'd jumped out of the car and paced up and down the side of the lonely road, trying to assemble a plan.

I told my audience how I'd called the sheriff's office and coerced Dispatch into transferring me to Detective

Inwood, who, I later found out, had been at home about to bite into a freshly grilled steak. I made a mental note to send him and his wife a gift certificate to Kristen's restaurant and continued my tale.

"The detective told me he'd spent the day making a case against Duvall and said he'd call Sheriff Richardson as soon as he got off the phone with me, and to go home, that they'd take care of everything."

Otto stirred. "But—"

Two female elbows, one from each side, jabbed him into silence.

I smiled at him. "But there was no way I was going to wait, not while Duvall had Eddie. When I told Inwood that, he told me to . . ." I paused, not wanting to repeat the detective's exact words. It was Sunday, after all, and besides, my aunt didn't approve of cursing at any time. "Let's just say my subsequent actions weren't sanctioned by the sheriff's office."

Kristen snorted, Aunt Frances sighed, and Otto chuckled.

Ignoring them all, I continued. "The detective told me they'd be there as soon as they could, and instructed me to wait until there was a police presence before approaching Duvall." I looked away for a moment, remembering and reliving. "But I couldn't do that," I said quietly. "He'd said an hour. I couldn't risk it, not when he had Eddie."

My aunt sighed again, but this time I could tell it was a sigh of understanding. She'd lived with Eddie all last winter and she loved him, too. Kristen cast a glance at the heavens and slouched down on the bench. She understood. Otto gave me a soft smile and a nod.

I told them about going down to the dock, about finding Eddie, about my short dip in the water to avoid being clonked over the head with a blunt object, and the appearance of the police to save the day.

"So," I finished, "it was a risk, but I knew help was on the way. And it all turned out okay, so there's no reason to tell Mom, is there?"

This last was to my aunt. Who, as my mother's sister-in-law, knew all about my mom's tendency to drama and overprotectiveness.

Aunt Frances gave me a keen look. "I hear you're dating Ash these days."

I closed my eyes briefly. How did she know these things? "We haven't been on a single date yet. Next weekend will be our first."

She *hmmph*ed and stood. "Maybe he'll do a better job of keeping you safe and sound than that doctor did."

Otto laughed and got up. He leaned over and whispered, "I think you're doing a fine job of that all by yourself, Minnie. Keep up the good work."

The two of them made their good-byes and walked off, hand in hand.

Smiling, I watched them go, then turned back to Kristen, who remained on the bench as if she meant to stay there for months. "What?" I asked. "We're going to be late."

"Details," she said, holding out her hands, palm up, and making "come here" motions with her long fingers. "There are more details to come and I'm not moving until I hear them all."

Though I'd glossed over my near death from hypothermia in the story I'd just related to my aunt and Otto, since Kristen was the one who'd picked me up from the hospital, she was aware of those particular circumstances. "What details?"

"That Seth, for one. I thought you'd thought he was a murder suspect. Say, did I ever tell you that I finally saw Tony Wartella?"

I shook my head.

"Oh. Well, I did. He and his wife came in the other day. I asked if he had a relative named Seth, and he said he did, a cousin of some sort. But Tony also said that since his dad had passed away, and that was years ago, he'd never once seen him."

I thanked her, but it hadn't mattered, not since Irene realized she'd mistaken a law enforcer for a lawbreaker. And I'd also heard, via Ash that morning, that Detective Inwood had tracked down Seth via his probation officer and made the appropriate inquires. "They checked," I said. "Turns out Seth had a solid alibi for the day Henry was killed."

"What about for the day Adam was almost run over?"

"Then, too."

Kristen nodded. "Good. Just wanted to make sure that Duvall can't wriggle out of this by having his attorney point the finger at anyone else. If they can't recover the audio from your phone, the prosecuting attorney might have a problem."

She had a good point, but the motive and the opportunity were so clear to me that I didn't see that happening. Even Felix Stanton had been ruled out as a suspect by Detective Inwood's Saturday investigations. It turned out that Felix had been meeting with potential investors the afternoon Henry died, and had been downstate trolling for new clients when Adam came so close to being hit by that car.

I held out my hand and hauled Kristen to her feet. "Remember Neva Chatham?"

"The lady with the gun? Sure."

"Turns out that the entire county except you and me knows that Neva's shotgun has been a squirrel's acorn cache since the Reagan administration."

My morning phone call with Ash had also revealed that little tidbit of information. And I'd learned, through Sabrina that morning at the Round Table, why Rachel Carter, the mother of the little boy who'd defended Neva, had never called back. There had been a family wedding in Hawaii, and they'd turned the event into a long vacation. "Lucky buggers," Sabrina had said, topping off my coffee. "The warmest place any of my relatives live is Escanaba. I'm the one who moved south."

Though I still didn't think it was a good idea for anyone to be waving around any sort of a firearm at harmless strangers—Neva might get herself into real trouble someday—now that I'd spent time in her kitchen, I could also see why there was a sort of tacit understanding in the community about her.

The one unknown still hanging out there was whether Duvall had tried to push those bricks onto Adam's head. Ash said that Duvall had sworn he'd had nothing to do with it, but they were looking into it. Not that it mattered, prisonwise. Duvall would stand trial for Henry's murder and the attempted murder of Adam and me, and would undoubtedly be imprisoned for the rest of his life.

My own personal unknown, a possible huge hike to my boat slip rental fee, was also still hanging out there, but I wasn't going to worry about that. It was too nice a day.

"Hey, know what?" I asked. We were walking along the waterfront now, and I pointed at a gorgeous wooden boat tied up to the city dock. "Aunt Frances is going to teach a boat restoration class this fall at the college."

"How nice," Kristen said.

I grinned. My friend, although she'd lived next to water most of her life, couldn't stand being out on it. "And you know what boat they're going to restore?"

"Haven't the foggiest . . . Hang on." She stopped and stared at me. "Don't tell me."

"Yep. They're going to restore Neva's boat as a class project. Won't cost her a dime."

Kristen gave a long whistle. "How'd you manage that?"

I smiled a little smugly. "Librarian magic." Well, that and a lot of fast talking. I'd called Neva ahead of time and invited her to the book fair to meet Trock. He was interested in local farmers, I told her, which was true, and while it hadn't been easy to get Neva and my aunt in the same spot at the same time, I'd managed to do so with Holly's help, and once I'd steered the conversation in the direction of boat restoration, everything fell into place.

Kristen and I, still talking, arrived at Josh's small ranch house. The yard was trim and neat, with low shrubs softening the foundation. Pale blue siding with white trim gave the house a friendly look, and the brass of the light fixtures that flanked the front door winked bright in the sunshine.

"I suppose," Kristen said, "that Holly is going to be here."

"Yes, and you're going to behave, just like you promised." For some reason I'd never quite grasped, Holly and Kristen, who had known each other since they were in kindergarten, couldn't be in the same room without sparks flying.

My best friend squinched up her face. "Did I really promise?"

"Absolutely," I said, and we went up to the front door and knocked.

The door opened to a smiling Josh. "Hey, Minnie. Hi, Kristen. Come on in." Behind him, there were a number of people milling about, drinks and plates of food in hand. Some of the people I didn't know, but I saw Kelsey, Donna, and a number of other library staff.

We stepped up and in, and I blinked at the color the living room walls were painted. "Isn't that—"

A female shriek from the recent arrival behind us made everyone in the room wince. "Josh Hadden!" Holly yelled. "You are such a jerk!"

Josh laughed. "Gotcha!"

Holly pointed at the walls. "This is the exact color I told you about, isn't it? Not a taupe, not an olive, not a brown, but something that's part of them all."

"Yep," he said.

She craned her neck around to see. "And your dining area. That's the same dark red I was talking about."

"And the kitchen is the sage green you picked out," he said, grinning. "I even painted the bathroom that pink you liked so much."

"You did not!" Holly said.

He shrugged. "It's just paint. I figured if I hated it, I'd do it over again in beige. Didn't turn out so bad."

Holly gave him a hug. "You," she said, "are the biggest jerk I know."

"But seriously good-looking," he said, combing back his hair with his fingers. "You got to admit that part, at least."

They started in on their siblinglike bickering, and Kristen and I eased away. "Food's in the kitchen," Donna said. "And you have to take a look at the bathroom. The color is gorgeous. I don't know how he had the guts to do that."

In the kitchen, ladling meatballs from a slow cooker onto a paper plate, was Mitchell Koyne.

"Hey, Mitchell," I said. "How are you doing?"

He looked at me, looked left and right, then looked back at me. It was a classic deer-in-the-headlights expression, but I had no idea why it was on Mitchell's face.

"Uh, hi, Minnie," he said. "Hey, Kristen."

An attractive woman came into the room and put her arm possessively around Mitchell's waist. "Hi," she said. "I'm Bianca."

Kristen blinked. I blinked. Then we recovered from the shock of seeing a seemingly sensible woman voluntarily attach herself to Mitchell and introduced ourselves. Once Bianca learned about Kristen's restaurant, the two immediately went deep into a discussion of arcane food preparation.

I spooned potato salad and meatballs onto a paper plate and was trying to decide which pasta salad to choose when Mitchell sidled over to me.

"You okay?" he whispered.

But, really, why did I have to choose at all? I dolloped both kinds onto my plate. "Why wouldn't I be?" I asked.

"Well, you know." He nodded toward Bianca.

I had no clue, actually. "She seems very nice," I ventured.

"The best," Mitchell said, a sappy grin on his face. "I just, you know, hope your feelings aren't hurt. I mean, I know you kind of have sort of a thing for me."

I'd just put a forkful of salad in my mouth, but I almost spit it out. "A thing?" I gasped, trying not to choke.

"Well, yeah." Mitchell shrugged. "That's why I haven't told you I was dating Bianca. I didn't want to hurt your feelings."

I summoned the deep reserves of strength I was rarely forced to draw upon, and didn't laugh. "Thank you for your concern," I said as seriously as I could manage. "But I'll be fine."

Mitchell peered down at me. "You sure?"

"Absolutely."

An hour later, Kristen and I were walking to the marina, and I was telling her the story. "Are you serious?" she asked.

"Yep," I said. "Remember he asked me out last summer? I'm guessing whatever I told him got misinterpreted."

"Wouldn't be the first time," Kristen said, grinning.

"And he said he didn't want to hurt your feelings?" Her laugh was loud and long. "Classic Mitchell. Creating problems where there aren't any around for miles."

"He was trying to be nice," I protested.

"And you're defending him," she said, still laughing. "No wonder he thinks you have a thing for him."

"Someone has to look out for people like Mitchell," I said. "Wouldn't the world would be a poorer place if we didn't have Mitchell stories to tell?"

"True enough." We had rounded the corner to the marina just as Kristen started to tell a story from high school about Mitchell and the physics teacher and a box of dry ice when she stopped short. "Isn't that your boss?"

"Can't be," I said. "He doesn't . . ." Then I looked in the direction where she was looking. "Uh-oh."

"Minerva," Stephen said, walking toward us briskly. "I must say I expected a phone call from you today."

"Oh." I couldn't think why. "My phone fell in the water last night."

"I see." He glanced at Kristen, who took the hint.

"There's a deck chair over there that has my name on it," she said, and left me alone with Stephen.

"Your phone isn't the only thing that went into the water, I hear." Stephen gave me a once-over. "But I can see that you came out without injury."

"Yes."

Our conversation, such as it was, languished.

"The book fair went well," he said.

"It did." Was this why he'd expected a call from me today? He'd made an appearance at the fair, and at that point he'd seemed agreeable to getting the final numbers for attendance on Monday, but maybe he'd woken up this morning and found that he couldn't wait. "If you're looking for the final numbers," I said, "I won't have them until tomorrow."

"Hmm?" He was looking at Janay Lake. "No, no, tomorrow is fine."

Then why was he here? I had things to do, friends to chat with, and cats to pet. I shifted from one foot to the other, trying to figure out what was going on and failing completely.

"Minerva," he said suddenly. "I am leaving Chilson."

"You . . . what?" This didn't make sense. Last winter he'd told me he would be retiring in about six years and that he'd been grooming me to take his place as director of the library. "But—"

"My plans have changed," he said. "I've been offered a job in Georgia, close to family, and it's an opportunity that seems tailor-made for me."

I realized that I knew very little about Stephen's personal life other than vague knowledge of a sister. I supposed he must have had parents, and there was a rumor that he had children, but some things are harder to imagine than others and I hadn't yet expended the energy it would take to envision Stephen diapering a baby.

"When?" I finally asked. "Are you leaving, I mean."

"They would like me to start the first of June." He kept his gaze on the lake. "I just notified the library board, and they will be starting the search for a new director next week."

"Oh," I said.

"I have also told them that they couldn't do better

than to select you." He paused. "There are a number of board members, however, who think there is an obligation to do a wider search."

No surprise there. Besides, they were probably right. "Thank you, Stephen."

"No need for thanks. The board has made no decision." He nodded toward the lake, started to walk away, but stopped and half turned toward me. "Good luck, Minnie," he said.

I blinked. Then, when I still didn't know what to do, I blinked again at his retreating back. "Well," I said out loud.

"What was all that about?" Kristen called from the marina's patio.

I held up my index finger, indicating I'd be right back, and went to the houseboat. "Hey, Eddie, are you awake?" When I'd left, he'd been curled up on the bed and snoring louder than I'd thought it possible for a cat to snore. "Eddie, where—ow!"

My cat looked up at me innocently, as if he hadn't just whacked my chin with the top of his hard head.

I picked him up and gave him a good snuggle. "Want to go sit outside with Aunt Kristen?"

"Mrr," he said, straight into my face. Cat food breath wafted over me, but I didn't feel like complaining, not after last night.

"So," I told him, "Stephen thinks I should become the new library director. Which sounds good in a lot of ways." One of which was money. I'd make not quite double what I was making as assistant director. And I'd be able to expand the children's programming, and I'd be able to do more outreach, and all sorts of other things that Stephen had resisted doing. "But what would I do about the bookmobile?" Because there was no way I'd have time to drive the bookmobile if I was director. "I love driving us around and—"

Eddie put his paw across my lips.

"You're right," I murmured as I rearranged him into a shoulder snuggle. "I'll think about it later. It'll all work out, won't it?"

"Mrr," he said, and started purring.

Sometimes the advice of a cat is the best advice of all.

Read on for a sneak peek of
Minnie and Eddie's next adventure,

CAT WITH A CLUE

Available August 2016 from Obsidian!

In my almost thirty-four years of living, I'd discovered that there were remarkably few things I absolutely had to do.

Yes, I had to feed and clothe and house myself, but besides those basics, there wasn't much that couldn't be put off for the sake of sitting for a few minutes in the morning sunshine, especially when said morning sunshine was smiling down on my very own houseboat, which was resting comfortably on the sparkling waters of a lovely blue lake alongside Chilson, a picturesque town in north-west lower Michigan that happened to be my favorite place in the whole world.

I lay flopped in my lounge chair, eyes closed and soaking up the sun, content with pretty much everything and everyone. Life was good and there wasn't much that could improve it other than making this particular moment last even longer. Peace and quiet reigned throughout my little land. There were things to do, but they could wait. Nothing I had to do that day was so important that it couldn't be put off for a few more minutes and—

"Mrr!"

Of course, my idea of what defined important didn't always match my cat's.

I opened my eyes and looked at Eddie, my black-and-white tabby, who was approximately three years old and who had placed his nose two inches from my face.

"You know," I told him, "if you'd gone out with us, you wouldn't have so much energy."

For the past few weeks, I'd actually been exercising. Sweating, even. I'd been meaning to start working out for a long time, but it had taken a number of gentle suggestions from Ash Wolverson, my new boyfriend, to get me to invest in some decent running shoes. A few more suggestions and I'd started hauling myself out of bed early three times a week to run with him. Luckily, he swung by the marina four miles into his own run, so he'd already had a good workout by the time we got together.

"Think about it," I said to Eddie. "You'll sleep even better during the day."

He blinked.

"Right." I patted him on the head. "You never have trouble sleeping during the day. It's the nights that are a problem. What do you think about going for a run in the late afternoon?"

"Mrr." Eddie pawed at yesterday's newspaper, which was sitting on my lap. I'd stayed at the library late the night before and had been too tired to do anything except reread *84, Charing Cross Road* when I got home. Since my boss, Stephen Rangel, had left his job as director of the Chilson District Library, I was interim director until the library board hired someone. This was stretching me a little thin, because in addition to my normal duties as assistant director, I also drove the library's bookmobile and was out of the building almost as much as I was in it.

"Which section do you want to hear first?" I asked, picking up the two-section paper.

"Sports, please," said a male voice.

I looked over toward my right-hand marina neighbor. Eric Apney, a fortyish male of undeniable good looks, was sitting on the deck of his boat, eating a bowl of cereal while a mug of coffee steamed next to him.

My left-hand neighbors, Louisa and Ted Axford, had spent summers in the slip next to mine for years and would usually be in residence by then, but a new grandchild had captured their hearts and Louisa had e-mailed me that they wouldn't be up until mid-July.

Eric, who lived downstate but spent as much time in Chilson as he could, was new to Uncle Chip's Marina. I'd met him a few weeks before and had turned down his invitation to dinner when I'd learned he was a doctor and, worse, a surgeon. I'd recently dated an emergency room doctor for almost a year and had learned that with doctors, dates were things that were made to be broken. Maybe I was being prejudiced, but my reaction had been instant and instinctive.

Luckily, Eric hadn't taken my rejection to heart. He'd laughed and said I was smart to stay away, and we were becoming good friends.

"Mrr," Eddie said.

"What was that?" Eric's spoon paused at the halfway point.

I looked at Eddie. "He's tired of hearing about the lack of depth in the Tigers bullpen and would rather hear the law enforcement report."

In a lot of ways, marina life was like being in a campground. Your neighbors were mere feet away, and if the wind was calm, you practically could hear them breathing. Politeness dictated that you didn't mention how their snoring kept you awake, but it was hard to maintain the fiction that you didn't know what the person on the boat next to you was saying while on his—or her—cell phone. From unintentional eavesdropping, I knew Eric was a huge baseball fan, just as he knew that I ordered take-out dinners more often than I cooked.

"Really?" Eric asked. Soon after we'd met, he'd heard me talking to my cat as if Eddie could really understand what I was saying. He'd laughed with only the slightest condescension, but when Eddie had replied, he'd stopped laughing and hadn't laughed since.

"No idea," I said, flipping newspaper pages. "But I know I'm tired of hearing about pitching problems. Okay, here we go. Ready for the good stuff?"

It hadn't been until I'd started dating Ash, a deputy with the Tonedagana County Sheriff's Office, that I'd become interested in the law enforcement tidbits that Sheriff Kit Richardson released to the newspaper. Ash said that what made it into print wasn't the half of it, and I wondered what half was missing, because the farcical half was certainly there.

"Mrr," Eddie said.

Eric shoveled in a spoonful of cereal. "Fire away."

"Do you want the funny stuff first or last?"

"Mrr."

"Last it is." I scanned the short paragraphs. "Here's a happy one. 'Lost six-year-old boy in the woods. Six-year-old boy was located and returned home safely.'"

Eric swallowed and toasted the newspaper with his coffee mug. "Score one for the good guys. What's next?"

"'Daughter called from out of state to have her elderly father checked on. The officer spoke with her father, who said he had turned off his phone because his daughter often calls too late at night, waking him.'"

Eric choked on his coffee. "Seriously?" he asked, coughing.

"I couldn't make this stuff up. Next is about a guy who called 911 to tell the sheriff's office that he'd been driving with his window down. A bee flew in, and when he was trying to get the bee out, he drove into a parked car."

"Good story," Eric said. "Wonder if it's true."

Thanks to my insider information, I happened to know that the man in question had been heavily intoxicated at the time. Of course, that didn't mean the bee hadn't existed. Smiling, I went back to the paper. "Here's someone who called 911 to report that someone had broken into her garage the night before her garage sale. Nothing was reported missing."

"Mrr." Eddie thumped his head against my leg.

"Yeah, I know," I said. "Not that good of a story, but they can't all be winners. How about this one? A woman taped her husband's mouth shut because he was snoring too loud." I looked up at Eric, but he was scooping out the last of his cereal and didn't notice. "And last but not least, 'Caller wanted to see an officer because her cat was being mean to her.'"

"Mrr!"

"Okay, okay," I said. "It was one sister being mean to another sister, and the mom took care of things before the officer arrived." I gave Eddie a long pet. "Just wanted to see if you were paying attention."

"Some kid really called 911 because she was fighting with her sister?" Eric held up his cereal bowl and drained the last of the milk into his mouth.

I averted my eyes, swung my short legs off the lounge, and stood. "Last week some kid called 911 because his mom wouldn't let him play all night with the video game he got for his birthday."

"Well," Eric said, "now that I can see."

"Mrr."

I turned around. Eddie was settling onto the newspaper, tucking himself into a meat-loaf shape. "Oh, no, you don't."

Gently, I rolled him onto his side and slid the paper

out from underneath him, like a sleight-of-hand artist pulling a tablecloth from under a tableful of china. Unlike the china, however, Eddie yawned and stretched out with his front feet, catching the paper with one of his claws, then yanking it out of my hand and making it flutter to the deck.

"Nice job." I crouched down to pick up the now-scattered newsprint. "You have a gift for making a . . ."

"A what?" Eric asked.

"Mess," I said vaguely, now standing with the newspaper in hand, looking at the page Eddie had opened. The obituaries. "Talia DeKeyser," I read to myself, "died peacefully in her sleep on Memorial Day. Born on May 24, 1933 to Robert and Mary Wiley, Talia married Calvin DeKeyser in 1955 — "

"Minnie, you okay?"

I folded the newspaper and tucked it under my arm. "Fine, thanks." I picked up a purring Eddie and tucked him under my other arm. "See you later, okay, Eric? I have to get to work."